"I don't stay in places long."

"Maybe it's time you did."

Josh touched Eve's face again, this time letting his fingers linger and trace the line of her jaw. His body ached with longing. He wanted to dig deep under that calm serenity and ignite the fire he felt in her. But he couldn't. "I'm a wanderer and you're a nester, and I would bet everything I have that you've never had a one-night stand, or one-week stand, and that's all I know. All I want. No complications."

He was lying. He did want more, he just hadn't known it until now.

But it wouldn't work. He would leave one day, and it could break two hearts. Maybe three.

He stepped back.

She gave him a long, steady look, then nodded. She started to turn, then stopped. "About Nick?"

"You can bring him over tomorrow afternoon." Bad decision, but the boy would be here with his mother. No temptation then. At least that was what he told himself.

"Thank you," she said softly, and as he closed the door he wondered exactly what she was thanking him for.

Dear Reader,

Most of my story ideas come from today's newspaper headlines. Life often holds more wonders than a writer's imagination.

All my writer's bells rang when I read a *New York Times* story about military dogs being retired because of post-traumatic stress disorder. Many are adopted by their handlers or the general public.

There were also news stories about veterans returning with PTSD and successful programs matching these vets and dogs rescued from the street. The matches often worked miracles for both.

My writer's "what if" mechanism shifted into high gear, and Joshua Manning immediately strode into my mind. He was a throwaway kid who'd raised himself and saw the military as the family he never had. But when a wound meant leaving the service, he had no idea of what to do or where to go. None except saving the military dog handled by a friend who'd died saving Josh's life.

And where better to heal than Covenant Falls, a fictional small town with a big heart and a lady mayor with an even bigger one.

Josh and his Amos, and Mayor Eve Douglas, her young son and their motley crew of rescues climbed into my heart and wrote their own story. I hope they will touch you as they did me.

Patricia Potter

PATRICIA POTTER

The Soldier's Promise

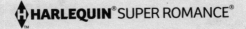

HARLEQUIN® SUPER ROMANCE®

Recycling programs
for this product may
not exist in your area.

ISBN-13: 978-0-373-60841-6

THE SOLDIER'S PROMISE

Copyright © 2014 by Patricia Potter

(H)HARLEQUIN®
™ www.Harlequin.com

Printed in U.S.A.

ABOUT THE AUTHOR

Patricia Potter is a bestselling and award-winning author of more than sixty books. Her Western romances have received numerous awards, including an *RT Book Reviews* Storyteller of the Year Award, a Career Achievement Award for Western Historical Romance and a Best Hero of the Year Award. She is a seven-time RITA® Award finalist for RWA and a three-time Maggie winner. She is a past president of the Romance Writers of America.

Besides writing, Patricia has a passion for accumulating dogs, specifically rescue ones. She's learned that you don't choose dogs, they somehow find you. She currently has two rescue Australian Shepherd sisters with two distinctly different personalities, but both overflowing with love.

In addition to dogs and books, she also loves travel and recently visited the magical, history-seeped Adriatic Coast, Spain and France.

Books by Patricia Potter

HARLEQUIN HISTORICAL

HARLEQUIN BLAZE

To our returning veterans and the dogs
that protect them.

CHAPTER ONE

TRACER BULLETS RIPPED through the night like shooting stars.

He hit the sand along with other members of his team. A rocket-propelled grenade exploded a few feet away, sending shrapnel slicing and burning his skin. Then the enemy poured out from rocks like locusts.

Adrenaline surged through him, smothering the pain. He slid behind a rock, called in copter support and aimed his M16 at the figures multiplying in front of him.

He cursed. Intel had said there was only a small group of Taliban here. One of their high-level couriers was supposedly passing this way.

He fired steadily but the enemy kept coming as his own men fell around him. The smell of gunpowder and the deafening sound of explosions filled the cold night air.

He glanced around. Four of his ten men were down. To his right he heard a steady return of fire. *Dave? What about the other four?*

Eric was down. *Trying to crawl for cover. Gotta go after him, get him behind rocks.*

Move. He sprinted toward his wounded teammate.

His leg exploded in agony and he went down as more bullets ricocheted off rocks around him. Everything was burning. He reached for the M16 he'd dropped.... Too far...

Someone lifted him. Dave. "No," he screamed. "Leave me!" Then he fell again, Dave falling over him, shielding him. He heard the sound of helicopters as everything went black....

Josh Manning jerked awake, the battle still alive in his head.

He reached for his gun. *It wasn't there.*

Then the adrenaline ebbed as his surroundings came into focus. Not a battlefield. A room. Familiar now after a few days. The rapid beating of his heart eased. He sat. *Breathe. Slowly. In and out.* His face and body were wet with sweat. So were the sheets.

Another damned nightmare.

Beside him, Amos whined and tried to inch under the narrow bed.

Knocking. That was what had woken him.

What time is it? He glanced at his watch. 1000 hours. Later than he thought, but he hadn't fallen asleep until dawn. He shook his head, trying to erase the remnants of the nightmare that so often cursed his few hours of sleep. Another knock at the door. Insistent. *Damn it.*

Whoever it was apparently wasn't going away. He looked to the floor. What he could see of Amos's hindquarters was quivering.

Josh knew he was in no condition to answer the

door. He was still wet from the nightmares, and he hadn't shaved in several days. He was wearing only skivvies in the warmth of summer. But more knocking would only exacerbate Amos's terror. He pulled on a pair of jeans, limped painfully to the front door and threw it open so hard it bounced against the interior wall.

He did not feel welcoming. He'd been beset with unwanted visitors since he'd reached the cabin a week earlier, and each one seemed to make Amos more fearful. Didn't make *him* happy, either.

A middle-aged lady stood at the door with an aluminum tin held out to him and a determined smile on her face. All he could think of was Amos's frantic retreat and the bone-deep pain in his left leg when he'd first put weight on it.

What in the hell did it take to be left alone?

He scowled at her.

Her mouth formed a perfect O. Then she thrust the tin in his hands and practically ran from the porch. She didn't look back as she scurried down the broken pavement that served as a driveway.

He must look a hell of a lot worse than even he thought. He went back inside, set the damned tin on a counter and grabbed a beer from the ice chest. He slugged it down and tossed the bottle in the garbage can. He reached for another, then stopped himself. *Drinking in the morning!* Damned bad habit to form. He'd never been a big drinker. No one in his unit had been.

But then he wasn't with the Rangers any longer. He wasn't with anything.

He swore in the silence of the room. He'd behaved badly. He must look terrifying with his scruffy face, uncombed hair and large size. A bare chest with scars probably hadn't helped.

All he wanted was to be left alone. He and Amos. *Amos*. He went into the bedroom and called his name softly.

No audible response. No wag of a tail. Not even a whine. Just heavy panting.

He gingerly lowered himself to the floor and started talking to Amos. "It's okay. Nothing there to hurt us. Just civilians. No enemy. No explosives."

He stopped, his breath caught by grief that was still raw. He continued in a low, rough voice. "I know you miss Dave. I do, too. But he wanted you safe. That's why he asked me to take you." He touched Amos's butt, the only part that wasn't under the bed. The dog gradually relaxed and finally eased from under the bed.

"Breakfast," Josh announced.

Amos was not impressed. He put his head between his paws.

Josh braced himself on the side of the bed to get up. He'd shed a cast six weeks after a third operation and threw away the cane two weeks after that. His left leg resembled Humpty Dumpty's after the fall, a result of the explosion that killed Dave. He could live with the injury, but he ached every time he looked at

Amos. Amos had been his best friend's canine partner, uncanny in finding explosives, unflagging on missions and ecstatic to play with his reward ball. He was a shadow of himself now.

Maybe it was a mistake coming here. Hell, he didn't even understand why Dave had left it to him, especially since he'd never mentioned it in the years they'd been friends. Dave had talked about Colorado and how they might start a camping and fishing business since their skills outside the army weren't much in demand. But a cabin? No. He'd racked his brain since an attorney contacted him in the hospital and said he was the sole beneficiary of Dave's estate.

From what the attorney had said, Josh had thought the cabin was somewhere deep in the woods, somewhere he and Amos could heal quietly and on their own.

He hadn't expected a parade of people invading his life and scaring the hell out of Amos. Perhaps a big No Trespassing sign would help.

He went to the door and looked at the deep royal blue of the lake that was several hundred feet from the cabin. It was the reason he'd decided to stay. At least for a while. That, and the mountain behind the cabin.

The small town of Covenant Falls snuggled on the side of a pristine blue lake and against forested mountains. The cabin was the last structure on a road that ran alongside the lake and dead-ended at the mountain. Shielded by towering pines and underbrush, the cabin was in dire need of repairs. It was apparent no one had used it in years, except maybe partying kids.

The attorney had told him a trust had paid the taxes and a certain amount of upkeep.

Not very much, from his point of view. Flaking paint, missing and broken appliances and rotting floors. The area in back was knee-high in weeds. But then he hadn't expected much. He'd mostly lived in on-base bachelor quarters or tents or slept on the ground these past seventeen years.

He had gone through the cabin, trying to decide what to do. It had good bones. Maybe he could fix it up. He didn't have anything else to do, and he'd learned a lot in the military about fixing things. When he finished, maybe he could sell the cabin. Find some someplace else to go.

He hoped it would be someplace without, God help him, curious neighbors.

His gaze caught the cheerfully painted tin on the cabinet. Now he did feel…chagrined.

Despite himself, he found himself taking off the lid. An enticing scent filled the room as he stared at rich, dark brownies that looked as if they'd just come from the oven. How long since he'd had homemade brownies? Not since some guy in the unit received some from his wife. They'd been stale and broken, but they'd been like manna from heaven.

He succumbed.

"THAT...MAN IN the Hannity cabin. June went over there to welcome him. He was practically naked, and he scared her to death."

Covenant Falls mayor Eve Douglas tried to pacify the caller. Marilyn Evans wasn't the first one in the past few days. Others had expressed concerns about the newest resident of their small community. Some were genuinely frightened. Others were offended at his rebuff of any welcoming overtures.

Marilyn ranted on for several minutes before Eve interrupted. "Has he done anything other than be rude?" Marilyn lived next to June Byars on Lake Road, three houses down from the Hannity cabin.

"Well, no," she admitted, then added ominously, "Not yet."

"You've complained many times that the Hannity cabin is an eyesore. If the owner is here, maybe he'll fix it."

"Fiddlesticks. Do you know he has a motorcycle?" Marilyn suddenly asked. "Maybe he's one of 'them.'"

Eve's body tightened and for a moment she couldn't breathe. Her father, then police chief, had been killed by a biker gang three years ago, and Marilyn knew that well. Eve knew she couldn't condemn everyone who rode a motorcycle, but still...the sight of two or more riders still sent shivers down her back.

"And he drinks," Marilyn continued in a lower tone. "Some bottles fell out of his garbage can when the truck came by."

Eve doubted they'd fallen out. More likely Marilyn had checked the trash herself. Marilyn contributed a weekly column to the *Covenant Falls Herald* and considered herself the town watchdog. "You haven't met him?" Eve asked, surprised that Marilyn hadn't shouldered her way inside.

"I tried," Marilyn said with a long-suffering sniff. "He didn't answer the door."

"Maybe he wasn't there."

"He was," Marilyn insisted. "The motorcycle and Jeep were there. Someone who really belonged here would answer the door. What if he's a serial killer?"

Aha. Therein was the problem, Eve thought. Marilyn was usually a good-natured, if overly inquisitive soul, but she took dismissal poorly. There was a silence, then Marilyn added stiffly, "I just thought you should know what's going on in your town."

"I appreciate that," Eve said. "But we can't send out officers without any reason."

"If anything happens...just don't say I didn't warn you."

Eve sighed. "I'll see what I can find out."

"And you'll let me know?"

"Yes," Eve said patiently, knowing she would also be telling the *Covenant Falls Herald*. "Thanks for calling, but I have a meeting, and I'm late. I'll talk to you later."

Although she hadn't met the newcomer, she understood both the curiosity and apprehension. No one had lived in the cabin permanently since Michael

Hannity had drowned in the lake and his nephew had been under suspicion of murder. Nothing was proved, however, and it was finally ruled an accident. David Hannity had left and hadn't returned. The property had been rented on and off for four years until some renters practically destroyed it, then it had been empty the past twelve years, although the taxes had been paid.

Rumors had started several days ago when the power was turned on. Then talk accelerated when several residents of Lake Road reported seeing a man in a Jeep turn into the driveway and enter the house. It rankled Eve that the new resident was so abrasive. Her town was friendly and welcomed newcomers with open hearts and hands full of goodies. She hated to see them hurt even if, she admitted, they could be rather aggressive in their attempted neighborliness.

There was also a dog. A big one, according to reports. And it wasn't on a leash. No one could describe it exactly because apparently the man and dog walked only in the middle of the night. And that in itself spurred more talk. Sometimes her small, eccentric town reminded her of a game she used to play when a child. Someone would whisper to the person next to her, and the secret would go around a circle, being embellished all along the way until a mouse turned into bigfoot.

As the beleaguered mayor of Covenant Falls, she didn't need this nonsense today. Not when this afternoon there was an informal council meeting. The council planned to discuss hiring a new police chief within the month. The council wanted to name one of the current officers, Sam Clark.

Over her dead body.

She looked at her watch. She had a few more minutes. She called down to Merry, who served as both city clerk and bookkeeper. "Have you heard anything from the county about a change in ownership on the Hannity property?"

"Not yet," Merry said, "but a Mr. Manning was in here around noon, asking about building permits for a porch. I told him we needed proof of ownership first, and he said he would provide it. He also wanted a copy of the property survey. I was so busy with the tax bills, I asked if it would be okay if I got it later in the day. He said yes, and he would be back tomorrow afternoon."

"Why didn't you tell me?"

"You were at lunch, then I was swamped with those bills."

"How was he?"

"Polite enough, although he didn't talk much. Looked a bit rough, but I liked him."

Eve had to smile. She had yet to find someone Merry didn't like.

She would probably like Genghis Khan. But it made Eve feel better. Obviously he was no squatter if he wanted a building permit and a land survey.

Ordinarily, she would have asked Tom MacGuire to quietly check out the newcomer.

He had been police chief for the three years since her father had been killed, and had been with the county sheriff's department as head of detectives before that. He was genuinely kind as well as efficient. But he was at home today, and she really didn't trust his officers to handle the matter with any finesse.

That drew her back to her immediate problem. Tom planned to resign because of heart problems. Finding someone to replace him was daunting, especially when small-town politics entered into the equation. There were less than three thousand permanent residents, and policing usually involved speeders, bar brawls and domestic conflicts. But there was the occasional fatal accident, lost child or robbery. She needed officers with diplomacy for domestic problems, and experience and judgment for the others. Tom had all that, and the affection and respect of the community. But he'd had a second heart attack, and his wife insisted he retire.

The problem was the city couldn't pay enough to attract someone like Tom. He'd served because he loved Covenant Falls. He was also a second father to Eve and honorary grandfather to her son, and she wasn't going to risk his life by trying to keep him.

She picked up her iPad and made her way to the small council chamber. Maybe she would visit the stranger in the morning. Quiet the rumor mill.

JOSH WORKED ALL morning on the interior of the cabin, and was just finishing cleaning the last room. The needed repairs were endless; the more he cleaned, the more problems he found. But he welcomed the work.

He'd temporarily fixed the roof and scraped most of the paint from the walls of the main room. He had to patch holes and sand rough spots, then prime the walls before painting.

He'd cleaned the windows, although he wasn't sure that had been a good idea. Blinds were a necessity since the community was so interested in his affairs, but the local hardware store had none that fit.

He also needed furniture. All he had now was a folding bed, a cheap chest of drawers, the cooler and an old sofa that had somehow survived years of neglect in the cabin. Probably only the fact that it was alligator ugly kept it from disappearing with the other stuff.

But even as it was now, the cabin suited him. It was as broken as him and Amos, and the work kept him from thinking. Remembering.

He quit at midnight. The cabin was hot, but nothing close to the brain-searing heat in Iraq and Afghanistan. His T-shirt was drenched with sweat, some from the heat, some from work and the rest from the pain that never left him.

Josh ran his fingers over his cheeks. Stubble partially covered a scar. It wasn't vanity that made him cover it, but he didn't like questions and he sure as hell didn't want sympathy. He didn't deserve it. He'd been team leader and had lost eight of ten men. Their faces haunted him every night.

He grabbed a beer and went to the window that overlooked the lake and considered his future. The army had given him the only family he'd ever had, and the Rangers had given him pride and purpose and confidence. And then three months ago, he'd been discharged with several useless medals and a bum leg. Bitterness—and drink—had almost destroyed him until he'd finally found Amos. Then he had a new mission. Dave had asked one thing of him before that last mission, almost as if he knew he would die. He wanted Josh to do what he could to help Amos, the military dog Dave had handled for four years.

He was doing a pretty damn poor job of that one. Amos usually ignored food and ate the minimum to stay alive even when Josh tried to tempt him with steak.

"We're a great pair," he told Amos, hoping for a reaction. A thump of a tail. A lifting of an ear. Anything.

Nothing. Just that empty stare.

He went out onto the porch. Clouds nearly hid a new moon and most of the evening stars. He smelled rain, and a cool breeze brushed over him.

Time to walk Amos. He preferred walking late in the night when no one else was around. He went back inside and called to the dog.

"Duty time," he said. Dave's words every time they went on a mission. He remembered when Amos had snapped to attention, eager to go. But now he stood slowly. Years of training said obey, but that was all he did. There was no joy in it. Only reluctance to leave a safe place.

Canine PTSD, according to the diagnosis at the Daniel E. Holland Military Working Dog Hospital at Lackland Air Force Base. Josh was told that after Dave's death, the dog had refused to obey any orders and cowered when approached. But Josh thought the behavior resulted as much from a broken heart as PTSD. Dave and Amos had been inseparable from the day they were teamed.

"Amos," he said with more authority, and the dog finally moved to his side. Progress. Small, maybe, but progress nonetheless.

With the moon entirely blocked now, the night was black. There was no light, but neither of them needed it. Josh's eyes were trained to see in the dark, or maybe he'd been born with that gift. He'd always been able to see better than his team members. They always said he was more cat than human, both for his night vision and the speed with which he could move.

With Amos plodding stoically at his heel, Josh followed Lake Road to where it ended in a path. He no longer moved like a cat, smooth and fast. Hell, an eighty-year-old great-grandmother could beat him in a foot race.

He walked until he feared his leg wouldn't make it back, then turned toward the cabin. He would read until his eyes closed. Maybe tonight he could actually sleep. Maybe.

CHAPTER TWO

JOSH SLASHED THROUGH the weeds as though they were the enemy. One particularly tall one came in for special attention. *Whack!*

"Wow," said a voice from behind him. "You really have it in for that poor weed."

He swung around, the scythe in his hands swinging with him, and found himself face-to-face with an attractive woman. He was really slipping if someone could move in behind him without his notice. He hadn't even heard a vehicle approaching. His attention had been riveted on clearing a path to an overgrown brick barbecue pit in back of the cabin. As far as he could tell, it was one of the few undamaged fixtures on the property.

He had gotten up at dawn. Made coffee, poured himself a cup then lured Amos outside. He'd instinctively started pulling the weeds that surrounded and nearly covered the pit. Finding it hopeless, he found the scythe he'd purchased the day before along with a number of other tools. Someone might have been mowing the front but they sure as hell hadn't cut the back for a long time. It was snake heaven.

"I didn't mean to startle you," the newcomer said,

and he realized he must have been staring at her. "I rang the bell," she continued, "but when no one answered I decided to try back here."

He went still and studied her. She didn't wilt under his gaze. A lot of people did. The lady yesterday certainly had.

"I wasn't expecting anyone," he said, hoping she would get the message, although she was certainly younger and prettier than his previous visitors. He rubbed his dirty hands against his equally dirty jeans. "What time is it?"

"Nine, or thereabouts," she said.

He scowled.

"Now I know why June ran away yesterday," the woman said, her eyes filled with something like bemused curiosity as her gaze ran over his sweaty T-shirt, stained jeans and, last, the sharp tool in his hands. Her eyes were hazel with flecks of green and gold. Mischief danced in them.

Damn, but she was fine to look at. He didn't much like the sudden hot rush of blood through his veins. He didn't need that. Not now. "I don't seem to have the same effect on you," he said wryly.

"No," she said. "Takes more than a scowl, although you have a good one. Do you practice it?"

He ignored the question and asked one of his own. "What *does* frighten you, then?"

"Not a Weedwacker. I approve. This place has been an eyesore."

He walked to the cabin's back door and placed

the scythe against it. He didn't need this new... distraction. He had a full day's work ahead. He had an appointment with the only vet in miles. He also intended to buy more tools and paint. Maybe he would get some fishing gear, as well. Once the barbecue pit was cleaned he could grill fish on it. He was growing tired of cold cuts from the cooler.

"You didn't say why you're here," he said. It annoyed him that he sounded boorish. But then he'd never been good at conversation. Surprisingly, the mischief didn't leave her eyes. "No," she agreed, "I didn't."

He liked the fact she wasn't intimidated. He couldn't say she was a beauty, not in the classical sense. Her features were not that regular. The wide hazel eyes went with a pug nose and high cheekbones. Her hair, the color of rich mahogany, fell to just below her shoulders. It was held back from her face by a clasp. Simple, but on her it looked good. His gaze fell lower. She wore a sky-blue sleeveless vest over a short-sleeve white cotton blouse and dark blue slacks. Neat. Practical in the heat, and yet they complemented her body. Which was fine, too. Real fine. Not reed thin like too many women these days. There were curves in all the right places. He suspected she had great legs under those slacks.

The worn briefcase she carried didn't quite go with the rest of her. An insurance saleswoman? That would be the ultimate joke. "You another member of the welcome wagon, then?" he said, sarcasm coloring the question. Sarcasm was his armor these days.

"No," she said.

"God, I hope you're not with the government."

"Hate to disappoint you, but actually I am." She thrust out her hand. "Eve Douglas. I have the dubious honor of being mayor."

He was stunned for a moment. Then he shrugged, brushed his right hand against his jeans to shed some of the dirt and sweat and took her outstretched one. If she didn't care about getting dirty...

A mistake. Her hand was slender in his large one, yet he felt calluses on her palm. That surprised him. So did the strength in her fingers. He found himself holding them longer than necessary as the very air around them seemed to spark with electricity.

He didn't like—or trust—the hot awareness he felt, the instantaneous attraction blazing between them. Or was it all on his part?

He didn't think so. Not with that startled, puzzled look in her eyes. He released his hold quickly, the warmth from her hand flowing up his arm. Their gazes met.

He *was* intrigued. She was holding her ground. He imagined he looked his worst, and his worst could be formidable as hell, or so he'd been told. But it didn't seem to faze her.

He waited, not speaking. A form of hostile intimidation, a psychologist told him when Josh perfected it during unwanted sessions at the hospital. Now it was for an entirely different reason.

She finally broke the silence. Her voice sounded stilted, unsteady, and he realized she was as shaken as he. "Merry, the city clerk, told me you had been in and wanted a copy of your property survey. She felt bad she didn't have time to find it then, so I said I would bring it over this morning. Save you a trip back into town. I also want to welcome you."

"Do you welcome every new resident this way?"

"Eventually. It's why I'm mayor. That and the hard truth that no one else wanted the job."

She said it wryly, and he found himself liking her. Combine that with the heat still lingering in his belly and he knew he was in trouble. He recalled how she introduced herself. Not as Mayor Eve Douglas, but simply as Eve Douglas who happened to be mayor. It said something about her that the title was of lesser importance than who she was.

He was only too aware of her eyes and the way they lit up when she smiled. He tried to ignore them. "I had a visit yesterday from a lady. I think I frightened her. Didn't mean to. She woke me up and scared the hell out of my dog, and I was a bit aggravated. Perhaps in the role of mayor, you can suggest that I came here for a little solitude."

"People in Covenant Falls are friendly. We like to think it's a plus, but obviously you don't," she said. "I'll try to put out the word that you're the hermit type and value your privacy." She said it without judgment and added with that quick, infectious smile, "Can't promise it'll work."

Concentrate, Josh. She was too damned disarming. He glanced down at her hands. She had a ring on her finger.

But it had been a damned long time since…

Down, boy.

He jerked back to the moment. "Mrs. Douglas," he replied. "You said you brought my property survey. And the building permit?"

She looked startled and for a fleeting second he wondered whether she'd felt the same awareness that was galloping through his body. Then she gave him a more cautious smile. "The survey was easy. There's a small problem with the building permit."

She met his gaze directly, and he noted that she was tall, only four inches or so shorter than his own just over six-foot-three height. Perfect height to kiss without contorting himself. A wisp of wind caught her hair and turned a curl loose. He found himself longing to tuck it back in. To feel that smooth skin and see whether her hair was as silky as it looked.

She sure as hell wasn't like any mayor he'd ever seen.

"And the building permit?" he asked, trying to divert the thoughts. *Mind over matter. Or body.*

"The city clerk said you didn't bring a copy of the deed, and she checked with the county. The property is listed as belonging to David Hannity."

"Dave Hannity is dead," he said, barely keeping

his voice steady. Even after nearly eight months, the words hurt like hell. "He left the cabin to me. An attorney in the county seat—Laine Mabry—just settled probate. The deed should have been transferred by now. I'll check with him."

"Good. Once we have a copy of the deed, there shouldn't be a problem."

He expected her to leave then, but she didn't, and he was surprised he really didn't want her to go. She challenged him. Intrigued him. He really *had* been too long without a woman.

Her gaze rested for a moment on the scar on his face. He could tell from her expression that she wanted to ask more questions. Still, she refrained, and that interested him, too, as did the way she stood her ground despite his scowl and lack of manners.

"The survey?" he prompted, silently cursing himself.

She lifted the briefcase and steadied it on the brick barbecue pit. She opened it and fished out a large piece of rolled draft paper.

Their hands touched, and he felt a surge of electricity streak through him. She suddenly backed away and bumped against the barbecue pit. He automatically reached out, steadying her. She smelled like fresh flowers, and he felt the calluses on her hand again. Oddly enough, that was sexy to him. Damn if she wasn't sexy in every way.

He didn't let go, and she didn't pull away.

A flame leaped between them. He felt its heat sear

him. She leaned against him for the barest of seconds, then pulled away. Confusion suddenly clouded her eyes.

What in the hell just happened? He must be more nuts than usual. She wore a ring, and he never played in someone else's yard. Never. He'd seen too many guys open Dear John letters and knew what it did to them. He was no angel, but he'd sworn never to cause that kind of pain. And he didn't think much of a woman who could. Maybe that was why he always preferred one-night stands with unattached women.

She looked at him with wide eyes now. He watched as she tried to compose herself. When she finally spoke, there was a catch in her throat. "Dave Hannity... I knew him years ago. Not well. He was older. Then he just seemed to disappear...."

That brought him back to reality. Dave was a subject he couldn't—wouldn't—discuss.

"You said inherited," she continued. "What happened to him?"

"Does it matter?"

"It matters that I didn't know. I liked him. I know my husband did."

He didn't answer immediately, hoping his silence would send her away.

When it was clear that it wouldn't, he said simply, "He was in the army. He died in Afghanistan."

"He must have been a good friend," she said softly.

"Excuse me, Mayor Douglas, but I don't know why that's any of your business."

She stiffened. "You're right, of course, Mr. Manning. It's not." She started to turn, then swung back. "You said you have a dog."

"Is that against the law?" He bristled again.

"Of course not." Her smile faded. "But we do have some ordinances regarding animals," she continued after a few seconds, as if she'd caught her breath. "Dogs have to be on a leash or…"

"Under the voice control of an individual," he finished. "Amos is under voice control when we walk."

The colors of her eyes seemed to change with her emotions. "I hope you'll learn to like us," she said. There was a not-so-veiled challenge in her tone. She wasn't *all* sweetness. There was some spice, too.

"Not bloody likely," he muttered, using an expression he'd learned from British counterparts. It was, he felt, appropriate at the moment as he tried to tamp down that sexual electricity that still hovered in the air. She looked so damn…intriguing. He sensed there was fire under that proper facade. He saw flashes of it in her eyes.

He reminded himself that she was married. And, God help him, a mayor. He'd never liked authority of any kind. Even in the army, he'd been a maverick and probably wouldn't have lasted long if an officer hadn't seen his independence as something that could be useful in Special Forces.

Mayor Eve Douglas was the last thing he needed.

He turned and limped inside, leaving her standing there.

But despite himself, he watched her through the newly cleaned window as she walked, ramrod straight, toward an elderly pickup truck. She stepped gracefully into the truck, not an easy thing to do.

A mud-splattered pickup truck? The mayor? Of course, it was a small town, but...

None of his business. He turned away. He tried to channel the persisting need into anger. Anger came easily these days. Right now, it was all he had to hold on to.

He went into his bedroom, where Amos still lay under the bed. The dog hadn't even moved to see who was outside. A year ago, he would have been at full alert, eager and ready to inspect the newcomer.

The two of them were aliens in this place. They were military castoffs, and neither of them knew how to adapt. Josh lowered himself to the floor and sat next to the dog. He put his hand on Amos's back and rubbed it. He knew it would be plain hell getting up, but right now he figured they needed each other.

"What in the hell are we doing here?" he whispered.

After leaving Mr. Manning's property, Eve sat in her pickup for a while. Waiting...for what? Then she saw movement inside the cabin. Drat, what was she doing? She started the truck and drove out onto Lake Road, resisting the temptation to look back. One thing for sure, Josh Manning was no squatter.

From the look of him, and what little she'd seen of the cabin, he'd been working like a demon.

She wasn't sure what else he was. Her hand still burned from his touch, and her heart was hammering. She couldn't remember that ever happening before. She was just flustered, she assured herself. He'd been rude and abrupt and...overwhelming.

She saw him now as he'd stood whacking at weeds, the ridges of his muscles straining under the damp T-shirt that clung to him, his sandy hair uncombed. There had been something elemental about him, something untamed and restless, and yet she'd also sensed control when he went to the trouble to harness it.

His face, partially covered with a beard the color of gold, was hawklike with guarded emerald-green eyes that assessed her as if she was prey. She completely understood why June had been frightened. He had nearly apologized about June, but not quite. It was probably as much of an apology as anyone would receive.

But she hadn't been frightened. Stunned at her body's reactions to him, yes, but physically afraid? No.

And why did she still ache inside? She hadn't been attracted to another man since Russ died four years earlier, nor even before that. And this man was the polar opposite of her husband. Russ had been her best friend as well as lover: warm and funny and very easy to love. He'd been everyone's big brother, and his students adored him. This man was a hostile loner. And a rather unkempt one at that.

When she reached the road, she drove past a few houses, then stopped the truck. She tried to regain her composure. It wasn't easy. She'd never been so affected by a man, and it didn't make sense. It certainly wasn't because she was lonely. Although she missed Russ with all her heart, she had a good life with her son, Nick, their small ranch and her job.

Still, she couldn't deny the attraction that had streaked between them when he had taken her hand and steadied her. So much strength there.

Nonsense. She didn't believe in looks across a crowded room…or a weed patch. And it wasn't that she didn't have enough problems already.

She realized she hadn't seen the dog Marilyn had mentioned. And it *was* strange that a large dog would not have barked at a stranger's presence. But Joshua Manning knew the law, had obviously checked into it, and she had no legal reason to demand anything. Especially with only Marilyn's vivid imagination to go on.

Go. Just leave. She turned the key in the ignition, but her thoughts went back to when he'd mentioned Dave Hannity. There had been pain in his eyes. It had been there only for the briefest of seconds, but in that time she'd felt its impact.

He hadn't said so, but she was sure he'd been in the service. That was probably why he limped. There was still pain in that leg. She'd seen that, too. She'd seen it in Russ when he'd been recovering from a football injury to his knee, the one that had ended his career as a college quarterback.

She wanted to look back, but she was too far away now. Her world had just been rocked, and she didn't know why or how. She only knew she had to stay away from him. He aroused feelings she didn't want or need. Her fingers tightened around the steering wheel until they hurt. Then she drove toward the main road. Going to the office.

To a safe place.

CHAPTER THREE

WHEN EVE ARRIVED at the office, Tom was waiting for her. Although it was only midmorning, he looked tired.

His appearance worried her. "Should you be here?"

"I'm going crazy at home," he said. "Maggie's hovering around like I'm an invalid. Hell, Eve, I'm not ready for a rocking chair. Two days of doing nothing, and I'm going nuts. Besides, I'm still chief until you replace me."

Eve was torn. Tom had been her father's close friend for years, and as a detective with the county sheriff's department had investigated his murder three years ago. A native of Covenant Falls, he had taken her father's place as police chief after the funeral and hoped to find her father's murderers, but he hadn't. She knew he still fretted about that.

In those three years, he'd become even more a member of her family, rooting for Nick at Little League games, serving as her sounding board and being part of every family celebration. He was someone she didn't want to lose. *Couldn't lose.* But she also knew him well enough to realize he would not do well sitting at home.

"You look a bit flushed yourself," he said. "Are you and Nick all right?"

She feared the flush was deepening. "Guess it's from running around this morning. And Nick is fine. Only two more weeks of school, then I'll be worrying all day long. I can't keep him off that bike."

"Your dad used to say the same about you."

She didn't have an answer for that.

He changed the subject. "I hear you couldn't agree on a replacement for me."

She sighed. The meeting yesterday had been contentious. One of the deputies vying for the job was the nephew of the council president. "In the first place, no one could replace you. But then Al, Ed and Nancy want Sam. I don't think he's ready. He's a little too fast to assume the worst." She didn't add that her husband had coached Sam Clark on the Covenant Falls High football team and thought him a bully.

"I agree," Tom said. "He has seniority over the other officers, but I purposely didn't promote him to sergeant because I question his judgment." He sighed heavily. "I think your father hired him for the same reason you have to keep him. You need Al's support for your budget, and he controls three of the five votes on the council. Or, I should say, owns them. I could keep Sam under control, but if we can't find someone too strong for the council to ignore, you'll have a fight on your hands."

Eve knew he was right. "You just have to find me

that person at a salary we can pay. We couldn't afford you if you didn't have the county retirement."

Tom shrugged. "You don't get paid nearly enough for all the work you do. Grady Dillard just sat in that chair and drank with his cronies. You've put life back in Covenant Falls."

"Our newest resident isn't very impressed." The words escaped before she could stop them. Why did Joshua Manning linger in her head?

Linger? No, dominate. It was annoying. Confounding. Maddening.

Tom raised an eyebrow and nearly looked like the man he'd been before all the heart attacks. "The guy at the Hannity place?"

"You've heard?"

"Marilyn called me, too. I don't take her too seriously." His face hardened. "Also had a burglary call this morning. That's why I came in."

"Where?"

"Maude's. Someone broke into her diner last night. Took the late-night cash. About three hundred dollars or so, she said."

Eve groaned. If she hadn't stopped at the Hannity place, she would have heard the news sooner. The amount wasn't much to a lot of people, but it was to Maude. And it was the first burglary in months. There had been vandalism in some of the cabins around the lake, but nothing more than that. Not in the past year.

"Could be teenagers," Tom said, "but most of the locals are good kids."

She suddenly knew who would be blamed. "Any suspects?"

He shrugged. "Not yet, but rumors are circulating, probably helped by Sam. He wants to talk to the new guy. I said no. I wanted to talk to you first."

"His name is Joshua Manning, and I talked to him this morning. He didn't say much, except he inherited the cabin from David Hannity, and that David had been in the army. I had the impression he's ex-military, too, although he didn't say so. He's fixing up the place. I can't see him breaking into a restaurant for a few hundred dollars."

"You have good instincts, Eve, but if you want, I'll quietly check him out."

Eve hesitated. She was reluctant to invade the man's privacy, and if it wasn't for the burglary, she would have said no. But she knew how rumors spread in town. Too many would put together the arrival of an unfriendly and admittedly scruffy-looking resident with the first major crime of the year. Better to quash them fast.

"You said you thought he was former military. Why?" Tom was a Vietnam veteran, and she knew he had a soft spot for other present and former servicemen.

She shrugged. Casually, she hoped. "He's not very talkative. In fact, he avoided saying much of anything about himself. Said it was none of my business, but everything points to it."

Tom looked quizzical. "He said that to you, and you didn't bash him?"

"Well, he was right. It really wasn't my business, and bashing wouldn't be very becoming of a mayor, would it?" She decided to change the subject. "But he does have a pronounced limp and a fairly recent scar on his face. It follows that he served with David."

"Or he's a relative," Tom said. "Didn't I tell you not to take things for granted?"

Something else she had learned as mayor. She nodded. "That could be." She winced at the memory of how Joshua Manning had controlled the conversation and how completely inept she'd felt. She hated that.

Not to mention that she still felt all tingly inside when she thought about him. That was unacceptable.

"Want *me* to pay a visit?"

"I think he's had enough of visits. Why don't you just check with the attorney who handled the probate? You know everyone in this county. And run a quick background check. That should satisfy Sam." She didn't like the idea of having to satisfy Sam, but she knew him well enough to realize he might go snooping on his own. Especially if Tom wasn't around to control him.

Tom nodded. "I'll do that."

"I don't want you to do too much."

"Just a few phone calls. I swear."

"If you feel…"

"I'll call the doc," he replied.

She hesitated, worried about burdening him more, then said, "And while you're at it, could you find out what happened to Dave Hannity? Russ used to run with him, and I would like to know. His disappearance was one of the town's big mysteries after his uncle drowned."

"Will do. I'm kinda interested myself."

"Maggie's not going to be happy about you sticking around here," Eve said, stating the obvious.

"I'll take it easy. I'll also put out the word to some of my friends across the state that we're looking for a police chief. Maybe someone who wants a second career in a nice quiet town will turn up. Having a good mayor is another benefit."

"I'll miss you around here," Eve said, hugging him.

"I'll be around. I don't plan to kick the bucket yet. I sent Sam out to Maude's. Maybe he can find something. At least it will keep him busy and out of Manning's way." He didn't sound hopeful as he rose slowly from the chair and walked out without his usual bounce.

She closed her eyes for a moment. She wasn't sure she should have encouraged him to make a few calls or delay his retirement even for a short time. But Tom was like an old warhorse, and she couldn't help but think he would live longer if he had a purpose.

She looked at the pile of papers on her desk. She had to work on the budget for the next fiscal year. Too little money. Too many needs. And in the current economy, a tax increase was out of the question. Her people were all struggling. A little juggling here, a small cut there. She just wished that Joshua Manning's face didn't keep intruding on the pages.

AFTER THE MAYOR left, Josh refreshed his coffee and fixed a bowl of cereal for both Amos and himself.

He had an appointment in an hour with the only veterinarian in the area. She'd already been contacted by the Lackland AFB veterinarian and had been faxed Amos's records, but Josh wanted to see her, take her measure. Hopefully, she might have some suggestions to help Amos.

He took a shower to cool the heat that still bedeviled him after his encounter with the mayor. A cold one. Then a hot one. After some repairs, the hot water heater was one of the few things that actually worked in the cabin. Then he dressed in a clean pair of jeans and soft cotton shirt.

He thought about shaving, then decided against it. He coaxed Amos out to his Jeep, but once in the passenger side the dog hopped back out and huddled next to the door. His entire body trembled, and Josh ached looking at him.

"Okay," he said. "I'll try to talk her into coming out here." He opened the front door and Amos headed for the bedroom and safety under the bed.

It was just as well. He had other errands to run. He needed paint for the walls and boards for the porch, as well as nails, screws and more large trash bags.

His first stop was to the vet. When he walked in, a bell jingled and a feminine voice from the back told him to take a seat.

He was too restless to sit. He walked around the office and peered at the bulletin board. Horses for sale. A lost dog. Puppies up for adoption. Advertisements for tick and flea medicine. After several minutes, an elderly woman holding an equally elderly poodle came out of the back.

He opened the door for her, got a "thank you, young man" for his effort.

"Hi," said a voice behind him. He turned around and faced an attractive woman in jeans and a white coat. "I'm Stephanie Phillips. Just call me Stephanie. You must be Mr. Manning." She looked around. "Where's Amos?"

"He objected," Josh said. "He started shaking, and I...wondered whether you could come out to the cabin." He hesitated, then added, "He was a basket case when I picked him up at Lackland and during the drive here. The only place he seems to feel even a little safe is the cabin. I understand the vets at the dog training center at Lackland sent you his records."

"They did. Extreme anxiety," she said. "Physically healthy, but Amos wouldn't respond to any trainers. Practically goes over the fence when there's lightning. Rest of the time huddles in the safest place he can find."

He nodded. "That's about it. I can take him for

short walks at night when there's no traffic. Most of the time he stays under my bed."

"Appetite?"

"He eats enough to stay alive and that's about it. This from a dog who used to gobble food like it was his last meal."

"You knew him before…?"

He nodded. "His handler was in my unit."

"Was?"

"He was killed ten months ago." It hurt like hell to talk about it, but talk he must. *For Amos.* "He was… close to his handler. Because we were often on the move and there weren't always kennels, Amos usually slept near him. Even when there were kennels, Dave found a way to keep Amos at his side."

She waited for him to say more. He was reluctant, but he knew he had to explain everything. *That's all that matters now. The promise.* "I was wounded, and Amos's handler was killed in the same engagement. I was sent to a hospital, but I heard from other members of the team that Amos had been sent to Lackland. Nearly starved to death."

"But he *does* respond to you?"

"Barely. Sometimes."

"After Lackland contacted me," she said, "I did some research on canine PTSD. It's not uncommon. I imagine it's worse when the handler is killed. Dogs grieve, too." She paused, then said, "I can come over in the morning. I have a mare about to foal this afternoon, and I'm not sure how long it will take."

He nodded. "I'll be at the cabin all day." He gave her his cell number, only the third person to have it. His shrink at the military hospital was one—he'd promised—and the other was Dave's attorney.

"I look forward to meeting Amos. I've never treated a military dog."

"One other thing. I would appreciate you not speaking to anyone in town about Amos's condition. People might think he's dangerous. He's not. I think it's more that he's missing his...handler. Amos wasn't with us the day Dave died. As far as he knows, he was abandoned."

"How long was Amos with him?"

"Four years."

The phone rang and she picked it up. "Excuse me," she said. "I have to answer this."

She walked to the other side of the room, said something then returned.

"The foal is coming. I have to go. I'll be over tomorrow."

He nodded, encouraged by her interest and questions.

He left and headed for the hardware store. He'd been there before to get tools.

Four people were in the store, two of them talking to an elderly man at the counter. A younger one had been there during his previous visits. Father and son, he surmised.

He went directly to the section with paint. He found a primer, then selected a color from the limited selection and took the cans to the counter. He looked at some thick pieces of lumber to temporarily repair the porch.

"Do you deliver?"

"Sure do."

"I live…"

"I know. End of Lake Road."

He should have known. "Maybe you'd better add an electric saw," he said.

"Got a real good one. On sale, too."

Josh nodded.

The man held out his hand. "Glad to have you in the community. I'm Calvin Wilson, and I own the store. Me and my son."

Josh had no choice but to shake hands. "I met him on my previous visit."

Wilson totaled the tab. Josh paid with his bank card and started to pick up the paint cans.

"My son will help you carry everything out," Wilson offered.

He wanted to say yes. The damn leg was hurting like hell after his work in the backyard. But he'd never asked for help before and he wasn't going to start now. "I can do it," he said, then added a belated, "Thanks."

He was suffering when he got everything into the dusty Jeep Wrangler, and he realized he'd been a damn fool. But he wasn't ready to depend on anyone else. His entire life had been built on self-sufficiency.

He'd never needed anyone, not since he was ten years old and he'd taken care of his mother rather than the other way around.

He sure as hell wasn't ready for women waking him with brownies or a mayor wandering into his backyard when he was working.

Even a very pretty mayor. To be honest, it wasn't her he didn't like, but rather the superheated attraction that had sprung so quickly between them. It scared the hell out of him. The last thing he needed now was complications.

He glanced at his watch. After two, and he was starved. Maybe he would try the diner down the street. Shouldn't be too many people there at this time. And he was tired of cereal and sandwiches.

He passed Monroe Real Estate and Insurance Company and glanced at the photos in the front window: several farms for sale, a ranch five miles out of town and a hunting cabin in the mountains. There were also several small homes.

Once he finished fixing the cabin, an advertisement for it would probably go up there, as well.

He stopped to pick up a newspaper from a rack in front of Maude's Diner. Reading usually kept people away. As he'd hoped, the restaurant was nearly empty. A couple of elderly men sat at the counter with coffee and two young guys sat in a booth chowing down burgers. A young woman behind a counter eyed him as he entered and hurried over as he sat down. "Good afternoon," she said brightly, holding out a paper menu.

He nodded and declined the menu. "You have a steak?"

"We do. Several of them. The sirloin is the best."

"Then I want one, rare, and a second one to go," he said.

"Comes with two sides. Fries or mashed potatoes, green beans, salad, corn, squash."

"Fries," he said. "And beans."

"And with the order to go?"

"Just a steak," he said. "Also rare."

She nodded and hurried off. He took up the newspaper. A weekly, and not much in it. The restaurant door opened, and he looked up. A youngish man in a deputy's uniform walked in. He came to Josh's booth, his eyes cold. "You must be the one living out at the lake."

Josh didn't answer. Just waited.

"Had a burglary here last night," the deputy said.

Josh raised an eyebrow and shrugged. "It happens."

"Not until you came to town. Mind telling me where you were last night?"

"I do," Josh said. "Unless you have more of a reason than I just moved here."

The deputy put his hand on his holstered gun.

Josh locked gazes with him. The door opened again, and Josh watched the mayor walk in. His stomach muscles tightened as she moved toward them, a frown wrinkling her brow.

"Mr. Manning," she acknowledged, then turned to the deputy. "Sam," she said, "Find anything?"

"No, ma'am. I just arrived."

"Then I suggest you talk to Maude."

"I was just asking this…person where he was last night. He refused to answer."

"Why don't you see if you can find some evidence first?" she asked patiently.

Anger sparked in his eyes, but he turned away and went to the back of the restaurant.

"I'm sorry about that," she said. "Sam's a little eager. There was a burglary here last night, and we're all a little protective of Maude. She cooks the best food around."

"Glad to hear it," he said evenly. "About the food, I mean."

"Your first time at Maude's?"

"You don't already know that?" he retorted.

"Well, I know you just bought paint in Calvin's store," she admitted. "I thought you might come here."

"And…"

"I wanted to explain about this morning. No one's lived in that cabin for a long time and…" She faltered as her gaze met his. He was suddenly warm, too warm. And he saw her stiffening as if bracing against something.

An almost palpable tension leaped between them. Time seemed to slow, and he wasn't aware of anyone else in the room. Heat simmered inside him like the sun hitting desert rocks.

The moment shattered when the waitress shoved a cup of coffee before him, as well as a napkin and utensils.

"How's Nick?" the waitress asked the mayor.

The mayor's face lit with that infectious smile, breaking the tension. "Doing great. He's going to pitch tomorrow night. You going to be there with Jamie?"

"Wouldn't miss it." The waitress grinned down at Josh. "Our boys play Little League together."

Josh stiffened. God, he should have remembered that ring. Not only was she married, but she also had a son.

He turned back to his paper. The signal was undeniable. *Leave me alone.*

The mayor started to turn away. "Enjoy your meal," she told him. Then said, "I'll see you tomorrow" to the waitress.

She left, and some of the light seemed to leave the room with her.

EVE WAITED AT the school to pick up Nick. It was two miles to her house and she'd resisted his pleas to ride his bike. She wasn't quite ready for that yet.

She needed the time to think. She was still unsettled by the meeting with Joshua Manning. Something slammed into her each time they met. She felt tongue-tied and unsure, and she hated that feeling.

She certainly didn't understand why she'd felt compelled to go into the diner when she'd seen Josh Manning inside.

Or why she'd lied when she went in.... She hadn't meant to apologize at all, but she'd been drawn inside like metal to a magnet. And then she'd just uttered the first thing that came to her mind. *Stupid.*

She told herself it was just to prove to herself that the attraction in the morning was her imagination. Or something fleeting.

It hadn't been, and that terrified her.

The sound of yelling interrupted her as kids poured through the school doors. Nick came running when he saw Miss Mollie—who could miss the old pickup?—and climbed in next to her.

"Got an A on my essay," he said with a relieved grin. "That means a dollar, right?"

"That's for an A on a report card," she replied, suddenly cheery that the love of her life was here. It had been a long time—more than four years to be exact—since he had stood beside her as his father was buried.

She put her arm around him and kissed the top of his head. She wanted to do more. She wanted to hug him with all the strength she had, but she knew he wouldn't like that. Not here.

She started the car and tried to relax. Just having Nick next to her made her feel better. Cleared her mind. He was everything that was important. And he was so like his father. Considerate, likable and always ready for a challenge.

She sighed, listening to Nick chatter about the essay. It had been about his father, and at first he had been reluctant to write it. But once he'd started he'd written like a whirlwind. He hadn't let her read it, although she usually helped with homework.

"Can I read it when we get home?" she asked.

He went silent for a moment, then nodded.

"I know you didn't want me to read it before you turned it in."

"'Cause I was afraid it wasn't good enough."

"And your teacher said it was?"

He nodded again.

Her heart nearly burst with love for him, and regret that he'd lost the father he loved so much. It was so wrong. So unexpected. A tear slipped down her face and she rubbed it away, relieved that Nick was looking in the other direction.

They were home in a few moments. They lived two miles from the heart of town and one mile from the lake. She and Russ had saved during the first years of their marriage, then bought a five-acre piece of land inside the city limits. Russ and his buddies had built a ranch house and barn, and she still had the two horses they'd bought together. She also boarded Stephanie's horse, which paid for her many vet bills.

A cacophony came from the house as Nick jumped out of the truck and waited impatiently as she unlocked the door. Nick opened it, and four dogs, barking madly, rushed out.

Braveheart, a mismatched pit-bull mix, hung back as usual. Badly scarred and terrified of people, he'd been found half-dead alongside the road. Nick had named him Braveheart because he thought the encouragement might help cure his fear.

Miss Marple—the part beagle and who knew what else—charged to the front. Eve couldn't help but grin at Nick's naming processes. Miss Marple was so named because she was always on the prowl for a misplaced sock. She, too, had been found along the road, but, unlike Braveheart, she didn't lack self-confidence. Captain Hook, a three-legged Chihuahua mix, added her high, piercing voice. Fancy, who was anything but Fancy, was probably the plainest dog Eve had ever seen, but she was also the most loving. Inside was Dizzy, a coon cat that spent his time chasing his tail.

Nick had named them all after much thought, and it said much about him the way he turned their weaknesses into strengths. Her son had been boisterous and curious and active until his father died. Then he climbed inside himself, but now he seemed to be emerging again. She watched as he gave each dog a moment of attention, then ran to the barn, the troop of dogs following him.

Lord, but he filled her with joy. She ached with it. She wanted to hold him so tight nothing could ever harm him. She knew how fragile life was. Russell had been all strength one day, and the next...

It didn't bear thinking about. Watching the dogs following Nick as if he was the Pied Piper reminded her that she hadn't seen the dog at Joshua Manning's home, the one that had Marilyn so upset. She suspected Marilyn used the dog only as an excuse to learn more about her neighbor. To tell the truth, once Josh Manning had mentioned voice control, she'd relaxed. She hadn't seen an ill-treated dog on voice control. And, truth be told, as rude as Josh Manning had been, she hadn't sensed meanness in him.

Who was he? If she was right about him being a soldier, it followed that he wouldn't want to talk about his experiences. But he seemed to carry it to the extreme. Or maybe she was wrong. Maybe he'd met Dave Hannity somewhere else. Or, as Tom had surmised, maybe he was a relative.

She wished she could remember more about Dave Hannity. His family had spent summers at their cabin on the lake. She'd met him at the annual Fourth of July picnic and other summer events for several years. He'd been a swimmer and runner, and Russ had known him better than she.

Now David, too, was dead, apparently in the service of his country.

They had lost other young residents in Iraq and Afghanistan. Too many for a small town, but then the military attracted small-town kids. There weren't many other opportunities.

As for Mr. Manning and Dave Hannity, maybe Tom would have some answers tomorrow, and she could reassure Manning's neighbors.

His image sprung into her mind again. His face was hard, the angles stark. It was…more interesting than handsome. There was a presence about him, an I-don't-give-a-damn attitude that perversely intrigued her.

"Mom, I'm hungry." She hadn't seen Nick approach from the back of the barn. Again he was followed by his four little tagalongs. She looked at him and hoped *he* would never have to go to war. She hugged him—hard—until he wriggled free. She didn't want to let him go. She never wanted to let him go. She wanted to protect him against grief and loss and disappointments.

He'd already had too many.

And, she suspected, so had Joshua Manning.

CHAPTER FOUR

JOSH WOKE WITH a start. Sunlight was streaming though his windows.

He stretched and glanced at the clock. A little after 0700 hours. It was the first time in days that he'd slept more than four hours without the nightmare. Or night sweats.

But then he had worked late into the night, first replacing the rotten boards on the porch, then scraping paint from the walls of the main room. Work, it seemed, was the best sleeping aid.

He thought about the day ahead and the growing list of things to do. Not for the first time, he wondered why in the hell he didn't just walk away.

He heard the soft snoring of Amos and knew why. Amos needed a safe place where he could learn to play. Learn to feel safe. Being dragged from one temporary place to another would not be helpful.

But, he admitted to himself, maybe part of him wanted to stay, too. A part hidden deep inside. He'd never belonged to anything but the army and his buddies, and that, he'd learned, had no permanence.

He needed a challenge, and the cabin was certainly a challenge. He hadn't known what to expect, but he sure as hell hadn't anticipated the amount of work needed. He welcomed it. Bringing order to chaos was something he knew.

And once this place was fixed, it wouldn't be half-bad. He envisioned a large porch that overlooked the lake and the mountains beyond. But then what?

Josh turned to the edge of the bed and ran his hand over Amos's back as he'd seen Dave do countless times. Amos would usually roll over and beg a belly rub. But Amos ignored the overture, merely looked at him with a gaze that held a sorrow and confusion that broke Josh's heart.

He'd read and heard about dogs like Amos. Greyfriars Bobby for one, the little Scottish terrier who wouldn't leave his master's grave until he died, or more recently tales of other service dogs who'd mourned for their handlers.

"Aw, Amos," he said. "One of these days you'll offer your belly to me, too."

He hoped. It was the least he could do for Dave—Dave, who'd had his own demons. Maybe that was why they'd bonded as much as two loners could.

Time to get up. The vet—Stephanie—was coming today. He needed to clean up as much as possible. He stood slowly, ignoring the pain that flared. He needed to do the exercises he'd neglected the past few days. But first Amos had to go outside.

"Come on, Amos. Latrine time." Josh pulled on a pair of jeans and opened the door. Amos reluctantly left the safety of the cabin and did his business, then returned immediately to the door. No sniffing. Or playing or wriggling with delight.

"What am I, chopped liver?" he asked Amos as he opened the door. Amos didn't bother to answer as he slunk inside.

Josh stayed outside and soaked in the cool breeze. The sun was a huge golden ball rising in the east, and the fresh, spicy scent of evergreens filled the air. He was beginning to understand the appeal of the cabin.

He needed his coffee. He brewed his in an old-fashioned percolator he had found in the general store. He'd had enough bad coffee to appreciate the good. He poured cereal into a bowl, got milk from the cooler and knew he had to do something about a fridge.

Josh spent the next thirty minutes on the exercises prescribed by his doctor and physical therapist. His leg would never be what it once was. New manufactured parts had taken the place of old ones, particularly in his ankle. There had been three operations, including two bone transplants and one to fuse his left foot where the main nerve had been severed. He would never have the old mobility, but he was grateful for what he did have. A lot of guys in the hospital had much, much less, and their courage was humbling.

He was sweating when he finished. He took a hot shower, then dressed in a clean pair of jeans and polo shirt before the vet arrived. The cabin was bad enough without his looking like a deadbeat. Amos could still be taken away from him if the army thought he wasn't being treated properly.

Josh stared at his image in the mirror and thought about the visit from the mayor. He needed a haircut. Bad. There were touches of gray in his sandy hair although he was only in his mid-thirties. Lines had deepened around his eyes and tightened around his mouth. He looked tired and cynical. *Face it. You look like hell.* It hadn't mattered for months but, for some reason, it did now.

His cell phone rang. He recognized the number immediately. His attorney. He'd called him yesterday about the deed.

"I got your message," Laine Mabry said. "The deed was been received by the clerk's office but not recorded. I raised hell and today it's official. I faxed a copy to the mayor and I'm sending you a copy."

"Thanks."

"There's something else," the attorney said. "The police chief in Covenant Falls called me. We're old friends. He wanted information about you."

"And what did you tell him?"

"That as far as I knew you were an upstanding citizen and anything else involved attorney/client privilege, as per your instructions."

"The police chief, huh? What time would that have been?"

"About eleven yesterday."

So the call was made after the mayor's visit. He felt like he had been kicked in a tender region. Yeah, he had been a smart-ass, but he'd liked her and thought she felt the same. More than liked her. If she hadn't been wearing a ring…

But then what would she want with a broken-down soldier with few prospects? "Thanks," he said.

There was a pause. "It's your business, but why not just satisfy curiosity? People in small towns are naturally curious."

"There's things I want to forget, that's why," he said. "I sure as hell don't want anyone to thank me for my service, not when it killed my best friend and a bunch of other really good guys."

"Understood," his attorney said, and hung up.

Josh put the cell in his pocket and wondered who else the police chief had contacted.

Maybe he shouldn't be surprised. He'd gone out of his way to be rude and avoid people. Rudeness hadn't worked with the mayor, and he'd found himself enjoying the verbal duel. And he was intrigued with her… even though she wasn't his type at all.

He tried to brush away the attraction he'd felt for the mayor, tried to do the same with the arousal that had an irritating way of returning when he thought about her.

It was nothing but the fact he'd been too long without female company.

The list. Back to the list. He had finished scraping paint and filling in holes on the living room walls. He planned to prime it today, then paint it tomorrow.

There was also the Harley outside, but that was at the bottom of his list.

Other than giving it a brief inspection, he'd hadn't had time to work on it since the bike had arrived from Georgia, along with his other belongings. It hadn't been used since before his last deployment to Afghanistan.

He missed it. It was one of his few big purchases, and he'd ridden across the country on it while on his leaves. It had been his only vehicle until he'd bought the used Jeep Wrangler to pick up Amos.

He sipped a second cup of coffee as he looked around. He wondered how the property had looked when Dave's family had owned it. Or why his friend had clung to it despite never coming back.

He finished his coffee and went into the smaller, second bedroom and searched through the cartons that had been shipped from Georgia. He hadn't gone back to the base to do it, just asked a friend to pack everything except his uniforms. He'd wanted those left behind.

When the boxes arrived, he'd discovered his off-duty clothes had been way too big after months of hospital food, and now he lived in newly purchased jeans and T-shirts. The other boxes included his stereo and CDs, a small television and a couple of paintings he'd bought to brighten his rooms in the bachelor quarters for noncommissioned officers.

Then there were the six boxes of books, everything from biographies to history to novels. He'd opened one of the boxes and was currently reading a suspense novel when he couldn't sleep.

Bookcase. He added that to the furniture list.

Then there was the box containing dog toys he'd purchased just before picking up Amos. Like other military dogs, Amos was trained with toy rewards rather than treat rewards, and he'd dearly loved his ball and rubber KONG toy that Dave had carried all over hell and back. But Amos hadn't been interested in the new batch. Still, Josh placed several toys in each room, then went back to work priming the living room walls.

The vet arrived at noon.

Stephanie Phillips looked around as she stepped inside, her gaze going to the primed walls, the cans of paint, the ladder and the fireplace. "You've been busy."

"Lots to do."

"You're going to stay, then."

Josh shrugged. "It needs repairs whether I stay or not."

"That's not a very definitive answer," she said.

"Maybe because I haven't decided yet."

"And it's really none of my business."

He let the silence answer for him.

"I hope you do. We need some new blood in town."

"Or at least a new patient." The ungracious words popped out before he could stop them. She'd agreed to make a house call, and he needed her. But the old protective wall had gone back up after discovering the mayor had had him investigated.

"Now, that's cynical." But her smile belied the cut of the words.

"And you don't deserve it. I apologize." He moved across the room to an open door. "Amos is in the bedroom." He turned and gave her a wry look. "Neither of us bite. It's safe."

"Didn't doubt it for a second," she said.

He led the way into the bedroom and watched as she knelt beside Amos, who had crawled halfway under the bed after hearing the door open.

"Dr. Phillips…"

"Stephanie," she corrected. She started talking to Amos in a voice so soft Josh could barely hear the words. Her fingers ran through his fur.

"You're a fine fellow," she said softly. "And you have nothing to fear from me. You just don't know who to trust, but that's okay. You'll learn. You'll like it here. Woods. Rabbits to chase."

Amos had tensed when she first touched him, but now under her gentle hands and soft voice, the dog started to relax.

"He's a very handsome dog," she said. "I've not seen a Belgian Malinois around here before."

"He's smart as hell. He saved a lot of lives out there. He deserves some peace."

"He was trained to detect explosives?"

"He was what they call a dual-purpose dog. He

could detect explosives as well as track enemy combatants."

"We always need trackers around here. People keep getting lost in the mountains."

"He's not ready for that."

"Not now, but…"

"I'm not concerned with anything but now," he said shortly.

She nodded. "He's thin. Too thin. What does he eat?"

"Not much of anything. I tried dog food at first. Some that the vets at Lackland recommended. He ignored it. I tried hamburgers and steaks on the trip. He would nibble after leaving it for a while, but never much. Same yesterday. I got him a steak from Maude's Diner. He couldn't be less interested."

"And those are good steaks," she said. "My dogs would die for them."

She whispered something to Amos, then stood. "Amos, can you sit for me?"

"Sit, Amos," Josh said, trying to reinforce the command.

Amos slowly moved his butt from under the bed. Amos usually cringed now when a command was given. Today was no different, but after a moment he obeyed.

"Good boy," the vet said. She took a small package from her pocket and pulled out a piece of cheese and offered it to Amos.

To Josh's surprise, he accepted it.

"Few dogs can resist cheese," she said. "Works a lot better than most dog treats." She continued whispering to Amos as she inspected his ears and then her hands checked the rest of his body. "Muscle tone is still good."

"I've been taking him for walks at night when there's no traffic. Sudden noises scare him. And any kind of loud noises. Knocking on the door, for instance."

"Is that why you've scared off visitors?"

"You've heard that, too?"

"Everyone in town has. I know you don't want to say much about your service. Or Amos's. But it would be a quick way to stop the visitors. They'll understand."

He shrugged. "We don't care if they understand."

She gave him a long, searching look, then turned back to Amos. "You're speaking for him?"

He had to crack a smile. "Guess so."

"From what you've said, his sitting is a big deal. Next step seems to be what you're doing. Walking him when you can. Try to stimulate him. I understand he was trained with dog toys."

"He has a box load of every kind of toy imaginable. Squeaky ones, long stuffed snakes, the KONG toys loaded with treats. He's just not interested."

She shrugged. "Give him time. Amos has had a lot of changes. And a huge loss. You said yesterday that you thought the problem was more a broken heart.

But he knew you. You were a familiar piece of his old life. That should help."

He had thought it might. But though Amos tolerated him, he'd reserved his loyalty and devotion for Dave, who'd always loved dogs and had worked hard to become a handler for the unit.

"I thought so, too, but Amos apparently is a one-person dog. He'd only had one handler."

Stephanie nodded. "You must have been a very good friend of the handler to take this on. I've discovered it's not the easiest thing to adopt a retired military dog. A lot of paperwork and a lot of time."

"I owed his handler."

"Why?"

"Dave was my best friend. He was killed...on my last patrol."

"David Hannity?"

He stared at her.

"It makes sense," she said. "From both what you said and didn't say."

He nodded. "Others died that day, too. An ambush." He didn't know why he'd said that. Especially to a stranger, but then she'd guessed most of it.

"And you feel responsible?" She paused, then added, "It's none of my business, and you can be sure I won't repeat anything to anyone. But I wanted to know your commitment to Amos."

"Dave saved my life that day. Do you know now?"

"I think I do," she said softly. "Start taking him on mountain trails during the day. No cars or loud noises there. Talk to him. Don't give up on the toys. If there's no progress in several weeks, then maybe we will try something else."

He nodded. "Thanks for coming."

"I'm not sure I helped much."

"None of the vets at Lackland could, either. Maybe time…"

She looked at him directly. "He's lucky to have you."

"Not so much. If he was lucky, Dave would still be alive."

She turned to leave.

"What about the bill?"

"I didn't do anything. No charge."

He walked her to the door and watched her leave. She walked with athletic grace. She was attractive, but there was none of that sexual electricity he'd felt with the mayor. So it hadn't been just a need for female companionship. He'd hoped that was the case.

The mayor, for God's sake. He'd truly lost his mind. Dave would have laughed his head off.

EVE RACED TO make her son's first softball game of the season.

Her in-laws, Abby and Jim, had picked up Nick after school and driven him to the baseball field since she wasn't sure whether she could make it in time.

It seemed everyone in town was there. No stands, but everyone seemed to have brought their own chairs. There was even a rocker for old Mrs. Evans.

The smell of corn dogs and popcorn floated across the field from a truck manned by mothers, as did the sound of laughter from younger children who played their own version of baseball in a smaller field.

This was why she loved Covenant Falls. It was stuck in a time warp. Sure, there was a problem with kids getting drugs, but it was mostly weed and alcohol. When the biggest news was a new resident, she felt herself lucky.

Abby turned to her. "I heard you met the man who is at the Hannity cabin."

"He owns the cabin," Eve corrected.

"Are you sure?"

"Yes," she said. "Because there was so much talk, I went against my better instincts and asked Tom to check on him. He has good credit, no record and a clear title to the cabin, and that's more than anyone needs to know."

Abby's hurt look stabbed her. Both she and her husband had always been wonderful to her. They looked after Nick when she had to work, Jim helped out at the ranch and they had loved her as a daughter. She was just so tired of all the suspicion surrounding the new resident.

But Abby was just voicing the gossip she knew was running around the community like wildfire.

A roar went up from the watching parents, and she saw a ball shooting through the air. Nick was running to first base. Second base. He rounded third as an opposing player caught the ball on the ground and threw it.

Nick slid into home plate and grinned at the cheers. Pride exploded in Eve. He was so much like his father. And that open, happy grin had been rare since first his father, then his grandfather, had died.

Maybe he was finally letting go, just as her mother-in-law had told her she should do. Memories were fine things, Abby had said, but not when they haunted the living.

She'd never been tempted, though. At thirty-three, she'd found that the good guys were already taken, and she didn't care much for those who were left. At Abby's urging, she'd tried a couple of awkward dates, but she couldn't wait to get home. Most wanted something she wasn't willing to give.

She'd had a great husband and she wasn't going to settle for less. Nor was she willing to lose someone again. And Nick? She didn't even want to think what another loss would mean to him.

It was, therefore, troubling—no, maddening—that Joshua Manning had been in her head all day. Flashes of his guarded but brilliant green eyes lingered in her brain, as did the sexual awareness that shook her to the core. She'd felt it like a bolt of lightning.

She tried to will it away, but the need was stubborn. Her skin warmed at the thought. He exuded primal masculinity. Control. Assurance. The memory of his chest straining against the T-shirt…

Go away.

"Anything wrong?" Abby asked. "You look a little flushed."

Drat him. "I've just been rushing all day," she said. Could everyone read her thoughts?

But Abby just looked concerned. "You work too hard."

"It's budget time, and we need a new police chief."

Another shout went up. One of Nick's teammates reached second base. She tried to concentrate. What inning was it? And what would they have for supper? Mundane things that were, nonetheless, important to her son, and that was all that should matter. Her son already had more losses than was fair for a ten-year-old. He deserved her full attention.

And he would get it, she promised herself.

Macaroni and cheese. That was what she would make. It was Nick's favorite, and she always kept the fixings available for emergencies.

She wondered if Covenant's newest resident liked macaroni and cheese. Despite that hard chest, he'd looked thin. Not thin. He was too corded for thin. But lean...

Quit it!

Then the game was over, and Nick ran up to her. "Did you see my home run?"

"I did, indeed. I'm raising a major leaguer."

"I wish Dad and Grandpa were here."

She hugged him hard. "So do I, slugger. So do I."

He looked up with an earnest gaze that pierced her heart.

"Let's head home," she said. "What about some mac and cheese tonight?"

His face lit up, and her heart flooded with love. He was all she needed. All she wanted.

CHAPTER FIVE

EVE ARRIVED AT her office early after a sleepless night. She kept second-guessing herself after authorizing Tom to run a check on Joshua Manning. She had never done such a thing before, never thought she'd let gossip influence her.

She would be furious if she went to a new town, then heard someone had started asking questions about her for no reason other than the way she looked or dressed. Or the fact she didn't wholeheartedly welcome strangers to her door.

But then that was his right. If it was because of war experiences, he had every right to his privacy, and his wishes should be honored. Even if it wasn't because of war, she still had no business questioning him. She had an apology to make. Even a bit of groveling. She would do just that this afternoon.

Her clerk told her that a copy of the Hannity cabin deed had arrived via fax. She would go bearing gifts: a copy of his deed and a building permit for his expanded porch.

That was the only reason she going. Absolutely the only reason.

She wondered if he knew she'd authorized a background check. She hadn't seen Tom this morning and wondered how far he had gone with it.

She phoned him. She didn't want surprises.

"Tom?"

"Sorry I didn't get back to you about Manning," he said, "but we've had another burglary. This time Gus's gas station. Gus swears he locked the door last night, and it was locked this morning when he went in. But someone got inside. Someone who knows his way around locks, and that lets out most of our possibles."

A knot lodged in Eve's stomach. Because there was so little crime in Covenant Falls, few of the merchants, aside from the bank, took security seriously. With the exception of the motorcycle gang that had roared into town three years ago and killed her father, Covenant Falls had few problems. It was far away enough from the interstate to miss that kind of crime.

"Any ideas?" she asked.

"None, but I suspect a number of people do."

"Joshua Manning."

"Right on. But I don't think so. The background check produced darn little except he'd been an army staff sergeant with an honorable discharge for medical reasons. The army wouldn't release anything else."

"Staff sergeant?"

"Pretty responsible job. Staff sergeants make the army work. Incompetent or dishonest guys don't make it. Don't even come close."

Eve wasn't surprised. It validated all her instincts. A dangerous man who'd lived on, and probably for, the edge. Nothing like her peace-loving husband or her father, who, despite being police chief, would go a mile out of his way to avoid trouble. Except for one time, and that one time killed him.

"Thanks. I think you should end any further searching."

"I agree. I'll steer Sam away from him."

"Good."

"But something like this burglary can escalate. The town will go into a frenzy if there's a third. I'm going to start Fred and Mike patrolling the downtown area at night."

"Good idea. If you need overtime I'll find the money. Somewhere. Do what you have to do."

"I think I'll process the crime scene myself and see what I can find. Are you going to be here?"

"I have that budget to finish and I plan to meet Stephanie for lunch so we can talk about the fundraiser for the community center. Then I have to leave early to pick up Nick for baseball practice, but you can reach me anytime on my cell."

She didn't tell him she planned to drop by the Hannity place sometime in the afternoon. She hoped Marilyn wouldn't be home, either. Because of the trees, Marilyn couldn't see the Hannity cabin from her house, but from the information flowing in, Eve would bet she had taken many walks down his way.

one you think could be a good father, and I'm not too keen on going that route again."

Eve knew Stephanie had been married twice, the first when she was young and a bit wild. The boy was killed while buying drugs. The second husband was the total opposite, a lawyer who'd liked the idea of an independent wife until he had one.

"Think about adoption?" Eve ventured.

"Not with my schedule. I never know when I'm going to be away all night with a sick cow or pregnant mare."

Mary came to take their order, although they usually got the same thing. Their guilty pleasure, they both agreed, and to be enjoyed once a week.

"Let me guess," Mary said. "Two patty melts with fries, and iced tea, one sweet, one without sugar."

"Got it." Eve beamed up at her. She would have a salad tonight and make Nick a hot dog. He ran all his calories off.

"I heard you went out to the Hannity place," Stephanie said.

"Marilyn again, I suppose," Eve replied with a deep sigh.

"Yep. I think she sits at that window all day long, just praying for more gossip fodder."

Stephanie nodded. "Mr. Manning came to my office day before yesterday to discuss his dog."

"And—" Eve held her breath "—was the dog as starved as Marilyn charged?"

"No," Stephanie said. "I can't talk about it. Mr.

Manning requested that I don't, and I won't. I can say, though, that he is a responsible owner and, hopefully, that will end the talk."

That shut down that subject. Eve had heard harsh words come from Stephanie when talking about owners who did not take care of their animals properly, and her defense of Joshua Manning told her a great deal.

She couldn't help but pry a bit more. "What did you think of him?"

Stephanie shrugged. "It's clear he's carrying a lot of weight on those shoulders. Don't know what, and it's none of my business, but I like him. He doesn't bullshit." She peered at Eve. "Rumor is that you went by his place."

"I did. I took him a land survey he'd requested."

"Do you usually do that?"

"I wish people would stop asking me that," Eve said.

"Ah," Stephanie said. "Same question you asked me, then. What did you think of him?"

"Prickly. Defensive. Secretive. Rude."

Stephanie's face creased into a smile. "And you liked him! I'll be hornswoggled."

"I didn't say that," Eve protested.

"Yeah, you did," Stephanie said with a big grin. "Not exactly with words but..."

Eve's face flushed.

"Okay," Stephanie said. "I'll drop it. But one small warning. He *is* attractive in a rather rebellious way, but he's a loner. I've seen them before. I know the type. My first husband was one of them."

Eve started to say something, then stopped. Why was she even carrying on this conversation? She'd had her love. It was as love should be: warm and caring and gentle.

And safe.

She wanted to tamp down the last word. But she knew there was some truth in it. Her mother and father had been passionately in love in the beginning, but they were entirely different. He loved the outdoors; her mother didn't. She was an Easterner who hated guns; guns were part of her father's life. He liked animals and wanted his daughter to have one; her mother believed dogs belonged outside. She'd watched her mother change through the years into a bitter woman and when Eve's father was killed in the line of duty, it had confirmed all her mother's fears and dislikes. The day after his funeral, she'd left Covenant Falls, never to return.

Passion, Eve had learned, was not enough for any relationship. Eve hadn't wanted to go through that, or turn into the person her mother was. She was grateful that Russ chose to be a high school coach rather than go into law enforcement or soldiering or some other dangerous profession. The irony was that he had died before her father. She shrugged. "He's definitely not my type, and I'm most definitely not his."

"Just how do you know that, my friend?"

"I just know it," she said. "This whole conversation

is ridiculous. My life is just as I like it right now. I have Nick. I have a great job. Well, most of the time. I like my independence. I don't need any problems, particularly a large, walking, talking one like Joshua Manning."

"I think thou doth protest too much."

Maybe she did. She didn't even know why he held such a fascination for her. She decided to change the subject, wipe that man right out of her mind, to put a new slant on an old song. "How's Sherry doing?"

Stephanie's eyes lit up. "Great. She's one of the best rescue dogs I've had. Head of the class at field training in Denver. Stryker, on the other hand, did not do so well. He has the nose for it but not the discipline."

"I hear you're doing an obedience training session at the fund-raiser week from Saturday. And donating your training services to the highest bidder. You think anyone in town will admit they have unruly dogs?"

"Why not? You do."

"What can I say? They had sorry puppyhoods."

"True. You're also a soft touch for anything with four legs and a tail. Which brings up a request I want to make. I need a volunteer for the obedience session. One of your tribe of little miscreants would be good. Nick can be my stooge," she said with a grin.

"I don't think he would care much for that description. Which specific miscreant are you considering?"

"I'll let Nick choose, although Miss Marple would be the biggest challenge."

"I can almost guarantee it will be Fancy. He wants everyone to see her for the gentle soul she is."

Stephanie grinned. "He would pick the plainest one."

"Well, Braveheart is certainly not ready to confront a crowd, and Captain Hook can't keep still for a second. Miss Marple wouldn't stay still long enough, either. Besides, Nick thinks Fancy is misunderstood because of her looks. He'll want to prove to everyone that she's charming."

"He really should be a vet," Stephanie replied.

"I wish. He's fixated on detective shows. He wants to be a cop like his grandfather and catch the guys who killed him. I'm trying to steer him toward a different path. Doctor. Lawyer. Rodeo clown. Anything but a cop. Or a soldier."

Stephanie shuddered. "Not a lawyer. Please." She glanced at her watch. "I'm late. I have some inoculations to do at the Morgan ranch."

"I'll see you Saturday, then, if not before," Eve said.

Then she was off. Eve paid the bill and left a hefty tip.

She was having second thoughts about another visit to the Hannity cabin. Steph had seen too much. More than she had. She needed to keep a distance. And yet she felt like a magnet drawn toward a lodestone.

Which made no sense. No sense at all.

CHAPTER SIX

EVE'S PLANS TO visit the Hannity cabin were thwarted by one of her least favorite people.

Al Monroe, council president, called an emergency meeting about the second burglary. He wanted something done. And he wanted a new police chief.

"Tom said he would stay with us until we find the right person," she said.

"He's turned in his retirement papers," Councilwoman Callaway said.

"I haven't accepted them," Eve replied. "He's willing to stay during this investigation."

"We have a perfectly qualified candidate now," Al insisted.

"You mean your nephew?" she said tartly. She was out of patience with Sam's maneuvering for the job.

"He's been with the department five years."

"And there've been complaints," she said.

Al frowned. "They were unjustified. You know they were all dropped."

"Tom didn't agree." Then, unfortunately, Eve's temper got the best of her. Al had pushed Sam on her father and had pressured Tom to keep him. She believed Al had intimidated—or bribed—complainants.

"And if he's so bright," she continued, "why didn't you keep him in your business?"

Al Monroe stiffened. "You know business has been slow. And Sam's always wanted to be a police officer. He's got a degree in criminal justice."

"That's very admirable, but we need someone with proved leadership skills to be chief."

"Young lady, you work for us."

Eve looked around the table. "I beg to differ. I was elected by the people in this town. I work for *them*. I will not support your nephew for chief. He's not ready." Then she reiterated her position to make it very clear. "We need a seasoned chief, someone with supervisory experience."

Al looked as if he was going to have a stroke.

"Now, Al, she's right," another councilman said. "Sam *is* young and, I must admit, a little hotheaded at times."

"Well, our current chief isn't all that good, or we would have the culprit by now. Sam thinks it's that new fellow out at the lake."

"Tom's already ran a check," she said quickly, "not that we had any reason to do so. Mr. Manning has full title to the cabin, having inherited it from David Hannity. He's rehabbing it, which should make all of us happy. He has an honorable discharge from the army, where he was a staff sergeant. There's no reason to suspect him."

"Nothing happened until he got here," Al grumbled. "Did Tom check his alibi?"

"He doesn't need an alibi. There's absolutely no evidence," Eve replied. "Anything else you want to discuss?"

"That's all anyone cares about," Al retorted. "Our business owners are scared."

Eve bit her tongue and shifted the subject. "Are you all planning to be at the fund-raiser a week from Saturday?"

Five of the six members nodded.

"Good. We need support. It would be great if you could donate some baked goods. We also need any books you can spare for the library and items for the garage sale. Crafts and services are welcome. For instance, Stephanie will conduct a dog-training session and donate free training services to the highest bidder. Cash would be good, too. We're going to list the donors in the newspaper."

A bit of blackmail proposed by Stephanie, but Eve wasn't going to mention who suggested it. Stephanie had a way of antagonizing the powers that be. Being the only vet for forty miles, she didn't have to worry about a boycott by clients.

She looked down at her watch. "I have to pick up my son. Anything else?"

Al glared at her as he left. The others followed without comment. So far, the council had skittishly refused to go along with him on promoting his nephew, relying on the fact that Tom had not officially left. They all knew Tom had more friends than any of them had.

She looked at her watch. Just enough time to go by the Hannity cabin if she stopped on her way from school to the baseball field. Nick would be with her then.

Maybe that would be a good thing. She would make a quick apology, drop off the copy of the deed and tell him the work to enlarge the porch could go ahead.

That way she would be safe from those feelings that had been so persistent. *Safe*. She was beginning to hate that word.

Nick was waiting for her at the school. He jumped in the car. "You're late," he said.

"I know. City business. And I have a quick call to make on the way. That okay with you?"

"Where?"

"The last cabin on Lake Road."

"You mean the guy with a dog. Awesome."

"What do you know about that?"

He shrugged. "All the kids are talking about it."

"What are they saying?"

"Maybe he robbed Maude's and the gas station."

"And you think going there is awesome?"

"You always tell me never to believe everything I hear. And you've been there. You wouldn't let me go if you thought he was bad."

Her son was ten going on forty. Not only that, but he would also make a good lawyer.

"You're right. I don't think he had anything to do with those robberies. But I'm just going to drop something off with him, and then we'll leave. I want you to stay in the car."

"Aw, Mom. I want to see the dog."

He always wanted to see the dog. Any dog.

She turned onto Lake Road toward the cabin. Mr. Manning was replacing some of the slats holding up the porch railing. She wondered why he bothered doing the work. Did he plan to stay? Fix the cabin and sell it?

Biggest question of all: Why did she care?

She didn't, she told herself. She grabbed her briefcase and looked at Nick, who was peering at Mr. Manning with great interest. "You stay here. You can get started on your homework."

"You said you wouldn't be long."

"I promise." She leaned over and kissed his tousled hair.

She took a deep breath. Maybe she'd been magnifying that attraction.

Maybe he would be even ruder than before. Maybe...

But Stephanie liked him. She was a good judge of character. Except, apparently, for husbands.

She walked up the steps. He straightened. His shirt was open and her gaze went to a hard, muscled chest sprinkled with golden hair. She willed herself to look at his face as she came toward him.

Also a mistake. Lord, but his eyes were mesmerizing. Particularly when they seemed to look inside her and see her errand for the sham it was.

"Mayor Douglas." His expression was grim.

"I received a copy of your deed and I have your building permit. I made copies of both for you."

"My attorney is sending me a copy of the deed," he said curtly. "He also told me that the sheriff had questions about me."

Eve felt her face flush. She hated that. "I'm sorry. It seemed a way to dispel rumors. But I shouldn't have authorized it. The questions should never have been asked."

"Discovered I'm not an ax murderer, did you?"

"Not as far as Tom could discover," she said. "He's our police chief. He was supposed to do this surreptitiously. He apparently didn't succeed." She tried a small smile. She almost gave him the other reason, namely that one of the deputies had needed stopping, but that would probably be insulting, as well. To both of them.

His grim expression didn't ease. His thick hair was combed, but he hadn't shaved. His eyes were just as cool as they had been during their first meeting. Cool and enigmatic.

There was pain in the hard lines around his eyes and mouth, reflecting experiences she couldn't even imagine.

There was definitely nothing easy about the man. Especially the raw sexuality that he exuded…and it slammed into her.

He moved to the door and stood aside, an invitation to enter. Frissons rocketed along her spine as she brushed by him and moved inside. She tried to concentrate on the cabin interior and not her sudden proximity to a man who sent all her senses spiraling out of control.

"I can't stay. My son is in the truck," she said. She handed the documents to him. Her hand shook slightly. *Stop it. You're not sixteen.* The smell of wet paint permeated the room. Newspapers covered the floor and two walls were painted a sand color, while another was half-done. The only furniture was a well-worn sofa that sagged in the middle.

"I would invite you to sit but, as you can see, I'm not exactly ready for the visitors who seem to keep coming."

"Will you ever be ready?"

"I doubt it," he said grimly, but she thought she caught the barest hint of humor in his eyes.

She saw a dog toy in the middle of the room. "My son loves dogs," she said. "Would it be okay if he met yours briefly? Then we'll have to go to baseball practice."

"He was out with me, hiding under the porch," he said, "and he was only there because I insisted. I can tell you he's even less tolerant of strangers than I am, so maybe it's not a good…"

A yell came from outside. The kind of yell that screamed fear and pain. Then there was loud barking.

Eve's blood turned cold as she turned and ran out the door. Nick, holding his right arm, stood next to the small porch. His face was white. "Don't come near," he said in a trembling voice.

A dog resembling a German shepherd growled next to him and moved around in attack mode.

"Amos!" Joshua Manning's voice was sharp and commanding, as he moved even faster than she had. "Stand down. Amos."

"No!" Nick said. "Not the dog. Rattlesnake bit me. The dog's trying to protect me."

Terror thrust through Eve like a spear. She knew from first-aid classes that the first rule after a bite was to stay still. She also knew how fast a snake-bite could kill, and that the snake could strike again. There had been several bites in the area in the past two years. Of three victims, one had died and the others had lingering effects. All those facts raced through her head as she saw the coiled rattler and made a move toward Nick.

"No! Stay still, damn it. You'll make things worse. You can't help him by getting bit yourself." A strong hand shot out and grabbed her arm, stopping her. She fought to get loose.

Eve wanted to grab her son and run to the car. She started to move again. But he tightened his hold. "You want to do something, get my gun. It's on the top shelf of the closet in the back bedroom. Ammunition is next to it."

He paused. "You know how to load a gun?" Before getting an answer, he turned to Nick. "You're doing good, boy. Real good. Stay totally still."

Reason fought against instinct. His eyes and voice made her listen. They came from someone used to being obeyed. Confident and competent. Still, the fear inside her was overwhelming. She couldn't lose Nick. *She couldn't.*

Her legs didn't want to move away from the one person in the world she loved with everything inside her. Nick looked so brave standing absolutely still, just as he was told. How could she be any less brave?

"Of course I can load," she said as she ran into the house, frantically searching for the room, then the closet, then the gun and bullets.

She lived on a ranch with snakes and coyotes and other unfriendly creatures. Her father had made sure she knew how to use a rifle and revolver. She loaded the gun and ran back out just in time to see Manning toss the snake with one of the slats he'd obviously torn from the porch. It landed six feet away from her son and the dog.

She aimed at the snake and fired. Once, twice. Again and again until the bullets were gone.

"I think you've killed it several times over," Josh Manning said. "Not bad shooting."

He took the gun from her hand with a gentleness she hadn't expected. "You've got one hell of a kid there. Kept his head. But I think Amos has been bit, too. He put himself between your boy and the snake."

Eve hugged Nick as hard as she could without squeezing his arm. "I told you to stay in the car," she said in shaking voice.

"I saw the dog's head poking from under the porch. I just wanted to see him," Nick said. "He tried to protect me."

Amos was still standing at Nick's side. But blood was coming from one of his paws, just as it was coming from small punctures in Nick's arm.

"Stand down, Amos," Josh said softly. "Well done." His voice was more gentle than Eve could ever have imagined as he ran his hands over the dog, seemingly looking for injury.

"We have to get your son to a doctor as soon as possible." He picked up Nick. "Try to keep that arm still," he said to him. "And a little below your heart." Then he turned to Eve. "The keys to my Wrangler are on a hook just inside. It has more room than your pickup. Get them. And soap up a washcloth and bring it out. I'll put the boy in the back of the Jeep." He paused. "Better take the gun inside, too."

He carried Nick to the backseat of the Jeep parked at the side of the cabin. Eve didn't want to leave Nick, not for a second, but Joshua Manning seemed to know what to do. She knew all the rules about snakebites as well, and he was doing exactly what she'd learned. Get safely away from the snake. Wash the bite to kill bacteria. Keep the patient calm. The less the victim moves, the less damage will incur.

She hadn't been very good at the calm part. She ran into the house, replaced the gun in the closet, quickly wet a washcloth and doused it with soap. She grabbed the keys as she ran out to the Jeep.

Joshua—she thought of him that way now—had a first-aid kit out and had already applied a compression bandage just above the wound. He was in the middle of splinting Nick's arm with a short stick. She handed him the washcloth, noticing that the arm was already red and beginning to swell.

"Stay as still as you can," Joshua was telling her son. "It's important."

"I know," her son said. "I'm a Cub Scout." He said it with bravado, but she heard the tremor of fear in his voice. He was also clenching his teeth from pain.

Eve ran to her truck and found the cell phone, then returned to the Jeep as she punched the number for Dr. Bradley. The number rang and rang, each ring seeming to last an hour. Then, after what seemed like forever, the nurse finally picked up.

"Janie, Nick has just been bitten by a rattler. Do you have antivenin?" The level of her voice raised with every word. She was choked with fear. She wanted to grab her son away and hold him tight. She listened, then hung up.

"The doctor's not in, but his nurse is trying to reach him," she told Joshua.

"We'll drive in. If he's not there, I'll call for a helicopter to get us the county hospital," Joshua said. "I'll drop Amos off at the vet's."

She stared at the phone, then wrapped her arms around her own body, hugging herself to keep from screaming, only to be jarred by his impatient voice. "Get in the backseat with him. You can put his head on your lap, just keep the wound area below his heart. I'll put Amos in the front seat with me. Call ahead to Stephanie, will you?"

"Of course. I have her number."

She maneuvered inside the car and raised Nick's head to settle on her lap, then arranged him so his heart would be above the wounded arm. She held his other hand and the Jeep moved. Her heart pounded. She saw Nick bite his lips and knew he was in pain. She wished it was her pain.

Her cell phone rang. *Dr. Bradley.* "Where is the bite?" She heard the urgency in his voice.

"The lower part of the arm."

"You're sure it was a rattler."

"I saw it. So did my son and Mr. Manning. It happened near his cabin."

"You're in luck. We had another bite a few weeks ago, and I ordered extra antivenin. The sooner he gets it, the better he'll be. Bring him in, I'll suction out the venom and give him the antivenin. Then I think you should take him on to the county hospital. Oh, and Eve, keep him lying down and still. The arm should be below…"

"I know. We're on our way," she said and hung up. She turned to Josh. "Doc Bradley has the antivenin. He said to bring him in as quickly as we can." She then called Stephanie and told her what had happened. Steph was in her office seeing patients and said she would be waiting for Amos.

Doc Bradley was standing outside his clinic when

they arrived. "Bring him inside. Did you bring the snake?"

"No," Josh said. "But there's no question it was a rattler. About four and a half feet long. Mayor Douglas shot it—" he looked at his watch "—fifteen minutes ago."

Only fifteen minutes. It seemed a lifetime.

Doc Bradley nodded his head. "Good. Can you carry him inside?"

Then he saw the dog lying on the front seat, shivering, and gave Joshua a questioning look.

"He was bit, too. I'm taking him to the vet right after I get the boy inside."

Doc Bradley hurried them into a treatment room. Joshua laid Nick on the treatment table and said, "I'll be back after seeing to Amos."

Dr. Bradley examined the fang marks, took blood from the area to determine the amount of venom then applied a Sawyer Extractor to remove as much venom as possible and slow the spread of the remaining venom in the arm. The arm was already swelling, and although Nick tried to hide it, she knew he was terrified as well as in growing pain. Being a Cub Scout, he knew as well as she how quickly a bite could maim and kill.

"We got it early, young man." Dr. Bradley said to Nick. "The prognosis is good, but I want you to go to the county hospital for observation. Just to be on the safe side."

Nick looked at Eve.

"Yes. Of course," she said.

"I think it's probably a good idea to go now. I'll call ahead and they will be waiting for him." He paused. "Do you have someone to go with you? He should still be lying down. I could call an ambulance, but that would be expensive and I don't think it's necessary."

"I'll take her."

She'd been so focused on Nick that she hadn't realized Joshua Manning had returned and was standing right behind her.

"What about your dog?" she asked.

"Stephanie has canine antivenin, but she wants to keep Amos overnight. She'll stay with him."

Eve considered his offer. Her father-in-law could take her, but it meant he would have to close the drugstore. She didn't know where Abby was and her mother-in-law never carried a cell phone.

She looked at him. "You've already done so much."

"I would just as well do that as paint," he said as his lips turned up in the slightest suggestion of a smile. "There's no hurry to do that. Besides, I feel responsible. It happened on my property."

"We were uninvited," she reminded him.

"So you were," he said with that trace of a smile. It lit the green in his eyes, softened the hardness she'd seen earlier. "I suppose you could still sue me, though." Charm was there, too, and it startled her. The rhythm of her heart quickened.

"Mom, please. I want Mr. Manning to drive me."

She still hesitated. "That's very kind. Let me call my father-in-law first and let him know what happened." She punched in his number at the pharmacy and quickly explained. "Nick was bitten by a snake. He's fine, but just as a precaution I'm taking him to County General."

"I'll take you," Jim replied.

"I don't want you to leave the store," she said. "Mr. Manning said he will drive us. I'll call as soon as I get there. If they want to keep Nick, I'll need you and Abby to go by the house, tend to the animals and pick up some clothes for us."

"Are you sure?"

"He saved Nick's life, Dad, and he's here, ready to go."

"Just let us know what you need, honey," he replied. "Abby will go to your house and take care of the animals and pick up your things." He paused. "I can run over there now."

"We're leaving right now. Doc Bradley really does believe he'll be okay. This is just a precaution."

"We'll wait for your call, then. And thank Mr. Manning for us."

"I will." She clicked off her cell and turned to Joshua. "Thank you, Mr. Manning."

"Josh," he corrected. "My name is Josh. I think we're beyond the Mr. Manning stage now."

The ogre of Covenant Falls had turned into a Good Samaritan, and an approachable one at that. He had clearly won her son's approval.

"I'm sorry about your dog," she said.

"He'll be fine." he said. "He's been through worse."

"Amos?" She hadn't paid much attention before when he'd called the dog's name. She should know. The dog might have saved Nick's life by preventing a second bite. "His name is Amos?"

"Yes."

He was back to short answers. The doctor appeared with instructions and test results to give to the hospital physicians. He eyed her companion with interest. "Welcome to Covenant Falls, young man."

Josh nodded but didn't say anything. He lifted Nick. "Come on, sport."

She took the paperwork and followed Josh to the Jeep. In the back of her mind, she sensed her world had suddenly turned upside down.

CHAPTER SEVEN

WHAT IN THE bloody hell was he doing?

"Bloody hell" was a pretty good description. Sometimes nothing else fit a situation, and this was one of those times.

Why did he volunteer to drive them?

He carried Nick to the back of the Jeep, opened the door and settled him there, then took the mayor aside. "What about the boy's father? Shouldn't you call him?"

"He died four years ago," she said flatly.

"I'm sorry.... Your ring..."

"No reason you would know," she said as she opened the rear door before he could and stepped inside.

The safety valve was gone. She was single and had been for four years. Surprising she had not been taken again.

"Is Amos going to be okay?" Nick asked. He was lying on the backseat, his head cradled in his mother's lap. "He saved my life. He kept the snake from me."

"He used to do that on a regular basis," Josh said.

"What do you mean?"

"He was a military dog. He saved lots of lives."

"Yours, too?" Nick asked in an awed voice.

"Several times," Josh replied.

Nick was quiet then, leaving Josh to his own thoughts. He ran through what he should have done to keep a kid and Amos from being injured. He should have mowed the area around the house, boarded off the crawl space beneath the porch and shouldn't have been distracted by someone he had no business being distracted by.

She was a widow. And a keeper. A keeper for someone who wanted a keeper. He'd never been one of those. And God knew he had little to offer except nightmares and flashbacks. He was a loner. A wanderer. He and the army were made for each other. He would go nuts if he stayed in this place very long. Everyone knowing everyone's business.

"How *is* Amos?" The mayor's voice was full of concern, and he realized he hadn't really answered her son's question. Maybe because he didn't want to think about it.

"Stephanie said we got him the antivenin quickly, and if a dog was to be bitten, the paw is the best place. She thinks he'll be okay."

That was the optimistic version of the vet's words, but he chose to believe them. He had wanted to stay but Amos was under sedation and needed quiet, and he felt responsible for Mayor Douglas and her son. He couldn't help Amos now, but he could help the boy.

The drive was seventy miles and usually took about an hour, but he aimed to make it in forty-five minutes. He figured if he ran into the highway patrol, he could convince them into giving him an escort. He had a pretty woman and an injured kid with a snakebite.

He had said everything he had to say, and the rest of the trip was in silence. Eve Douglas called the hospital when they were minutes away, and a gurney was waiting when they drove up to the emergency doors. The kid was whisked inside and he stood with...Eve. They followed a nurse to a desk in front while another rushed Nick into a treatment room.

"That's a gutsy kid," he said to break the tense silence. He realized she was barely holding it together.

"Too gutsy," she said in a trembling voice. "There was someone in Covenant Falls who was bitten last year. She was in the hospital for weeks and lost the feeling in her hand. The doctor said she was lucky to be alive." A tear trailed down her cheek. "You try to keep them safe," she murmured, "and you can't. I told him to stay in the car and..."

And then Josh couldn't help himself. She was in pain, and he felt responsible. She was a widow, a much too young one, and now she needed someone. His arms went around her and held her close as her body shook with emotion. She had been great when the danger was real. She'd done everything he'd asked, then shot the snake as efficiently as he could have. *Almost.*

His arms tightened, and then he didn't know what to do. He hadn't really comforted a woman before.

He'd never stayed with anyone long enough to reach that level in a relationship.

Comfort. That was all he was doing. Offering comfort. A body to lean into for a few seconds. Then she looked up at him and he was lost in those hazel eyes that were misty from tears. There was sheer agony there, and his own personal demons faded. A tenderness he hadn't known before filled him.

"He'll be all right," he said softly. "We got him here fast."

"He loves dogs," she said. "He usually obeys, but he can't resist one."

"Amos isn't usually out," Josh said. "It's a battle of wills just to take him for a walk. But I thought while I was working… I should have mowed around the porch first." His thoughts were a jumble, his words nearly incoherent. Where was that coolness his team teased him about?

He felt helpless now. Inadequate. He was saved when a doctor entered. "The blood test indicates a minimum of venom still in him," he said. "Your doctor did a good job. The suctioning helped. His arm is going to be swollen, discolored and painful for a few days, but then he should be fine. We want to keep him here, though, for a few days, just to make sure."

The doctor looked at Josh. "Are you his father?"

"A friend," Eve said before he could respond. She turned back to Josh. "I'm staying here. I'll call my father-in-law and he can bring some clothes for the two of us in the morning. I know you want to get back and check on your dog."

Dismissed. Neatly. Well, wasn't that what he wanted? He didn't know a damn thing about kids. Or this type of woman. He couldn't even take care of a dog. He nodded. "You sure you'll be okay?"

"As long as Nick is," she said. "Thank you for everything you did. Please keep us posted on Amos."

He nodded and turned. Nothing else to say. And he did want to see Amos. For a few minutes anyway, Amos had returned to the alert protector he'd once been. He could only hope it was a breakthrough, but hopes and prayers hadn't been very helpful in the past eighteen months.

This time they had to be. He couldn't lose Amos like he'd lost his team. He was out the door but looked back. She was still talking to the doctor, her stance rigid as if she was about to shatter. But she wouldn't. She obviously had a strong core.

He slid into the Jeep. He felt helpless, and he hated that. He couldn't save the kid, and he couldn't save Amos. He had to rely on others, and he wasn't very good at that. He started the vehicle and drove toward Covenant Falls, his temporary place of residence.

EVE SPENT THE evening in Nick's room, checking his arm every hour. It was swollen, had turned several shades of purple and he couldn't move it without whimpering. He was nauseous and didn't want to eat anything, a condition that was highly unusual. He was also running a slight fever.

He was sedated now, but his body twitched occasionally. She wanted so badly to take the hurt away.

She looked at her watch again. After 1:00 a.m. She had changed from her work clothes to the sweats her father-in-law had brought. His pharmacy assistant had locked the store for him. Jim had stayed an hour, then returned to town to take care of the motley crew and horses. Both he and Abby planned to come in the morning.

Eve had called Stephanie just after Josh left, and asked about Amos. She knew it would be Nick's most urgent question. Stephanie assured her the dog was doing well and that Josh was on his way over to check on him. Then Eve called Merry to tell her where she was in case of an emergency. As Nick slept, she kept her eyes on him. Oh, Lord, but she wanted to hold him. Never let him go. She put her hand over his. Lightly so as not to wake him. She had lost her heart the moment she'd first felt him move inside her. She remembered the day he was born. He had been a few weeks early, but he still had a mass of black curly hair and the bluest eyes she'd ever seen. He'd been a tiny duplicate of his father, who had adored him.

Nick took after his father in other ways, as well. He was a natural caretaker. He loved animals and younger children. He stood up to bullies who intimidated other kids. He was also athletically gifted. And he had Russ's curiosity. He wanted to know every-

thing about everything. Nick had tottered behind his
father as soon as he'd taken his first steps.

Her heart shattered every time she looked at him
and knew what he'd missed by his father's death. She
tried to make up for it as much as possible, but she
saw the longing in his eyes when he saw fathers and
sons together.

He was her life.

If she had not gone to Josh Manning's cabin, Nick
would not be lying in a hospital bed. She'd allowed a
momentary attraction to put her son in danger. She
should have known he wouldn't stay in the truck.
How could she have been so irresponsible?

She blinked back tears. He was going to be all
right. But what if…

She occasionally dozed off but woke at his slightest
movement. One time, he whimpered and her hands
went around his and rubbed them. She tried not to
wake him, but wanted to let someplace inside him
know she was there.

She felt alone. She knew Jim would have stayed
overnight if she had asked, but then she would have
felt the need for small talk, and she didn't think she
could bear that. Maybe she just wanted to keep Nick
all to herself. Scare off the demons of fear on her
own.

And no matter how much she tried to banish them,
images of Josh Manning invaded her thoughts again.
She tried to shut them away, but she still felt his
warmth and gentleness as he had held her down-

stairs. She never would have expected it from him, not the tenderness or the quiet competence that had kept her fear under control. His strength had flowed through her, and it dismayed her that she had desperately wanted him to stay.

She didn't want to care—much less love—again. She couldn't risk another loss. There was too much pain. For her and her son.

BEFORE GOING BY the clinic, Josh stopped at his cabin to make sure it—and the gun—was secured after their hasty departure. The cabin, as he'd feared, was unlocked. He changed clothes, grabbed one of Amos's toys and drove to the vet.

Instead of putting Amos in the kennel cages, Stephanie had spread out a blanket and put him in her office, where she could keep her eyes on him. The first eight hours after a rattler bite were critical, she said.

Amos raised his head when Josh entered and even licked his hand when Josh leaned down to pet him. "That's the first time he's done that since Dave died," he said.

"He licked you before his handler died?"

"Not often, but sometimes. When Dave wasn't available I would feed him, make sure he had water, and he would give me a little thank-you."

"Have you ever owned a dog?"

"No."

"You're learning. You got him here fast."

"Then he's going to be okay?"

"I think so. After biting Nick, the rattler may not have had much venom left. And it's good that Amos was bit on the leg, not the mouth. He looks good and tried to get up several times, but I managed to convince him to stay down."

"He might have saved the mayor's son from a second bite."

"He's a hero, and I think he knows it," she said. "There's more life in his eyes than when I first saw him. I think he knows he did good."

"He doesn't look much different to me."

Stephanie shrugged. "He licked you."

"That's true," he said with a small smile.

"Oh, you *can* smile." Stephanie grinned. "Can't wait to spread that around."

"I would appreciate it if you didn't. It would ruin my obviously dismal image."

"You work hard enough at it."

He liked her. She was easy to be with. He suspected she had her own problems in town with her quick tongue. He looked at his watch. "You and Mrs. Douglas are friends, aren't you?"

"Yes."

"Can you call and see how her boy is?" He didn't know why he was reluctant to do it himself. Or maybe he did. Today he had become entwined with the Douglas family, and part of him was fighting it.

"Why don't you?"

"I don't have her number."

She raised an eyebrow. "I talked to her just before you came. The doctors say it looks good. He's feeling some effects, but the amount of venom in his system is treatable. They will probably stay until Monday. I have her number," she added with an impish grin.

"Thanks, but you told me what I wanted to know." He changed the subject. "Have you had supper?" he asked.

"Nope. Been a little busy around here."

"Is Maude's open?"

She looked at her watch. "For another half hour."

"I'll get us some food. What do you want?"

"A patty melt. Maude has the best ever. I have soft drinks and coffee here."

"Fries?"

"Why not live it up?" Stephanie said. "You might get a cheeseburger for Amos. He deserves it."

"A vet recommends a cheeseburger?"

"Only on special occasions."

Josh made the trip just in time. It took fifteen minutes to fill the order, then he left with his hands full. It was summer, when days were long, but shadows were now falling on the town. Only a few people were visible on the street. The businesses, with the exception of the grocery and Maude's, were closed. One older man was locking up the pharmacy.

When the man finished, he looked up and hurried to Josh and studied him for a moment. "I'm Jim Douglas," he said. "Nick's grandfather. I understand we owe you thanks. Your quick action might have saved my grandson's life."

"Mrs. Douglas and Nick were doing just fine without me," he said.

"Well, we won't forget it. How's your dog?"

"Dr. Phillips thinks he will be fine, but she wanted to keep an eye on him overnight."

"That sounds like Stephanie. I was at the hospital earlier, but now my wife and I are in charge of taking care of their animals."

"Animals?"

"Two elderly horses, one boarding horse, four needy dogs and a dysfunctional cat," he replied with a rueful smile. "My daughter-in-law is probably Stephanie's best customer."

Bloody hell. He was falling for someone with a zoo. And in-laws. And a son. And a job as mayor. He needed to run for the hills. Sell the infernal cabin. Now.

After Amos was out of danger.

He nodded to Jim Douglas, tightened his hold on the bags of takeout and headed to the veterinarian's office.

"Welcome to Covenant Falls," the man called after him.

When he returned, the door to the clinic was unlocked. Dangerous. Even in a small town like this.

What did he know about living in small towns? He crossed the reception area to Stephanie's office.

"Mmm, I smell it," she said with a wide smile. "I

didn't realize how hungry I was. I usually save patty melts for special occasions except for Thursdays with Eve. Then we both splurge."

"Thursdays with Eve?"

"We meet for lunch and discuss the goings-on in town. We've been friends since I moved here."

"You moved here of your own free will?" That was a surprise.

"Didn't you?"

"Long story," he said.

"Here, too, but the nub of it is a divorce. My ex-husband didn't want a working wife. He wanted one who would help advance his career. I figured he didn't know me very well, and I hadn't known him at all. I divorced him and wanted to get as far away from Boston as possible. To make a long story short, a friend told me about this small practice in Colorado, so here I am. I like it. I like large-animal medicine. I like being outside, and I like the mountains. I don't like the gossip. And the sacred cows."

"Mayor Douglas said her husband died four years ago." It more a question than a statement.

Her eyes gleamed for a moment. "Interested?"

He wished he hadn't said anything. "Just learning the battlefield."

"Covenant Falls isn't exactly that kind of battle-field, although there are skirmishes. As for Eve, her husband was a coach with the high school. Coached baseball, football and basketball. He died before I arrived, but from everything I've heard, he was some kind of hero around here. Everybody loved him, especially Eve." She gave him a sidelong glance. "They were high school sweethearts. Never was anyone else for her, not before and not after he died."

She paused, then continued, "He died suddenly on the football field as he ran with his team before a practice. Some heart defect that had never been detected."

Josh didn't know what to say. This was not exactly what he wanted to hear. But then what *had* he wanted to hear? That her husband drank too much? That he had been careless?

Why did he even care how the man died?

He'd opened the door for questions, and Stephanie walked through it.

She asked a few questions about him but he had even fewer answers. Where was home? "Army bases." Family? "None." And a big one: What did he plan to do in the future? "Finish the cabin."

"You are not a very informative man," Stephanie said.

"Notice that, did you?"

They finished their food in silence. Amos slept as they ate, and Stephanie said she would give the meat in the cheeseburger to him when he woke. She looked at her watch. "It's late. Why don't you go home? I often rest here on the couch when I have a patient I need to watch. You can pick him up in the morning."

He hesitated.

"He's breathing normally. I found one puncture but there's no swelling around it. He got lucky."

"Then why do you want to keep him?"

"An overabundance of caution," she said.

"I don't want to leave him," he said.

"I'm going to keep him sedated through the night. He won't know if you're here or not. He won't be alone, and you might want to clear the area where you found the snake before you take him home."

She made sense. At first light he would do just that.

"You will call if there's any change?"

"Of course."

He ran his hand around Amos's ears. The dog didn't move. "You did good today, Amos. Dave would have been proud." Then he turned back to Stephanie. "Thank you," he said, meaning it.

"Glad to have another rebel here," she replied as she closed the door behind him.

CHAPTER EIGHT

THE CABIN WAS dark when Josh arrived home. And it didn't look inviting.

Wasn't this what he wanted? A place to hide and nurse his wounds.

A broken place for a broken soldier and his broken dog.

He walked in, turning on the interior light as he did. The porch light was broken. Something else to do. It hadn't mattered yesterday, or the day he arrived. Now, for some reason, it did.

Without Amos, the cabin felt lifeless...empty. That surprised him, considering the fact that Amos had been none too convivial a companion. Maybe it was because he had no one to care for. Loneliness struck him like a mortar round, ripping apart all the protective armor he'd built around himself.

He closed his eyes, willing away the feeling. He had a lot to do, and a good book waiting for him. And tomorrow Amos would be back.

Only then did he realize the enormity of his loss if anything happened to Amos. The dog was his connection to the only life he really knew, to the one friend he knew as well as he knew himself. Except he hadn't known Dave as well as he thought or he would have known about this cabin.

He went to the cooler he'd filled with ice earlier and took out a beer. He then went out and sat on the steps he'd repaired earlier that day. The midnight-blue sky glittered with as many stars as shone in Afghanistan. But here the air was sweet, not sweltering hot in the day and freezing at night. He could breathe here.

He saw some kids walking along the narrow beach. Holding hands, then stopping to embrace. Pain bored a hole in his heart. He watched like a voyeur until they disappeared, and then he went inside.

EVE STILL SAT next to Nick as the sun came up and filtered through the window. The swelling in his arm seemed better but the color was just as angry-looking. She wanted to kiss it and make it well, just as she had promised when he was a toddler and fell down.

And now he still looked so young and vulnerable huddled under covers in a hospital bed. If she had not gone to Josh Manning's cabin, none of this would have happened.

She clutched his uninjured hand, and it seemed even smaller because the other one was so swollen. She thought about Josh and his dog. She remembered the worry in Josh's eyes and the protective way he'd carried Amos. In her opinion, Josh's behavior with the dog said a great deal about him.

Her thoughts were interrupted by a brief knock on the door. Nick's grandparents, Abby and Jim, looked in, their faces lined with worry. Eve put her finger to her lips and walked silently out the door, closing it behind her.

"How is he?" Abby asked after hugging her. "Jim couldn't keep me away."

"His arm is still swollen and sore, but the doctors think he'll be fine within a few days."

"Thank God," Jim said. "I met that Josh Manning last night. I was checking on the store after Riley locked up for me. Manning was going to the vet clinic. Seems like a nice young man. Kinda quiet."

"It's my fault it happened," she said. "I stopped at Mr. Manning's cabin with a building permit on our way to baseball practice. Nick was supposed to stay in the truck, but you know…your grandson. He had to meet Mr. Manning's dog, which was outside. When he approached the dog, the snake bit him, then bit the dog when it tried to protect him."

"He said the dog is doing well," Jim said.

"And your dogs are fine," Abby added. "I let them out for a few moments and fed them while Jim cared for the horses."

"You must have been there at daybreak."

"We stayed at your house overnight," Jim said. "Just seemed best for the animals, and we packed more clothes for you. Also bought a thermos of coffee and some sweet rolls Abby baked."

She gave them both a hug.

A technician came to the door and the three of them went into the room with him. Nick was still asleep, and Eve gently woke him. He looked confused for a moment, then saw his grandparents and a wide smile spread across his face.

"I got snake bit," he said proudly to Abby. "I didn't move. Josh tossed it away with a stick and mom killed it with Josh's gun."

Josh. Where did he get that? "Mr. Manning," she corrected.

"He said I could call him Josh," Nick said.

"When was that?"

"When you were talking to the doctor. I called him Mr. Manning, and he said no one called him Mr. Manning. He said he was just plain Josh."

Nothing plain about him at all. "Well, it's still Mr. Manning," she said.

"Oh, Mom," her son said. "I like him."

"You can like 'Mr. Manning' just as well. And how are you feeling?"

"My arm still hurts."

The technician finished taking blood and left. Eve knew the nurse wouldn't be far behind to take his blood pressure.

"I brought some of the cinnamon rolls you like," Abby told Nick, and Eve knew she must have been baking late into the night. Which was something Abby would do. She was convinced that baking solved all the problems in the world. And if everyone cooked as well as she, it probably would.

She took the small suitcase Jim held, and Abby said, "I brought you two changes of everything, but I can bring you more if you need it. And tell me about the mysterious Mr. Manning. Jim said he drove you here." She hadn't stopped to take a breath.

"Between you and me?" Eve asked.

"Promise."

"He's very…efficient when there's an emergency. Otherwise, he's more like a bear who has just been awakened in his cave. Early."

Abby looked disappointed. "Is he good-looking?" Abby had been urging her to date again despite Eve's protests. She'd had one great marriage. It was too much to ask for two. And she didn't *need* another, thank you. She had learned to be independent and she liked the feeling. Besides, she didn't have time even if she was interested, which she wasn't.

"Interesting looking, maybe," she finally said.

"Why don't you invite him over to our house for supper?"

"Because he would run for the hills."

"Hmm," Abby said, but dropped the subject. Instead, she went to Nick and planted a kiss on his forehead. "Playing with snakes, huh? Trying to scare us to death." She dropped the bag of cinnamon buns in his lap.

"He's been nauseated," Eve said.

"I feel good now," Nick said quickly, his good hand grabbing inside the bag.

Abby turned to her husband. "See, I told you they would work." She beamed.

Just then the nurse came in. She was one Eve

hadn't met. "You have company, huh? And those rolls look good."

"There's enough for you," Abby said.

"I don't think it's included in my diet, but thank you," the nurse replied. "I'm Sheila. I'll be this young man's nurse today."

She quickly checked the blood pressure, temperature and oxygen level. "All good, young man," she said. "Heard you got a rattler bite."

Nick nodded. "And I did everything right. Josh—I mean, Mr. Manning—said so."

Sheila removed the dressing from the wound area, examined it, then redressed it. "Still looks tender, but it doesn't appear to have been spreading. You are a very lucky boy."

"When can I go home?"

"That's up to the doctors."

Eve felt better when the nurse left. Surely there would be a change in vital signs if there were complications. Still, the image of the snake and the fang marks on his arm wouldn't leave her head.

Neither would that of Josh Manning holding her son.

"I can stay here with Nick if you have to go to work," Abby offered.

Eve shook her head. "I want to be here when the doctor comes by."

"I would like to stay with you," Abby said.

"We would love your company," Eve replied.

"Good," Abby said and took a thermos out of the

large tote she was carrying. "Have a cup of coffee with the roll."

Jim nodded. "I do have to open the pharmacy. Call me as soon as you know anything more. Riley can fill in for me this afternoon and I'll get Reggie to drive Miss Mollie up here so you two have transportation. I can drive him back."

"Miss Mollie can be temperamental."

"Tell me about it. I think Reggie can handle it."

"Thanks," she said. One of the not-so-good things about a small town was that everyone knew your business. One of the really good things was that everyone was willing to help when needed. Reggie was a mechanic at the garage, and she had gone to high school with him. He'd had a crush on her then but later married one of her good friends.

Jim took Nick's hand and squeezed it. "You get well real quick now, and we'll go fishing."

Nick brightened. He loved going fishing with his pa-pa.

Jim left. Abby took a deck of cards from her magical tote that always held everything but the kitchen sink. "Now, what about a good game of hearts while we wait for the doctor?"

Some of the tenseness eased from Eve's body. The color in Nick's face was back to normal, and though his arm was still black-and-blue and he grimaced when he moved it, some of the swelling had gone down.

Now, if only Josh Manning's dog's recovered, as well...

She spent the rest of the morning playing hearts with Nick and Abby.

Nick had lunch and went to sleep, and she and Abby had lunch in the cafeteria and swore they wouldn't eat there again. Eve's truck, Miss Mollie, appeared later that afternoon. Reggie, followed by a friend in another car, had driven it to the hospital. The friend drove both Reggie and Abby home but not before saying hello to Nick, teasing him about his lack of ability as a snake charmer and handing him a model motorcycle. Nick was elated by the gift and she was touched.

To her amazement, a bouquet of balloons and cookies also arrived, this time sent by Al Monroe and the city council.

But Nick was worn out by midafternoon. He was still receiving sedatives, and he moved between sleep and sluggishness. When his eyes closed, his body twitched occasionally. But the doctor was more encouraging and said he should be able to go home Monday morning.

Stephanie called with good news about Amos.

"Josh Manning stayed several hours last night until he was convinced that his dog would be okay. He even bought me a patty melt and met your father-in-law. I like him. He's spare with his words, but he's no one's fool. I found him rather comfortable."

Comfortable was not the word Eve would use to describe Josh Manning. In fact, she didn't think anything about him was comfortable. "Are we talking about the same man?" she asked.

Stephanie laughed. "Maybe it's because we were both worried about his dog. He's very gentle with him."

"He told me Amos was a military dog," Eve said, trying to pump Steph without showing too much interest.

But Steph changed the subject. "I heard your in-laws are taking care of the animals. I'll pitch in if you need me."

"I think they are more than happy to help, Nick being their only grandson, but I'll tell them."

"How long will you be there?"

"Over the weekend. Hopefully we'll be back Monday. It depends on whether he has a fever or the arm looks worse. Nick's taking it better than I am."

"Let me know if I can do anything."

"I will." She hung up.

Stephanie mentioned Josh's name easily while Eve was still trying it out. And Josh had mentioned Stephanie several times. Not as "Dr. Phillips," but "Stephanie." Unexpected jealousy streaked through her. She didn't like the feeling. But she couldn't forget the warmth of his body, the tenderness when he'd held her.

But he was obviously a loner and here only temporarily. She would be a fool to let him into her life. And especially Nick's.

CHAPTER NINE

Eve drove Nick home on Monday after spending three nights in the hospital. The swelling in his arm had gone down, although its color was still an ugly mixture of purples. There was some lingering pain, but Nick shrugged it off.

He bubbled with anticipation. He had a tale to tell his classmates. "Wait until I tell them about Josh tossing that snake and you blowing it to pieces. Wish I had its rattles."

"Today you rest, tomorrow we'll see," Eve said. "Depends on whether you have a temperature."

"But there's only four more days of school."

"Nonetheless, the doctor said you were to keep quiet if he was to let you go home. And quiet you will stay today. Not only that," she added, "your grandmother said Braveheart has been hiding behind the sofa, Captain Hook is running around in circles and Miss Marple has brought kleptomania to a new level. Time to stop the mayhem."

"But…"

"Plenty of time for you to share. You have all summer."

Nick grinned. "Okay. But can I see Josh and Amos soon?"

She winced at his use of *Josh.*

"He's really busy, Nick."

"You think he'll come by and see me?"

"I don't know, but Stephanie said he asked about you."

"I like him."

"You like everyone, kiddo."

They reached her house and she turned the ignition off. Nick ran for the house. "Walk," she yelled.

He slowed, but then Abby opened the door and the dogs spilled out. They swarmed over Nick first, then Eve, licking and barking and jumping with joy. Then there had to be a trip to the stables. A box of sugar cubes was waiting for Nick to give to the horses.

When they finished saying hello to Beauty and the Beast and Stephanie's horse, Shadow, Abby was waiting inside with Nick's favorite casseroles.

"Can you stay for a few more hours?" Eve asked. The proposed budget had to be published in the weekly on Thursday, and she still had a few bugs to work out. Then there would be a public hearing and finally, hopefully, approval by the council.

"Of course. You know I love to spend time with Nick."

Eve ate quickly and hugged Nick. "Stay quiet," she said, recognizing the fact that he probably wouldn't.

"I want to see Amos."

She had been wondering when that was coming.

Stephanie had told her that Amos had gone home, and she had reassured Nick, but he wanted confirmation. Amos was his hero.

"Tell you what," she said. "You stay quiet today, and I'll call Mr. Manning and see if you can visit Amos tomorrow after school."

He looked disappointed.

She looked at all the animals gathered around his chair. "You wouldn't want to hurt their feelings," she said, knowing it was a low, though effective, tactic. Guilt usually worked with Nick. "They've been waiting for you."

"Okay, Mom," he responded, but there was disappointment in his voice. And she knew her son. If she didn't arrange a meeting, Nick would.

She hugged him again. She could never hug him tight enough. She felt tears coming, but she didn't want him to see them.

"I'll be home early," she told Abby. "Thank you for taking care of this crew."

Abby nodded. "Nothing makes me happier. Nick reminds me so much of Russ."

"I know."

Eve left before more tears came. She had never been much of a crier. But she had been an emotional wreck since the snakebite.

She had sworn that she wouldn't lose her heart again. She couldn't do it to her son or to herself. The pain was too deep. She had to stay away from Josh Manning, who stirred feelings she'd thought gone forever. But how was she going to do that when he had become Nick's hero?

MONDAY. THREE DAYS since he'd seen Eve Douglas. Three days since Amos had come home. Odd how time had suddenly become important.

He'd spent part of Sunday on a trip to Pueblo, where he'd bought flooring. He'd chosen bamboo for the main room and vinyl tile for the kitchen, both of which were to be delivered Wednesday.

Then he had made another stop at a furniture store for a fridge and stove, his two most immediate needs. But going through the store, his gaze had caught other items and he'd gone on a buying spree: a sofa for Amos and a lounging chair for himself, along with several lamps, a bookcase, a desk and a small dining table with two chairs.

Delivery for all this would be Saturday morning, which meant he had to finish painting and flooring. A daunting job. He would finish painting the kitchen tomorrow, then tear out the kitchen floor and replace it Wednesday and Thursday. At least that was the schedule. The living room floor would come next. He figured he might have to hire someone to help him with the flooring. He wasn't that good on his knees yet.

He figured he could double the value of the cabin by a good month's work and minimal investment.

Josh had to admit, though, that the place was growing on him, and that was before he'd had a chance to explore the forest behind it. He was even getting used to the town's curiosity. There was something to be said for the friendly greeting at Maude's, the vet's easy friendship as she continued to check on Amos, the view from his windows at sunset.

And Eve Douglas.

Amos spent more time with him rather than hiding in the bedroom. Josh thought about simply closing the door to the bedroom to keep Amos from retreating, but decided it was something Amos had to do in his own time. He, too, had wanted to withdraw from the world when he'd emerged from unconsciousness and discovered that nearly all his team, including Dave, had died in that last battle. Then he'd learned he'd been left the cabin and, in a way, Amos. He owed a debt, and he'd never reneged on one.

But that was all he'd intended to do. He hadn't meant to care so much for Amos or get involved in the lives of civilians. He certainly hadn't expected to find himself befuddled by the mayor. He had called once to see how the boy was, and it had taken all his willpower not to drive back to the hospital.

No sense in getting involved when he would leave sooner rather than later. And Stephanie's words about Eve's husband had only deepened his resolve to stay away. *Never was anyone else for her. Everyone loved him.*

He worked through the day, stopping only when the pain in his leg became too bad. Then he would grab a bottle of water and a sandwich and rest for thirty minutes.

It was four o'clock when he heard a knock on the door and he limped to answer it. *What now?*

Eve Douglas stood on the stoop as if she'd been summoned by his thoughts. He didn't believe in sorcery, but...

"Hi," she said. "I tried to call you, but..."

"I forgot to charge the damn thing," he said, holding the door open. "Come in if you don't mind the smell of paint." He paused, then asked, "How's Nick?"

She stepped inside. "Doing well. We came home this morning, and he's staying home today with Abby. He's not happy. He wants to tell everyone at school about his adventures."

She looked around. He'd finished painting the walls and ceiling of the living area. She went on to the kitchen. "I'm impressed."

"Just trying to make it livable."

"And then?"

"I don't know. Sell it, maybe. I've never stayed anywhere long."

"Where's home?"

He shrugged. "Army bases, mostly."

"Then where were you raised?" she asked patiently.

He stilled, then shrugged. "Atlanta."

"I hear it's a good place."

"I suppose."

She looked at him with questioning eyes, but he

didn't feel like explaining. How do you explain a mother on crack, a series of temporary "stepfathers" who were abusive and finally having to live on the streets while trying to finish high school in order to join the army?

"I stopped by to thank you for everything you did for us. You and Amos. Nick wants to thank Amos. Can we stop over tomorrow after school? Just for a few moments?" She said the last words in a rush. Their gazes met. She looked so earnest. Tenderness swept through him. He touched her hair and pushed back a curl, then let his hand drop to his side.

He knew he shouldn't touch her at all. She'd just been through pure hell after Nick was struck by the rattler. She was vulnerable. But then their hands brushed and his enclosed around hers. She leaned into him and suddenly she was in his arms, and their lips met, tentatively at first. Her lips parted slightly and her eyes, always alive and curious, misted. He stopped. It had been a long time since he'd been with a woman and he'd never felt the potent mixture of tenderness and passion as he did now. It stunned him.

The need was insistent. A connection with another person. He had been running away from that most of his life, but now it was irresistible. His arms went around her, and she trembled against his body.

She felt good, so damn good. She attracted him as no other woman had. But maybe these feelings were like fireworks: great explosions of light and then they fizzled out as they fell to earth.

He reminded himself that she was vulnerable after the scare with her son. And he didn't want sex that way. Not from her.

He leaned down and kissed her, slow and gentle, then held her against him. It went against all his instincts not to take the next step. Maybe tomorrow. Or the next day, when she'd had time to unwind from the scare.

She looked up at him. Her eyes were glazed, her face flushed and her breath came in short bursts. "I don't usually fall into men's arms," she said softly.

"I know. I usually back off."

"I know," she replied, some regret in her voice.

"Besides, everyone in town probably knows you're here," he said drily.

"Probably," she agreed.

"And the longer you stay…"

"I didn't think you were the type to worry about that."

"I couldn't care less for myself. It's you I'm thinking about. You and the boy." He let a few seconds go by before adding, "It's good to know he's doing well. I know you were frightened."

"Terrified." Her voice shook slightly, and he knew the nightmarish afternoon was still with her. "Nick doesn't really know how bad it could have been."

"Maybe he did and didn't want to scare you." He paused, then added, "There's something to be said for being young. When something doesn't kill you, it becomes an adventure."

She smiled at the truth of that. "He keeps asking about Amos. I know him. If he doesn't see for himself that Amos is fine, he'll find a way to get here. Probably by bike. I thought I should warn you."

Her gaze was locked on him, and the color of her eyes seemed to be changing. Damn, but they were beautiful, particularly when they were swimming with emotion.

"I appreciate it," he said and stepped away before he grabbed her and carried her off to bed. He'd placed a wall between them. Invisible, but he knew she sensed it.

"What happened, Josh?"

Her voice was soft and caring, and he knew she wasn't asking about the snake or the cabin. She was asking about the months and years before, about the part of himself he protected.

Her eyes were so searching, he almost told her. About his rotten childhood, when he'd learned not to trust anyone. About how when he did learn to trust the members of his team, he'd betrayed them. He'd gotten them killed. He was a Jonah, plain and simple. He couldn't even take care of a damn dog without it getting snake bit.

"Josh?" The question again. The one he didn't want to answer.

Just then Amos barked, and Eve seemed distracted.

She tipped her head. "I'm so glad he's okay, too. He's such a beautiful dog. Stephanie told me that he had gone home after an overnight stay."

"Did she say anything else about him?"

She shook her head. She stepped closer, put her arms around his neck and those wide hazel eyes looked up at him questioningly. "Tell me about him."

"I told you he was a military dog. Dave was his handler for four years, and they were close. Because we were often in places without kennels, they slept together, ate together. Then one day Dave didn't come back. Amos wasn't with him on that particular mission because his paw had been injured. Amos waited and waited and waited. He wouldn't respond to anyone. Barely ate. He was sent back to the States for retraining, but that didn't work. He simply refused any command and was put up for adoption."

"Were you there when Dave was killed?"

She saw too much. He nodded and he knew his voice was rough when he said, "I promised him earlier I would take care of Amos if anything happened." He stopped, closed his eyes.

She waited, silently, for him to continue. "I was injured in the same battle," he said huskily, "and after a stay in Germany I was sent to a military hospital stateside. Then I started looking for Amos." He didn't tell her everything, not about the months of pain and operations and, worse, the guilt that never faded.

She didn't say anything but her arms tightened around him and she rested her head against his heart. No words, but he didn't need any. She'd known loss, too, loss deeper than his own. *Someone everyone loved.*

Change the subject.

"I think in trying to save your son, Amos might have saved himself. Stephanie tried to tell me when we first talked about Amos that maybe he needed a purpose. I thought he had withdrawn because he missed Dave, and I still think that's a very large part of it, but then I looked at what happened to Amos the past year. He was mourning, probably thought he'd been deserted by the person he loved most, then was shipped off alone to kennels stateside." He paused. "Maybe he found a purpose Friday. At least made a start."

"Maybe his owner should take a lesson from that?" Eve said. "I can't believe what you've done with this cabin in the time you've been here. Those skills are needed."

He shook his head. "I'm learning as I go along," he said, "and, like I said, I don't stay in places long."

"Maybe it's time you did."

He touched her face again, this time letting his fingers linger and trace the line of her jaw. His body ached with longing. He wanted to dig deep under that calm serenity and ignite the fire he felt in her. But he couldn't. He shook his head slowly. "I'm a wanderer and you're a nester, and I would bet everything I have that you've never had a one-night stand, or one-week stand, and that's all I know. All I want. No complications."

He was lying. He did want more, he just hadn't known it until now.

But it wouldn't work. He would leave one day, and it could break two hearts. Maybe three.

He stepped back.

She gave him a long, steady look, then nodded. She started to turn, then stopped. "About Nick?"

"You can bring him over tomorrow afternoon." Bad decision, but the boy would be here with his mother. No temptation then. At least that was what he told himself.

"Thank you," she said softly, and as he closed the door he wondered exactly what she was thanking him for.

CHAPTER TEN

SHE HAD BEEN ready to fall into his arms.

It was frightening how much she'd wanted that. Even now she ached for his touch.

She'd almost told him that, almost said that maybe all *she* wanted was a one-night stand, too. But it would be a lie, and he would know that. He'd pegged her right. She *was* a nester, a forever kind of girl.

Russ had been the only man she'd ever slept with. She wasn't a prude. She knew the world had changed. It was just that she hadn't ever had the desire for another man before or since Russ. Oh, sure, she was human. She could lust as well as anyone over Hugh Jackman, but that was just fantasy. Perhaps because her life had been so full, so busy, these past years, she'd never given anyone even a sideways glance.

Her marriage hadn't been perfect. Russ was always gone. Covenant Falls High School was small, and he taught history as well as coached. In the summer, he ran the Little League program. A kid had a problem, Russ would try to work it out.

She couldn't even begin to count the number of dinners that had gone cold, the events they'd never made or invitations they'd never accepted. But when he *was* home, he was warm and loving and a great father. He loved to grill outside and cook huge pots of spaghetti and chili and other "specialties." He never seemed to stop moving....

Josh Manning reminded her of him in that respect. Despite his limp, he moved with purpose and even quickly when necessary. He certainly had moved fast when tossing the snake away from her son. She'd seen a tightening of his lips several times when he moved, though, and knew that it hadn't been painless.

But neither that nor abstinence explained the way her world rocked when he was within arm's reach. Nothing explained that. All things considered, she still knew very little about him.

She tried to dismiss him from her mind and headed for home and her son. She'd finally completed the budget, and Merry was checking it for errors. Some of it would meet resistance from the council, particularly the ten thousand dollars for the community center. After Merry reviewed it, Eve would go over the corrections, then it would go to the newspaper to be published Thursday. The budget was always big news in Covenant Falls, a subject of great debate, and she knew she had to be ready to defend every line in it....

When she arrived home, Nick was on the sofa covered by three dogs. The fourth, Braveheart, was huddled next to it. Eve was happy to see her son resting, not so happy to see he was watching a detective story on television. He had been obsessed with them since his grandfather's murder.

"Hi," she said. "How you doing?" Not exactly grammatical, but Nick certainly didn't mind.

"Grandma says I don't have a temperature. Can I go to school tomorrow?"

She looked at his arm. There was a small bandage where the fangs bit into the skin, but the area around it had lost the angry purple and was mostly the color of a three-day-old bruise. And it was blessedly cool. "Looks good."

"Grandma's cooking spaghetti," he said. "Why don't you ask Mr. Manning for supper? Grandma said it would be okay."

"I stopped over there, and he's busy painting a room," she said, "but he wants to see you, too. I said we would stop over there tomorrow afternoon after school. No baseball practice for you yet."

"Maybe we can take something over to him," Nick persisted.

"There's the rolls I baked today," Abby suggested. "You could take those over."

Nick's face fell for a moment, then he nodded. "Yeah."

Nick giving up his beloved cinnamon rolls was a really big deal. She was impressed. And worried. She didn't want Nick to get too attached to someone who would probably be leaving soon. "Okay, then, cinnamon rolls it is," Eve said. Anything to end the conversation. She feared her face flushed whenever Josh's name was mentioned.

She decided to divert attention. "Anything going

on I should know about?" Because Jim talked to so many people at the drugstore, Abby always had a pulse on what people were saying.

"Folks are still upset about those burglaries."

"Has someone else been robbed?" she asked, alarmed.

"No, it's just that Al Monroe is spreading his poison all over Covenant Falls about how we need a new police chief. I told him off when he said something loud at Maude's. Isn't a better person alive than Tom, but I'll tell you, Eve, the businesspeople are worried. Jim is real worried because of the drugs the store carries."

"The other two targets had bad locks," Eve said. "Jim has a strong security system."

"But I don't like it when he fills a prescription at night. He should just tell people he's closed, but you know him."

"Tell you what," Eve said, "I'll alert the deputies on night duty. When Jim has an essential prescription, he can call them and they'll escort him. It's usually quiet at night anyway."

Abby looked relieved. "I don't want anyone to think we're getting special favors."

"They won't," Eve said, wondering how many other residents were equally worried about safety. "I'll make the offer to any business open past dusk."

Jim arrived shortly after seven and ate with them. The four of them then played hearts for an hour. Jim and Abby packed up at nine, leaving a plate of cinnamon rolls behind when they went out the door.

Eve followed them out and thanked them for taking care of the animals while she and Nick were gone, and for staying over today.

"You know how much we love that boy," Abby said. "The dogs kinda grow on you, too. Especially Fancy. Followed me all over the house when you were gone. Jim even let her sleep on the bed."

Abby got a nudge from her husband.

"I wasn't supposed to tell you that," Abby said. "He likes everyone to think he's a tough guy."

She gave Eve a quick hug. "I couldn't ask for a better daughter-in-law. We are all so proud of you. Russ would have been, too." She paused, then asked, "Do you know where he came from yet?"

Eve didn't have to ask who "he" was. "Only that he's an army veteran and his dog was a military dog. I know he's a hard worker—it's miraculous what he's done with that cabin in little more than a few weeks. More than ten years of dirt and grime gone. Basic repairs made. He's painting. He's cleared the area in back."

"Do you think he's going to stay?"

"I doubt it," she said and wished that observation wasn't accompanied by a sick feeling in her stomach.

"Too bad. Jim said he seemed like a nice young man."

That made her smile. "Nice young man" didn't quite fit her experience with him.

She decided she didn't want to explain that thought so she just nodded. "Just to let you know, we won't be going to baseball practice tomorrow. Nick still needs to take it easy."

"There's a big game Saturday. Will he be able to play?"

"I'm not sure. I'll check with Doc Bradley first."

"Then he'll be out of school. He can stay with us during the day while you work," she offered hopefully.

"He's going to day camp at the community center, and I'm going to try to do some work at home. But we'll certainly need you."

Abby beamed. "Anytime."

They swapped hugs, and Jim and Abby left.

After closing the door, she played a game of chess with Nick, losing as usual. She had too many other things on her mind to concentrate, and Nick had learned from Tom. It was humiliating being beaten by a ten-year-old, even if he was hers.

After he went to bed, she went out to the barn. Jim had cleaned the stalls and put down fresh hay. The water trough was full, and she could tell the horses had been fed. She gave them each an apple. "We'll go riding Saturday," she promised. They were restless, she thought, and then realized that she was restless, as well. Jumpy.

She went to the corral fence and leaned against it. There was nothing more magical to her than a clear Colorado night sky.

Her mother, though, had hated it. A big-city girl from the East, she had fallen in love with Eve's father when he was in Philadelphia as a witness. Her mother's father was the prosecuting attorney, and Eve's father, then with the county sheriff's department, had captured the prime suspect in a Philadelphia murder. Her father had been a long-limbed, good-looking man with a Western drawl and quick wit. But her mother had hated the isolation of Covenant Falls.

She had stayed with Robert Douglas because of Eve, but the marriage had been tense and unhappy, and she had left the day after her husband was buried. She hadn't returned.

Eve had learned then that love didn't conquer all.

Attraction didn't, either. She refused to believe there was anything more than that between her and Josh.

She heard the soft snort of one of the horses, probably Beauty, in the barn, and it was a good sound. A familiar sound. This was home. The only place she wanted to be.

EVE WOKE UP with a jerk and realized she hadn't set the alarm. The sun streamed through the windows. She glanced at the clock face. *Seven o'clock.* She had to get dressed, wake Nick and fix breakfast, feed and water the horses and get Nick to school by eight.

She sprang up and went to start the coffee. To her surprise, Nick had already started it and was sitting at the table eating cereal and drinking orange juice.

"I woke up in the wrong house," she said. "Who are you?"

He giggled.

She put two slices of bread in the toaster, grabbed the orange juice and filled a glass.

"You really should eat a proper breakfast," Nick said with a huge grin.

How many times had she said those words to him? "You're pretty chipper today. Especially for a boy who's been bitten by a rattlesnake. Does it still hurt?"

"It itches."

"And you know not to scratch it? No matter how much you want to."

He nodded.

"Remember, you promised not to run. Okay?"

"Okay." He finished his cereal. "I'll help feed the horses. I already filled the water bowls for the dogs."

She munched on the toast as they left the house. He grabbed his backpack and box of cinnamon rolls and tossed them in Miss Mollie before following her to the barn. They filled the water buckets and put out oats. Her father-in-law had already cleaned the stalls yesterday.

They put the dogs in the house and she locked the door. She didn't always lock it, but after the recent burglaries it seemed a good thing to do. She suspected a lot of people felt the same.

She had just started the truck when her cell phone rang. It was Tom. "We had another robbery last night," he said. "The Boot Hill Saloon. Same M.O."

Very professional. No one saw anything. It didn't close until 3:00 a.m. Austin went in early to accept a delivery. Considering what's been happening, he hadn't left any cash there, but the thief took eight cases of his most expensive liquor. His estimated losses total a couple thousand dollars. I was out there this morning. The lock wasn't broken. That means whoever did it is a pro. I dusted for prints but I don't have much hope of finding any useful ones."

"Let's talk at the office," she said, "but we might want to do a survey of business security measures in town and take at least one officer off day duty to patrol businesses at night."

Nick looked at her curiously, but she had taught him long ago that as mayor she might not always be able to answer his many questions.

They reached the school and he jumped out the second they stopped. Despite the fact he had two more tests in the next three days, he was excited to tell tales of rattlesnakes.

Her day would be full of tales of burglars.

And then, of course, there was the promised visit to see Josh Manning.

This was not going to be an easy day.

FIREFIGHT. EXPLOSIONS. DAVE covered in blood. Josh woke suddenly. He must have yelled because he felt a furry face nudging him. He opened his eyes to see a pair of canine eyes staring back at him.

"Hey, buddy," he said. "Thanks." He touched the

dog's head, then Amos moved away, sat and just kept staring as if he wanted something and Josh was too stupid to understand.

His body and bed were soaking wet again. Sweats. The same he'd had so many nights. He looked at his hands. They were shaking.

He stood painfully. He'd been on his feet all day yesterday and his leg ached. He took a cold shower and dressed in jeans and a dark blue denim shirt, then brewed a pot of coffee, poured himself a cup and went outside to drink it.

The day was perfect, the sun ascending into a clear blue sky. The morning air was fresh. Images of the ambush, the smell of gunpowder and chill of that night faded in the daylight. He looked down at Amos, who stood at his side.

He scratched the dog's ears. "Good dog. Good Amos."

Amos didn't wag his tail, but he had come out on his own. He wasn't shivering and he didn't shy from him. Josh tried not to be too optimistic.

"We have a job to do, Amos," he said. He went back inside and found a pair of gloves and his Swiss Army knife, then limped out the rear door and walked toward the overgrown path that led into the woods.

Amos hesitated, then followed when Josh called his name.

They walked to the spot where he'd thrown what was left of the snake on Friday. It wasn't easy to find since it blended into the rocky soil. It was Amos who found it, as if he knew what Josh was looking for. Josh leaned down with his knife and cut off the rattles. In addition to bullet wounds, the snake looked as if it had been injured before the attack. Maybe by an eagle.

He buried the snake. He had no anger toward it. It had done what snakes do—tried to protect itself.

He carefully walked farther into the woods. The trees almost immediately closed around him as the path disappeared upward. He wondered where it led. But right now he wasn't sure whether his leg was ready for that.

And the cabin awaited him. The work blotted out other thoughts. It also exhausted him, and that was good. It was productive work. Bringing order out of chaos. He was smart enough to know on some level he was trying to bring order to his life, but he wasn't ready to fully admit that yet.

He wondered if he would ever be there. Until he was, he knew he should keep away from Covenant Falls's pretty mayor or he could bring disaster to both of them.

The fact was, he no longer had confidence in himself or anything he might do. He had trained half his life to be a leader, and he was a leader who lived when his men died. Dave. Dragon. Kelly. Mac. Eric. Men who depended on him. Trusted him.

He went back inside. He washed the rattles in disinfectant, dried them and placed them on the counter. Then he ate breakfast and knew it was time to start painting again. The furniture would be delivered Saturday.

He touched the primer he'd applied to the kitchen walls. Dry. He mixed the paint, a soft yellow for the sun to play off. He taped around the two windows that looked out over the lake. He glanced out and saw a police car move slowly along the road to where it ended, then turn around and head back. It seemed to slow as it passed his house, then sped up.

Probably a routine patrol. He brought his portable stereo into the kitchen and turned it on. He'd picked up an appreciation for jazz—the early smooth Chicago stuff—and he hadn't heard it lately.

He erased everything else from his mind and started painting. Anything to keep from thinking. From remembering.

CHAPTER ELEVEN

HOW WAS SHE going to handle this? Shivers of anticipation ran through Eve as she drove to the school to pick up Nick. The box of Abby's cinnamon rolls was beside her.

Her hand had been forced. She had promised Nick she would take him by Josh's cabin. Or had she promised not because of Nick, but because she wanted to see Josh again and was looking for an excuse?

She couldn't remember when last she had been so confused. She always thought things through. She was practical. Realistic. She was none of these things now.

What did she want? Certainly not romance. Certainly not the complications that came with it. Especially with a man like Josh, who obviously was fighting battles of his own. Yet, like a lemming, she kept running toward that cliff.

She was late. She'd had to sit through yet another rant by Al about the most recent burglary and the need for a new police chief. But it was what he said at the end of the conversation that had struck her hard.

"I hear you've been visiting that Manning guy," he'd said.

"I took over his building permit."

"Isn't that unusual? Taking a permit by hand."

There was a leer in his eyes she didn't like. Marilyn, apparently, had been busy spying lately. "No," she said. "I usually try to visit new residents and welcome them."

"Several times?"

She wanted to smack him for his suggestive remarks. "I don't report to you, Al, about my comings and goings."

"There's talk, Eve. Just thought it was my duty to bring it to your attention."

"And now you have, and I can say it is none of your business."

His face turned red. "You're mayor," he said. "You should be aware of appearances."

"I'm very aware, Al. I would suggest you do the same. Nepotism is not usually considered a good thing."

She was making an enemy, but right now she didn't care. She was tired of his bullying. He had power because of his wealth and the fact that he had financial ties to many of the businesses not only in town but also in the county.

She needed this job, she needed it for her son, but if she had to fight Al for what was right, she would. This wasn't about her visits to Josh's cabin. It was all about his nephew and her refusal to appoint him police chief.

His brow smoothed out. "I was just trying to give

you a piece of useful advice. He's a newcomer, and there were no burglaries before he arrived. Just be careful."

"I appreciate your advice," she said ironically and left.

She wasn't going to be intimidated. The burglaries were concerning, though. Each one seemed to escalate in the amount of financial damage.

Tom was discouraged, as well. There were no clues to any of them. No eyewitnesses. No fingerprints. No evidence left at the scene. Tom didn't think it was an amateur.

Even worse, he'd concluded it had to be someone in Covenant Falls. Someone who knew routines. Someone who knew who would have money or items of value available. Someone who knew the weaknesses of each establishment.

It made Eve sick to think about it. She knew suspicion was concentrating around Josh. He was an easy target. He was seen as unfriendly. It was easier to blame Joshua Manning than someone everyone knew, even though he didn't have the intimate knowledge of the town Tom thought the perpetrator must have.

Tom didn't agree with common opinion for that reason, but he had no leads and Al was on a tear.

All those worries evaporated when Nick jumped into the car, all his energy on display. His face was full of excitement.

"You're supposed to be quiet," she said.

"I was. I didn't play ball during recess."

She swooped down and gave him a kiss. "Good for you. How did the day go?"

"Everyone was jealous," he said.

She raised an eyebrow. "Jealous of getting a snake-bite?"

"Sure, no one else has had one, and I told them about Josh and his dog and how they saved me. I told them Josh was a really good guy and my friend," he finished in a rush. "Can we go see him now? You said…"

"I know what I said, and we can, but just for a few minutes. You have that last test tomorrow."

"Yeah, but it's English and I'm good at that."

"This coming from a boy who says *yeah*."

"Sorry, Mom."

She looked down at his earnest face. The color was back in his cheeks and his eyes were clear and excited. It had been a long time since she had seen him this happy. And she was happy, too. Just worried. Nick and Josh had met only once, and he had already made Josh his hero.

More to the point, the dour Josh Manning had the same effect on her.

"We can't stay long," she said. "I want to look over the budget one last time tonight before it goes to the newspaper, and Mr. Manning is very busy."

"I just want to make sure Amos is all right. And thank him. And Josh," Nick added shyly.

"I know," she said. "And it's a good thing to do. But

we can't stay long, okay? And you give him Grandma's rolls. It was your idea."

He nodded. "But maybe later he can meet Braveheart and the crew."

Poor Braveheart. Amos, as retiring as he was, would probably scare the pit bull to death. But she didn't say anything.

"I brought a dog biscuit," Nick offered.

"Don't be disappointed if he doesn't eat it, okay?"

"I won't," he said, but she knew he would. He had a magic touch with animals and he rarely failed to make friends with one.

They arrived at the cabin. Josh's Jeep was in front. She saw the covered motorcycle to the side. He must be home. She beeped the horn to alert him, then climbed down from Miss Mollie. Nick scrambled out the other side and started to run up the porch steps. "Slowly," she said.

He slowed a little and knocked on the door.

She followed behind. Nick's possible disappointment that Josh might not, in fact, be home was the only reason her heart hammered. But then the door opened and there he was, dressed in snug blue jeans and a paint-splattered blue shirt with the sleeves rolled up, displaying heavily muscled arms. A paintbrush was in one hand. Her heart didn't just hammer now, it thundered.

"Is this a bad time?" She barely managed the words.

Nick's face fell.

"Not for Nick," he said, looking directly at the boy, who beamed back up at him with hero worship. "I think Amos would like to know how you're doing."

He held the door open, and the three of them walked inside. The smell of paint was strong. The world's ugliest sofa dominated the middle of the room. Once inside, Nick stammered for a minute, then said solemnly, "Thank you for saving me from the snake."

"Your mom killed it."

"But she's my mom. She's supposed to do stuff like that."

"Not all moms do," he said, and Eve heard a sardonic note in his voice.

She started to say something but Nick broke in. "Where's Amos?"

"In the bedroom. Go straight down the hall to the end room. I want to see how Amos reacts," he said. "Amos headed for the bedroom when he heard your pickup."

With that, he started down the hall, his limp more pronounced, but it was late in the day and from what she could see of the walls, he'd been working all day.

His bedroom was as Spartan as everything else in the house except for several dog toys. They looked untouched.

Nick knelt next to Amos, whose butt stuck out from under the bed, and started telling him what a fine dog he was. A hero. Before long, Amos had inched out from the bed and licked Nick's hand.

"He's been going outside with me," Josh said, "but then he heads for the bed when he hears a loud noise."

"He looks happy now," she said. The dog had turned over on his back for a belly rub. Nick complied, and Amos practically purred with pleasure.

Eve looked at Josh's face. It was stunned at first, then she saw the dawning of a smile. She was entranced by it.

"Is it okay if I give him a dog biscuit?" Nick asked. "I want to thank him, too."

"I think you already have, champ, but I think he would appreciate it."

Amos did. He took the biscuit gingerly, then crunched on it. He didn't seem to mind three people watching every bite.

"I have something for you, too," Josh told Nick.

"You do?" Nick scrambled to his feet, more excited than she had seen him in the past few years.

Eve took in the image as Nick and Josh walked into the kitchen: the tall, lean man with the limp and the young boy trying to match his steps. Josh handed him the rattles from a snake. From, apparently, *their* snake.

"A souvenir," he said. "A badge of courage. You deserve it."

Nick looked stunned, then said, "Awesome." He hesitated, then switched the present to his left hand and held his right one out. A man-to-man shake. "Thanks a lot."

"You're welcome," Josh said and took Nick's small hand in one of his large ones.

It was said with a sweet sincerity that made Eve ache inside. She had liked Josh from the moment they'd met. She hadn't known exactly why. Now she saw another side of him. Thoughtful and kind beneath that gruff exterior.

"We have to go," she said before she did something stupid.

"Aw, Mom."

"You have the test tomorrow and I have to work."

Nick looked up at Josh. "Can I come back?" he said. "Maybe even bring Braveheart?"

"Braveheart?"

"Our pit bull who needs some confidence," she said. "He's like the cowardly lion in *The Wizard of Oz*."

"I question whether Amos is the greatest role model at the moment," Josh said.

"He's the bravest dog ever," Nick argued.

"Now, that I can agree with," Josh said.

"We do have to go," Eve said, before she started crying. Nick looked so happy and proud.

"The rolls," Nick said suddenly. "Grandma's rolls."

She had forgotten all about them. "Why don't you go get them?" she said. "Slow, remember."

When he was out the door, she turned back to Josh. "That was very thoughtful to give him those rattles. He'll treasure them."

"He deserved them. He did everything right.

And today's the first time Amos has licked anyone since…"

His voice dropped, and she hurried to fill the void. "He's always been that way with animals. His dad… He was, too. As for the rolls, my mother-in-law sent some of her prizewinning cinnamon rolls. I dare you to eat one without eating a second. And a third. Abby placed second in the bake-off at the state fair. Second to another lady in town. You might say Covenant Falls is the cinnamon-roll capital of Colorado."

"You don't have to dare me." He gave her a half smile that was devilishly attractive. "I'm tired of my own food, particularly without a working stove and fridge." He sat down on the sofa, and she could hear the intake of breath as he spread out his legs.

"Should you be on them so much?" she asked, knowing it was probably an unwelcome intrusion. It was none of her business anyway.

"I wasn't made to sit," he said. "I would go crazy. And the more I use my leg, the stronger it gets. At least that's the theory."

He was far more open than he had been. *Nick's magic.*

"And it's really nothing compared to some of the training exercises in the army. *That* was pain."

"What were you in?" she asked.

He raised an eyebrow. "You don't know?"

She flushed. So he knew, or guessed, that Tom had done a background check.

"Rangers," he said without waiting for an answer. "You go through hell to become a member."

Nick came back in then, holding the box of rolls as if it were a trophy. Josh took them, studied them then teased Nick, "Did you make these?"

"Grandma did, but I didn't eat them," Nick said earnestly, and Eve couldn't help but smile.

"Considering how they smell, I think that's a terrific accomplishment," Josh said solemnly. "Thank you for not eating them, and tell your grandmother I thank her, too."

Nick waited patiently for him to taste one. Josh grabbed a roll and took a bite, mostly, she realized, for Nick's sake.

Eve watched as appreciation passed across his face. Had he never had homemade cinnamon rolls before?

Nick didn't wait for him to finish. "Grandma wants to meet you. Maybe you can come over and meet Braveheart, Miss Marple, Fancy and Captain Hook. Do you play baseball?" The words ran together in his enthusiasm. Eve had to smile at his excitement. Surprisingly, for a man without a family, Josh knew just how to talk to him. Or maybe he did have a family somewhere. She was reminded how little she knew about him.

"I'm...sorry," she said, apologizing for Nick's questions, but Josh shook his head.

"Played baseball a little in the army," he said.

Another snippet of information. Nick was the only one that seemed to be able to elicit any. Josh suddenly seemed…approachable. Even open. Nick had disarmed him in a way she had not.

But she didn't want to wear out her welcome.

She also recalled Al's words about visiting Josh. She wasn't going to let him tell her what to do, but she was only too aware of how fast gossip ran through Covenant Falls and how Al could twist it to get his way.

"Enjoy," she said. "There will be more this weekend. The city's sponsoring a fund-raiser for our community center. Abby is baking cinnamon rolls for sale, along with pies. You think her rolls are good, just try her cherry pie. There will be other food, too." She eyed the sofa and raised an eyebrow. "And a rummage sale. You can also probably get some good buys in used furniture."

"Are you maligning my sofa?" he asked with a crooked grin that took her breath away.

"Never," she said with a grin of her own. She hurried on, hoping to interest him into attending the fund-raiser. If everyone else met him like she had, attitudes would change. "Stephanie is auctioning a dog-training class, and she's going to have an example obedience class featuring none other than Nick and one of our dogs."

"Please come," her son begged.

"Sorry," he said, "I would like to, but I'm expecting some deliveries Saturday morning."

Nick looked at Josh with wide eyes.

"Hey, I really need a stove and fridge. You don't

want me to starve to death." It was an apology of sorts, and it surprised her.

"It's going to be in and around the community center in the big park at the lake," she said. "We're trying to raise money for computers for kids and books for the library. Drop in if you get through. And now we really do have to go."

He nodded. "Thanks for the rolls."

"Say goodbye to Amos," she told Nick, who, she knew, was about to protest.

After one look at Eve, Nick leaned down over the dog, who had hovered near him, and gave him a big hug. Amos tolerated it.

Eve thought she saw the smallest smile on Josh's face but wasn't sure.

She did know that nothing had calmed the tingling feelings inside. They were still there. Even stronger. But now there was something else, something even more dangerous. She *liked* Josh Manning. She liked him very much.

And she prayed he wasn't aware of it. Forcing herself not to look back, she hustled her son out the door.

CHAPTER TWELVE

JOSH QUIT PAINTING at midnight, only because his leg wouldn't hold out much longer. It was time to walk Amos before it stopped working completely.

He put the brushes away. The kitchen was mainly done but there was still finishing trim needed in both the kitchen and main room. Then there were the two bedrooms, a hall and a bathroom to go.

Amos had remained in his bedroom, probably offended by the smell of paint. Josh called to him and was relieved when Amos poked his nose out the door with a "do I have to?" look.

"Latrine time," he said.

The night was cooler than in past few days. A half moon drifted in and out of clouds. He started down the road. The house next to him was dark.

He limped to the side of the road when bright headlights moved toward him. The patrol car again. He wondered whether it would stop, but it continued slowly past his cabin to the road's end. Then it turned back. Its lights suddenly went bright as they approached him. Josh thought for a second that it might stop, but it continued its slow way past him, then sped up. He didn't like the clammy feeling that ran down his back. He'd felt it before when danger threatened. But there shouldn't be danger here.

Amos did his canine duty and Josh picked up after him. They reached the end of the road, then turned back. Josh didn't want to walk on the main road on a dark night, and his leg was complaining bitterly. "Okay, Amos, time to return to base."

Amos looked at him, then wagged his tail. He knew he would get a nighttime treat, but still, this was the first time he'd greeted the comment with any sign of enthusiasm. Josh thought about young Nick's request to bring another dog. Maybe that would be good for Amos. *Four dogs. Eve had four dogs and other assorted animals.* He had trouble with one.

He counted the ways they were incompatible. He got to five and stopped. They reached the cabin and Josh reprised his now almost normal routine of a cold shower, then a hot one. The cold water somewhat dissipated the sexual tension still very much bedeviling him and the heat soaked some of the pain away. He sat down on the bed, and Amos relaxed close by on the floor. Josh felt a jolt of satisfaction. Amos wasn't hiding tonight. He wasn't the dog Josh had known with Dave. Not at all. But there were small steps.

He'd realized today he would need help tearing up the floor and laying down the tiles. Kneeling most of the day would be awkward and slow. He didn't want to contact Eve…or maybe he did, and that was why he shouldn't.

He could call Stephanie for a name, but he had

another idea. One that might improve his reputation in town. He didn't much care what others thought of him, but he realized he might be hurting Eve, and that was the last thing he wanted.

As physically tired as he was, he knew sleep wouldn't come easily. It never did and never left gently. Too many memories. Too many debts. He picked up the book he'd left on the pillow. A biography of Thomas Jefferson. Some might think it dry, but somewhere along the way he'd picked up a love of history. He would read until he drifted off. The sound of Amos's soft snoring helped. He turned off the light at two, hoping tonight would be one without demons.

AT 9:00 A.M., Josh changed from work clothes into a new pair of jeans and a green shirt. He'd already been up for hours, finishing the trim on the two rooms he'd painted. He would start peeling wallpaper in the bathroom after the flooring was installed in the kitchen and living room.

He shaved closely and even trimmed and combed his hair. Then, holding an empty tin that once held a dozen brownies, he straightened his back and resolutely left the sanctuary of the cabin.

The sky was clearing now, but there had been heavy rain during the night. The thunder had jerked him awake at dawn, and for moments he'd thought he was back at camp in Afghanistan. Amos had crawled up on the narrow bed, shivered and whined. It had been uncomfortable, sharing a narrow bed with a big, furry animal, but satisfaction had overrode discomfort. It was a giant step for Amos. Maybe he needed to take one, as well.

He walked two doors down the road, approached the neat white cottage and rang the bell. He saw someone peek out the window, then the door opened and the plump elderly woman who had brought the brownies a week earlier opened the door, a quizzical look on her face.

He held out the tin. "Ma'am," he said, "I want to apologize. I was inexcusably rude the other morning. My leg hurt late into the night and I had just gotten to sleep when you came." He tried a repentant smile, although he had damn little experience at it. "I can't tell you how grateful I am for the brownies. They were truly a work of art."

Her face softened. Sympathy flooded it, and she opened the screen door and took the tin. "I heard you and your dog saved young Nick Douglas. That family has had so many troubles. I'm grateful to you. Would you come in and have some coffee?"

It was the last thing he wanted to do, but he was on a mission to make amends. "Thank you, ma'am. I will, but I can't stay long. I'm expecting some deliveries today and have some painting to do."

"We're certainly glad someone is fixing that cabin," she said. "Now, you just come into the kitchen." She hustled him inside. "Jim Douglas said you were busy fixing the cabin. He's the one who told me about that snake. Nearly scared the wits out of me because I have a garden out back."

He went by a framed photo on the fireplace mantel and stopped as he saw the large photograph of a young man in uniform.

"My son," she said. "He was killed in the last days of the war in Vietnam."

"I'm sorry," he said, guilt now piling on top of guilt. He'd hurt this woman who'd lost a son.

"Lots of folks around here have lost sons," she said. "Kids here don't have many opportunities. Don't see much of life beyond this town. Jesse wanted to see the world. Instead, he died in a godforsaken country. Guess you would know something about godforsaken countries."

He must have looked surprised.

"I had you pegged for military the first time I saw you," she said. "That's why the brownies. But I knew when I saw you that morning that it wasn't a good time. I'm sorry for intruding."

He was stunned. He had come to apologize. Now she was apologizing to him after suffering the worst loss a mother could. At least some mothers.

"I'm Josh Manning," he said, "and you're right. I was with the army."

"Officer?"

"Sergeant," he said.

"Jesse had just made sergeant." Sadness filled her voice.

Josh didn't know what to say. He had written letters

to new widows and other loved ones when he'd lost a member of his team. It had always been his most difficult responsibility, and he'd always felt inadequate. He felt just as inadequate now.

He needed to change the subject. "I was hoping you could do me a big favor," he said.

"If I can," she replied instantly.

"I'm tearing up the floors in the kitchen and main room, and I need some help. I figured you probably know everyone and might be aware of someone who would like the job."

She smiled. "Bless you, of course I do. Betty Rowland's son, Nathan. He lost his construction job in Denver. He's a hard worker and honest as the day is long. Here," she said as she picked up an address book and wrote down a number. "Tell him June Byars told you to call."

She poured coffee into a cup, then asked, "Cream or sugar?"

"Neither, ma'am," he said. "Black."

A plate of cookies appeared along with the coffee. Chocolate chip, he noticed. To be polite, he took one. The coffee was good, the cookie even better. He took a second one, and Mrs. Byars beamed. Then her face turned serious. "I knew David Hannity. He used to love those cookies. Can you tell me what happened to him?"

It was the question he dreaded. From anyone. But he liked this woman, and she apparently had known Dave well.

"He died in Afghanistan about nine months ago. He was a good soldier and a good friend."

"I'm so glad he had one," she said softly. "He had one tragedy after another. I worried about him. Kept hoping he would come back, but I guess there were just too many bad memories." She paused, then added, "You need any more help, Mr. Manning, you just come to me."

That was exactly what he had intended to say to her, to offer help if needed. "Josh," he said. "My name is Josh."

"Josh. I'm happy to have you as a neighbor."

He finished the second cookie and stood, thanking her. Before he could leave, she thrust a cookie tin in his hands. He mumbled his thanks and stumbled toward the door. Once there, he turned back. "If you ever need any help, just call me."

"You seem busy enough now," she said, "but I always enjoy a visit." There was a twinkle in her eyes.

He left the cottage with the tin of cookies, thinking maybe civilians weren't so bad after all. There was Eve, Nick, Stephanie and now Mrs. Byars.

Maybe he'd misjudged Covenant Falls. Maybe he might stay longer than he'd planned. Probably not a good time to sell anyway.

When he returned to the cabin, he called the number Mrs. Byars had given him and made an appointment to meet Nathan Rowland the next day, Thursday, at noon.

THE BUDGET WAS to be published Thursday, but it had gone to the publisher Wednesday and word had leaked out. Eve fielded calls all morning asking why this project was in it and that one was not. Why there weren't funds for paving for Oak Street when Front Street was scheduled for resurfacing. The school budget was cut. Not much, but it meant an employee raise that was half of last year's. Teachers felt betrayed by the widow of one of their own.

The police department also came in for a cut. She would have to cut one dispatcher. That meant only one officer and one car at night while the other night officer manned the phone, but she left uncut an open position as patrolman. They had been running one man short for four months.

Tom would not be happy about the loss of a dispatcher. He came in her office, a frown on his face.

"You don't like the budget?" she said.

"No, but I understand priorities." He walked around the office.

She knew that meant trouble. "Okay, Tom, what's wrong?"

"Sam Clark says he has a witness who saw a Jeep in back of the Boot Hill Saloon on the night it was robbed. He said it was a dark green."

Her heart jumped a beat. Josh's Jeep was green, and there weren't that many Jeeps in town. In fact, she didn't know of another one. "Who's the witness?"

"Tim Waters."

She knew Tim. He had been on one of Russ's football teams and had hopes of a college football career. Russ had said he had the talent but not the discipline. He'd been thrown off the team for drinking before games. The first offence had put him on probation, the second had knocked him off the team for the season in his senior year. His family had blamed Russ when he wasn't offered a football scholarship.

She wouldn't trust him with a candy bar, and said as much.

"I know," Tom said into the silence. "That was my reaction, as well. He's been in jail several times on drunk-and-disorderly charges, but lately he seems to be on the right track. Cliff Barber, his boss, says he's been on the wagon for years now."

"He says he saw the Jeep Saturday night."

Tom nodded. "I'm going to have to talk to Mr. Manning."

"He didn't do it," she said.

"How do you know?"

"You said he had a good army record. You're taking Tim's word as your only evidence to accuse someone? Maybe he did it and is trying to throw the blame on Manning."

"I checked a little deeper. Manning was a Ranger. Tough outfit and highly skilled in getting into difficult places."

"That's all?"

His face flushed. "We can't ignore the fact that we didn't have robberies until Manning came."

She found herself getting angry. She tried to hide

it. Tom was under pressure about the robberies. And
he had a heart condition. He shouldn't even be working.

But she felt Josh was just beginning to like—or
maybe tolerate—Covenant Falls. She knew the effect questioning would have on him. He would retreat
again, just as he was beginning to open up.

"I'm sorry, Little Bit, but I have to at least talk to
him. I do, or Sam will do it, and I'm a hell of a lot
more diplomatic."

It had been a long time since he had called her
"Little Bit." That went way back when she was six,
and Tom was her father's best friend. "Can't you stop
Sam?"

"I could, but the council is up in arms. There are
definitely grounds to question him now that Waters
has come out publicly. I wouldn't be doing my job
if I didn't. The other members of the council are on
the edge of firing me."

"They can't. That comes under my job description."

"They can take the money for the department out
of the budget. And they will." He glanced around her
office, then said, "What about grabbing a few sandwiches and drinks and driving down to the lake?"

Bad news was coming. She could feel it. Taste it.
"Okay."

"Where?"

"The Dairy Queen," Tom said. "Maude's is too
crowded."

She nodded. "Miss Mollie's outside. Better that than the chief's car."

It was a short distance, but she didn't want him walking more than necessary. They walked together to the pickup, then she drove the few blocks to the Dairy Queen, the hangout of every kid in town. It was empty now, but it would be filled at three. It was, after all, the next-to-last day of school. Graduation ceremonies would be next week.

She ordered a burger and fries. He sighed and ordered a grilled chicken sandwich without the bun. "Doctor's orders," he said sadly.

"I'm proud of you, Tom."

He grumbled.

They were the only ones in the park and headed for a picnic table. From here she could see across the lake to Josh's cabin. It was too far to see details or know whether his Jeep was there. It was usually parked under a pine tree as protection against the bright sunlight.

Tom hesitated, then said, "I know this Manning helped your son, but you don't know that much about him."

"You always tell me I'm a good judge of character, and don't tell me you're buying in to Sam's theory."

"No, I'm not," he said.

"Then why bother Mr. Manning?"

"Because I don't have any proof Tim Waters is lying." He hesitated. "I think Al is planning to run against you later this year, using me and these bur-glaries as a reason."

"But why? He had his opportunity three years ago."

"I know he's been talking to some folks. Telling them you're wasting city money on the community center, that he thinks taxes should be lowered and the city needs a strong police chief. Not, he makes a point to add, that I haven't been one, but, well, I'm getting on in years and the department needs new young blood."

"The salary is hardly worth the headaches," she said.

"Not if you're honest," he countered. "If you're not…" He shrugged. "I just read about a city clerk who stole more than a million dollars from a small town without anyone suspecting her."

"And he's using Josh as a weapon?"

"Maybe. Like I said, rumors. I know he's had some business losses. Hell, most small businesses are in trouble, and you know how he feels about Sam. I think he promised the job to him when he gradu-ated with the criminal justice degree. Sam's just been waiting for an opportunity to prove he could be po-lice chief. Remember all the rumors when Manning first moved here? Sam could have figured him for an easy patsy. He could solve the crime, get the commu-nity's gratitude and slide into my job. And get some cash, as well."

"Is he that smart?"

"More like calculating," Tom said.

"Then we should warn Mr. Manning."

Tom shook his head. "That's only one possibility. There's two others. One is that Manning *is* our thief. My source said he's been highly decorated. His superiors tried to get him to go for officer training and he refused. Wanted to stay with his team. Rangers see a lot of intense action. Someone like that would find it hard to settle down, to adjust to a place like Covenant Falls. It wouldn't be the first time a vet went bad."

"No one would put that much work into a cabin and then steal a few hundred dollars," she said.

"Maybe not, but some warriors just can't give up that adrenaline."

"You said three possibilities," she persisted.

"Could also be some hunters up in the forest. There's been some poaching. We've had trouble with them before." He paused. "The fact is we don't know, and I haven't met Manning. I wouldn't be doing my job if I didn't talk to him."

"I still think it's Sam," she said.

Tom was silent for a moment, then said, "Right now all I have against Sam is some roughness with motorists and poor judgment in several disputes. He's careful because he knows I've been watching him. But if he gets control of the police department and Al is elected mayor, Covenant Falls is going to be in trouble. I can't give the council a reason to fire me."

"If Al wants a war," she said, "he'll have one. And it's not about Josh Manning. It's about this town. And

I can fight as dirty as they do. I can veto any attempt to give Sam your job, even if I have to dissolve the department and contract with the county to provide services."

"If he thinks he's under suspicion, Josh Manning might pick up and leave. And this town would be right back where it was. The burglaries would stop. Everyone would think he committed them and fled, and Sam would be a maligned hero because you didn't listen to him.

"Or maybe Manning could help us," Tom added cautiously. "If Sam has anything at all to do with this, or suspects who does, he'll make a move to cast more suspicion on Manning."

She knew Tom didn't have to follow big department rules but acted on instinct, just as her father had done. She suddenly realized he had been feeling her out.

"And you might use Josh as a tethered goat?"

"Maybe. It might be the only way to learn the truth." He slumped on the bench. "Or maybe I should just let go."

A lump caught in her throat. She felt torn. Loyalty against…against what? A stranger who probably wouldn't stay long. And what if Tom was right? Sam as police chief, particularly if Al was mayor, would be a tragedy for the city. If he was responsible for the thefts, there was little he wouldn't do.

"No," she said. "If you're right, we have to know and have to have proof."

"I know you like him," he said. "I haven't seen that sparkle in your eyes for a long time."

"*Like* is the word," she said. "Nothing more. He's a loner. He's made it clear this is just a short stop along his way."

He gave her a long, searching look. "Are you really okay with this?"

"No," she replied, "but for now I don't see an alternative."

She suddenly realized why Tom was hanging on to his job despite his wife's objections. She knew he'd been opposed to any promotion for Sam, but she hadn't known how deep his concern was.

How could she not tell Josh? Trust was just beginning to build between them.

Because eventually he would leave, but Covenant Falls and its three thousand plus people would still be here.

Her heart pounded. Was she doing the right thing? She nodded. "Okay."

CHAPTER THIRTEEN

JOSH HAD STARTED pulling boards from the kitchen floor when he heard the sound of an approaching vehicle. He looked at the clock. It was only ten o'clock, and Rowland had told him that, while he'd been eager for the job, he couldn't arrive until noon because of another commitment this morning.

Josh decided to begin without him. The tiles and bamboo flooring had arrived yesterday as promised, and time was running short before delivery of the furniture on Saturday. The kitchen was particularly important since he wanted to hook up the new fridge and stove as soon as they arrived.

He went to the door. A tall gray-haired man in uniform stepped from a patrol car emblazoned with *police chief.*

He waited for the officer to come up the steps, then he stepped outside. "Is this an official visit or another hello?"

"A bit of both," the caller said. "I'm Tom Mac-Guire. The officer thrust out his hand and after a second's hesitation, Josh took it. Strong grip, but not one meant to intimidate. He relaxed slightly and waited.

"Wanted to come by and talk to you about a few things," MacGuire said. "Mind if I come in?"

"The place smells of paint," Josh said, "and there's not much to sit on."

"Doesn't matter," MacGuire said and waited.

Josh felt trapped. He opened the door. "I warned you," he said as MacGuire went inside. Amos had already made for the bedroom.

He watched as MacGuire's gaze took in the new paint, the newspapers still spread out on the floor. "You've been busy. Yard looks good, too."

"Not 'good,'" Josh corrected. "Controlled."

"I heard about the rattler. Fast thinking."

"Not really," Josh said. "It had been hurt in some way."

"Maybe. But you made some friends here in Covenant Falls."

Josh decided that directness was the best course. "My attorney said you had called him for information. You could have just asked me."

"I'd hoped to do it quietly," the chief said. "We've had three burglaries in the past few weeks. The first was a week after your arrival here and people here don't want to believe any of their neighbors were involved."

"Is that a warning? Or an accusation?"

"An observation," MacGuire said. "One I don't share, by the way, especially after my queries."

"That's comforting." Josh couldn't hide the sarcasm.

"I hoped to quell the rumors, but your service record is your business. I told my officers that I was satisfied you were not involved, but I haven't said any more." He paused, then added quietly, "I came home from Vietnam. None of us wanted to talk about what happened. I respect that."

Josh understood that. No one he knew went around talking about what they did, especially if they were in Special Forces. He relaxed slightly and got right to the point. "Is this the hello or the business part of the visit?"

MacGuire chuckled. "I see why Eve likes you. She doesn't do well with bullshit, either."

Josh felt an unexpected jolt of pleasure at the comment but tried not to show it. He waited for the chief to continue.

"Okay, that was the hello. Now for the business. Someone saw a green Jeep in the back the Boot Hill Saloon, the night it was robbed earlier this week."

"I would ask you what day it happened," Josh said, "But then there's no point because my answer would be the same if you're asking my whereabouts at the time. I've been here every evening since the day I arrived, except for Friday night when I spent the evening at the vet's office with my dog. You can ask her about that. And no, there were no witnesses to confirm I was here all that time, but there is all this paint. I've been too busy to discover who has what in this town, much less plan to steal it. And then there's the patrol car that has been passing here nearly every night. You might ask the driver. He probably saw my Jeep. I can tell you it hasn't been in back of a bar."

"I had to ask," the chief said.

"Any other Jeeps in town?"

"Not anyone in town. Could be renters in some of the summer cabins around here. Or campers."

"Interesting," Josh said. "Anything else?"

"Nick said you had an 'awesome' dog."

"Amos is resting at the moment," Josh said wryly. "He's not as friendly as I am."

MacGuire laughed, but then his face grew serious. "How long were you in the service?"

"Seventeen years."

"A lifer?"

"I thought so. At one time. Not much use for a soldier with a bum leg."

"There are desk jobs."

"Not for me. Not in the Rangers."

The lawman squinted. "When I came home from Vietnam, I didn't want to see anyone. Particularly civilians. They simply couldn't understand what war was like or how you had build walls to survive." He hesitated, then added, "Sometimes it got damned lonely. You need anything, call me."

Despite himself, Josh found his guard lowering. There was something in the policeman's voice that rang true.

"I would appreciate a tour," the police chief continued after a brief silence. "Eve said you've done wonders."

Two weeks ago, he would have refused. Maybe he had mellowed. A little. "Not much to see. I fixed the leaks on the roof." He led the way into the kitchen. "Just finished painting the kitchen and this room. I plan to install flooring in the kitchen today and in the living room tomorrow."

He opened the back door so they could see where he'd cleaned out the weeds and mowed the lawn. Then he showed the bathroom, which needed new wallpaper but was army clean. His bedroom was next. Amos had retreated to his haven under the bed.

MacGuire stooped and ran his hand around Amos's rump. "So this is the awesome Amos. He made quite an impression on Nick."

Amos didn't seem impressed. He didn't move.

"He doesn't care much for strangers," Josh said. He didn't add that he shared that view.

Josh noticed how the police chief's gaze never stopped moving. It covered every inch of the room, including the closet. "There's a Glock in there, but you probably know that. Eve used it quite effectively."

The chief didn't look embarrassed, merely said thoughtfully, "I was here a few years ago. Some kids used the cabin for a party. Pretty well trashed it. I made their parents have the kids clean their mess, but the cabin was already a mess. You've done a lot in a short time."

The chief left the room, leaving Josh to follow. "Thanks for the tour. You need anything, call."

Josh had absolutely no intention of doing so, but he nodded.

"Try me," MacGuire said and went out the door.

Josh watched the chief stride to the police car. He was in equal parts bemused and irritated. If being new in town was cause for suspicion and a visit from the police, he didn't want to stay long. He was through fighting for causes. All he'd wanted in coming here was peace. Quiet. Healing for Amos. Maybe for himself.

An illusion, it seemed. He decided he would hurry his efforts to put the cabin in decent shape for sale. Then get out the hell out of Dodge.

NATHAN ROWLAND ARRIVED at twelve sharp.

A good sign, Josh thought. But it was the only good thing about the day.

The man immediately asked Josh to call him Nate. "Only my mom calls me Nathan." He accepted coffee as Josh described the job and made what he thought was a fair offer. Nate accepted and said he could start immediately.

The afternoon went quickly. He and Nate tore out the worn boards to find an uneven and cracked floor. Nate continued to work while Josh went to the hardware store for more supplies.

When he returned, they used concrete leveler to smooth out the floor. Then it was nearing nine o'clock, and they both were dirty and tired. Josh decided to wait until the next morning to condition the surface, spread the mortar and place the tiles. Then they would start on the living room floor.

Nate asked whether he wanted to join him for a beer at the Rusty Nail, one of the bars around town.

Josh's first instinct had been to refuse, but he agreed. He wanted to know more about the police chief, and he wanted to hear it from an unbiased source. He liked Nate. The man was certainly competent. They worked well together. Neither of them were talkers. If he'd planned to stay longer, he would have liked to know him better. But he wasn't planning to stay. Especially after today.

"Sure," he said. "Give me a few minutes to clean up and feed Amos."

"My nephew got excited when I said I was coming here. He's in Nick Douglas's class and heard all about the dog. Is it okay if I bring him over? My brother and his wife are thinking about getting him a dog."

"Anytime, but I can't say how social Amos will be." Josh said. He went into the bedroom, grabbed a clean shirt then headed for the bathroom to wash. When he finished in there, he returned to the living room.

"I'm going to take Amos out and feed him. Use the bathroom if you want to wash up."

Amos cooperated without complaint this time. He went out willingly but avoided Nate on the way back inside. Josh filled his dish with dog food and several small pieces of cheese. Amos sniffed, ate the cheese then sat in front of the dish contemplating it.

"So that's the famous Amos," Nate said. "He's a handsome dog."

Amos regarded him suspiciously but made no move to go back into the bedroom. Nate stooped and offered Amos his hand to sniff. To Josh's surprise, Amos didn't shy away. He seemed to understand that Nate belonged here.

Josh grabbed his wallet and keys and locked the door as he left. "I'll follow you in my Jeep," he said,

Nate nodded. "It's four miles north of here."

Josh had noticed it when he'd driven into Covenant Falls. "I heard a bar was robbed a few days ago."

"Not the Rusty Nail. Johnny Kay, who owns it, lives above the bar and would blow away anyone who messed with it. Most of the townspeople go there for a beer. Good bar food. Boot Hill Saloon was the one that was robbed. It's farther out of town and attracts the cowboys and ranchers and the wilder crowd. Has country music and dancing on weekends. There's a third bar connected to a small motel just outside the city limits."

Josh didn't have to ask questions about that one. He just nodded, and he went to the Jeep while Nate went to his pickup truck. Josh had already decided his limit was going to be two beers, particularly now that he knew he was under scrutiny. He probably shouldn't go at all, but he was tired of his own company. And he wanted information.

The Rusty Nail was a typical bar. For a workday, there seemed to be a large number of cars in the gravel lot. Nate led the way inside and found a table in the back. After they both ordered a draft and a cheeseburger, they sat back and relaxed. "You a native of Covenant Falls?" Josh asked.

Nate nodded. "And lived here most of thirty years. Went to Covenant Falls High School. Then went to work at a construction company in Denver. I was a construction foreman, but the company went bankrupt three years ago, and I haven't been able to find anything steady since. Now I get odd jobs in Covenant Falls and surrounding areas."

"Married?"

"I was. Lost her when I lost my job. Figured it was no big loss if she skipped out the first time there was trouble."

Josh clinked his glass against Nate's. "Saw a lot of that in the service. Kinda turned me against marriage." Josh changed the subject. "Did you know Dave Hannity?"

"Yeah, but not well. No one here did, really. Several of the cabins around the lake were owned by Denver families that came down here in the summer. Now most of them are owned by people who live here year-round. Got them for a song where the market tumbled. Mrs. Byars is the exception. She's lived on the lake forever. I do know David had a pretty tragic life. His parents were killed in a small-plane crash, and he lived with his uncle. One day his uncle went fishing and didn't come back. He drowned in the lake." He hesitated, then added, "There were rumors, but then there's always rumors around here."

"I've discovered that," Josh said ironically. "What were these rumors?"

"Dave was an athlete. He could swim across that lake twice and never breathe hard. He said he was out running when it happened, but there were questions."

"Such as?"

"He was seen in the boat with his uncle earlier. They were arguing."

Why hadn't he heard any of this before? Probably because he hadn't talked to many people, and Eve wasn't the type to spread rumors. Neither, he suspected, was June Byars, but she probably had more information. He remembered her few cryptic words about Dave. He wished he'd pursued it then. And then again, it was really none of his business if Dave hadn't mentioned it.

But the question eating at him was why Dave had hung on to the cabin, paying the taxes and maintenance all these years, and then why he'd left it to Josh. Of course, it was part of the small estate he'd received, just as Dave would have received Josh's.

But there was something different about the cabin. It was as if Dave was prodding him from the grave.

"Wish I could help you more," Nate said, finishing off his beer. "He was your friend?"

More like a brother. Josh nodded.

"In the military?"

"Everyone know about that?"

"I don't know about everybody, but I know ex-military. I was in Iraq myself. Lot of us in Covenant Falls were. A great adventure," he added ironically.

"Was Sam Clark in the military?"

"Hell, no."

"You don't like him?"

"Not many people do. He likes to parade that badge and bully people. Wouldn't have the job if his uncle didn't get it for him."

"The police chief can't do anything about it?"

"Al Monroe owns the insurance company, the real estate company and a big share of the bank. You don't cross him if you want a loan or don't want your insurance canceled."

"Why isn't he mayor, then?"

"I think he thought he could control Mayor Douglas."

"And he doesn't?"

"No, but two other members of the five-member council are his puppets. Truth is, most of the people are with Eve Douglas. She's done a lot for the town. Singlehandedly started the community center. She has a way of maneuvering people into helping others. I've worked on more than a few roofs for no pay. She put the city back in the black without raising taxes. Cut her own staff, never asked for a raise. She's trying to attract business, but the council isn't helping."

"Maybe there needs to be an uprising."

"You volunteering?"

"Me? I'm an outsider who's leaving the minute I sell the cabin."

"Is that so?"

"Yes."

"Then why so curious?"

"I always like to know the lay of the land."

"Okay. Subject closed," Nate said. "By the way, you do good work."

"You learn to do a little of everything in the army."

"What unit?"

"The Rangers. Seventy-fifth. You?

"The Twenty-fifth Brigade," Nate said.

"Strykers?"

Nate nodded.

"They did a damn good job."

Nate shrugged and took a big sip.

Josh ordered a second beer. And the last. Now that he seemed to be on Sam Clark's radar, he certainly didn't want a DUI. But Nate was proving to be a fount of information. And he liked him. For a few minutes, anyway, it was like being back in uniform.

They sat and enjoyed the beers, united in the moment by shared experiences but unwilling to talk about them. They didn't have to.

"What more are you going to do with the cabin?"

"New porch. One you can sit on and look through the trees to the lake. I'm painting the other rooms and wallpapering the bathroom."

"You need any more help after we finish the floor, I'm your man."

"I'll need you," Josh said. "I have to order materials for the porch, then I'll call you."

"I know you plan to leave when you finish, but there's a roofing party Saturday after next. Sort of like an old-fashioned barn raising. Widow lady with a pittance of social security needs a new roof real bad. A bunch of us have volunteered to install it. One of Eve's projects. She sweet-talks a roofing company into donating the shingles. She's a hard lady to say no to."

"She hasn't mentioned it to me," he said. It certainly wasn't an answer to the implied question, but he wasn't ready to get involved any deeper with Eve or the community. He was still rankled by the visit by the police chief this morning.

He tossed down the rest of his beer once he'd finished his food. "I have to get back," he said.

Nate stood with him. "Me, too."

"See you tomorrow," Josh said, and headed for the door.

CHAPTER FOURTEEN

THE FUND-RAISER ON Saturday was a great success.

Drawn by a Little League game, food and craft booths and games for the kids, there was a larger than expected crowd. In fact, Eve thought, nearly every resident of Covenant Falls was there. Everyone but Josh.

Stephanie's dog-training session was a huge hit. Nick had his way and had convinced Stephanie to use Fancy rather than Miss Marple and, Eve had to admit, he'd been right. Fancy refused every command Nick gave her until the last thirty minutes of Stephanie's session. Then a miracle happened. Fancy charmed everyone by obeying every command. The bidding on Stephanie's dog-training service skyrocketed.

Nick's baseball team won a resounding victory without him. But he promised his teammates he would play next week. He was everywhere, looking for Josh Manning.

"He will be here, won't he?" he kept asking.

"I don't know. He's working hard on his cabin, and remember he told you he had some deliveries today."

Nick looked disappointed as he held Fancy's leash. But the dog was practically preening. Then a couple of boys came up to see his rattles from the snake, and he got to tell his story all over again. He was a happy boy.

At the end of the day, there was still no Josh, but they had raised more than two thousand dollars. It was a fortune for Covenant Falls, and it meant five new computers and three printers she'd arranged to purchase at cost. The frosting on the cake was a bin filled with donated books for the library.

But best of all, the day brought the community together. Not once did anyone mention the robberies. Most were excited about the center offering computers. Volunteers had already been recruited to teach computer lessons. Eve particularly wanted to target older adults.

But still, she, like Nick, had looked for Josh all day.

The depth of her disappointment frightened her. How had she become so involved in a total of two weeks? She packed up the paperwork, sealed the money and checks in an envelope after asking the city clerk to count it with her. Now that she suspected Al Monroe might run against her, she was going to be careful every step.

After she finished, she looked for Nick but didn't see him. Nor did she see Fancy.

She had brought his bike in the pickup. He wanted to bike with the other boys, and he had been so cooperative all week she'd said yes since he couldn't play in the baseball game. But he was supposed to stay within the five acres of the community center and park.

She went inside the community center. No Nick. She started to panic. How long since she last saw him? An hour, maybe. Nick was usually responsible. But he was only ten years old.

Her heart pounded faster. She was too raw from last week. And Nick should have known that. She looked for his bike. And for Fancy. No trace of either, and immediately she knew where he had gone.

Josh's cabin was little more than a mile down the road. But there was traffic on that road, especially Saturdays. She reached Miss Mollie and turned onto the street, fighting to keep her speed under the limit. But what if she were wrong? What if Nick hadn't gone to the Hannity cabin?

What if. There were a million what-ifs running through her head. Nick didn't have a cell phone, nor did she know Josh's number. *Please, please, please let him be there.*

THE FLOORING IN the kitchen had been completed late Friday, and the fridge and stove were delivered and installed Saturday morning. The other furniture had been stored in the second bedroom until he and Nate finished the flooring in the main room Monday.

Josh regarded his new possessions with mixed feelings. No more refilling the cooler with ice, and he looked forward to going to the grocery store to stock the fridge. That part was good.

What wasn't so good was what having new things here represented. Permanence. Sure, he had bought materials to make the cabin sellable. But this felt different. He'd realized there was a time he would finally have to settle down and supplement his savings and army disability pay, but he hadn't been ready for that. Not until he'd met a pretty mayor who was a bundle of energy and good works.

But then the police chief had dropped in, and his opinion of the town had plummeted. Time to talk seriously with a real estate agent about listing the cabin when he finished. The police chief's visit had spurred that idea, as did the growing attraction between the mayor and himself. He was bad for her and her reputation. She was bad for him. Sticking around would only hurt them both. And Nick.

Still, he had considered going to the fund-raiser, mainly, he told himself, for the kid. Or maybe he would just take today off and sort through the boxes of books sent from his base in Georgia.

He had just started sorting the books when Amos barked.

Amos was barking?

He went to the door and saw Nick leaning his bike against a tree, holding a small animal. Josh opened the door as Nick mounted the steps, cradling what resembled a dog but a decidedly homely one.

"Who is this?" he asked.

"This is Fancy. She was the star of Aunt Stephanie's class. She and me, too. We did good."

"I bet you did," Josh said as Amos sidled out the door and sat next to Nick. Josh couldn't help but smile at the way Amos sniffed the little dog, then licked her.

"What *is* Fancy?" he asked with real curiosity.

"Mom says she's a little bit of everything, including Mexican hairless. I think she's beautiful."

"Then she is," Josh said. "Beauty is always in the eye of the beholder, and I think she's quite fetching."

"Mom says that, too. The part about the eye of the beholder. Not that she's fetching. What does *fetching* mean?"

"It means… Where is your mom?" Josh suddenly realized the boy was alone.

"She's at the community center," Nick said. "She's real busy."

"Does she know you came here alone?"

The eagerness in Nick's face faded. "No," he said, ducking his head, "but I wanted Amos to meet Fancy."

"Come inside," Josh said. He opened the door for Nick, who still held the little dog. Amos followed. Josh located his cell phone and asked Nick, "What's your mother's number?"

He punched it in, and she answered immediately. "Nick's here," he said. "He rode over on his bike."

He heard her let go of her breath. "Thank God," she whispered. "I thought he might be coming your way. I'll be there in a minute."

She hung up, and he put the cell on the table, sat down on the sofa and looked Nick in the eyes. "She sounded worried sick about you," he said. "It wasn't fair you didn't ask whether you could come here. She was really scared last week when you were bit by the snake. She hasn't recovered from that, and now you've put her through that kind of fear again."

Nick hung his head. "I didn't think about that. I ride my bike all the time."

"But your mother, or your grandparents, know where you're going, right?"

"Yes, sir."

"You're old enough now to be responsible, and that means not scaring the hell out of your mother. If you were in the army, I would have to write you up for disciplinary action." The minute the words left his mouth, he knew he shouldn't have said *hell* and probably should have left out that last comment.

"I'm sorry."

"I'm not the one you need to say that to," Josh said, feeling like an ogre. "I like you, Nick. I'm happy to see you, but only when you have your mother's permission."

Nick looked up at him. "I can still come here?"

"I think that's up to your mother," Josh said. Then, looking at Nick's crestfallen face, he added, "You've been very good for Amos. He hasn't been very happy because he doesn't know where he belongs, and he lost someone he loved. You've helped him care again."

"Really?"

"Really. You're a natural dog man. It's a fine thing."

Nick beamed.

"That doesn't mean I approve of you worrying your mother. You're very lucky to have one who cares so much about you," Josh added. "I guess sometimes it's difficult to understand the why of rules, but I would have given anything for a mom like yours."

"Don't you have a mom?"

"No."

"Did you ever?"

"Not like yours."

Josh didn't know if Nick understood. But the boy tipped his head to one side. "I really am sorry about today," he said, and this time Josh knew he meant it. "I didn't think. I just wanted Amos to meet Fancy."

They heard a vehicle outside, and Josh struggled to his feet. His leg was particularly painful this afternoon after so many hours working on the kitchen floor.

Nick went out to meet his mother, and Josh limped to the door and watched.

She leaned down and gave Nick a huge hug, then an obvious scolding. She came to his door. "I hope he didn't bother you."

"He's one visitor who doesn't. I told him, though, it wasn't a good idea to come without telling you."

"Thank you."

He couldn't take his eyes off her. Her cheeks were flushed. Her eyes were warm. She looked both vulnerable and lovely. He fought the longing inside him. "You're welcome," he said coolly.

"We have to get home. Nick is going to be grounded for years." But she didn't move.

Neither did he. "Sorry I didn't get there today, but the fridge and stove finally came." That wasn't the entire truth.

"It went well. We made enough to buy new computers."

"I've had more company," he said after a pause. "The police chief. On Thursday. He invited himself inside to look around. Is that common practice for a new resident?"

Her gaze met his, and he knew immediately that she had known about the visit, maybe even in advance. Maybe approved it.

He wasn't quite prepared for the kick in the gut he felt. He had hoped the police chief had acted on his own.

"I have some errands to do," he said in a voice that went from cool to frigid. It was a clear invitation for her to leave.

She looked as if he'd slapped her. "Thanks again for looking after him," she said in a strained voice. She took Fancy from Nick and took her to the truck. Nick slowly followed her. She then went for the bike.

Josh limped out and picked it up before she could and carried it to the back of the pickup.

"Thank you," she said, "but I could have done that."

"I don't doubt it."

They looked at each other for a moment. So much

passed between them. Regret. Anger. And still...that damnable attraction. He swallowed hard, nodded and turned back to the cabin. He knew she was watching his every step.

Then as he reached the front door, where Amos waited, he heard her engine start. When he went inside and looked through the window, the truck was gone.

SUNDAY MORNING AND it was time for church. Usually Eve looked forward to it, but not today. She'd had a sleepless night.

Josh had been distant yesterday, but then she'd been every bit as cool toward him. She'd been angry and upset and scared to death for the second time in two weeks. And the underlying cause of both instances was one Josh Manning.

To be fair, neither time was really his fault. He didn't lure Nick out of Miss Mollie when she'd stopped by with the a copy of the deed. And he hadn't invited her son to bike over to his cabin. But he was like the Pied Piper to Nick.

And she hated to admit, to herself, as well.

She hurried Nick, who was taking his time finding his good pants and a clean shirt. Jim and Abby would be at church, too, and then they usually went together to Maude's for chicken and dumplings, as did so many other Covenant Falls residents. Sunday was Maude's busiest day.

She wondered what Josh was doing today. More

work? He never seemed to pause for a break. A man on a mission.

So he could sell the cabin and leave?

She thought about her conversation with Tom, and guilt racked her. Nick had told her what Josh said to him yesterday, and he had apologized to her again and swore never to disappear without telling her. Evidently Josh, with a few words, had made an impact that she hadn't been able to make.

"Do you think Josh will be at church?" Nick asked.

"I wouldn't expect it," she replied.

He sighed. "I want him to meet Captain Hook and Miss Marple. Maybe we can ask him for dinner."

She had to stop this. Josh was becoming all too important to him.

She sat down and pulled Nick to her. "Hey, guy," she said gently, "Josh has made it clear he doesn't plan to stay in Covenant Falls. I don't want you to get too attached to him. I don't want you hurt."

"I know, Mom." But she saw the hurt in his eyes. How had this happened so fast? She knew he missed his father. But why did he have to latch on to a laconic loner?

Why had she?

She hadn't. He was just different. Unlike the other men who had asked her out or expressed interest. There was a strength in him that reached out to her. And gentleness. She had seen it in his interaction with Nick. A gentleness he went to great lengths to conceal. "Come on, let's go. We'll be late for church."

When they arrived in Miss Mollie, Nick met some friends and sat with them. She found a seat next to Jim and Abby and tried to concentrate on the service. On leaving the church, several people came over and commented on the fund-raiser and how much they enjoyed it. June took her aside. "Sold out of my brownies and pies. You get those computers and I might try my hand at this World Wide Web thing."

"That's one of my goals," Eve said. "You can't even imagine what you might find there. An endless number of recipes for one, and gardening tips for another."

"You don't think I'm too old?"

"Not you, June. You're probably going to outlive all of us."

June smiled at that. "That nice young man from the Hannity cabin came over to see me," she said. "He apologized for the time I tried to welcome him. We had a nice chat. I like him, but he seems lonely. Probably needs a good woman."

Eve nearly choked. Was the whole town talking about her? And Josh? She had been at his cabin only a few times and never at night. She was going to have to careful, especially now that Al might be after her job.

Was it worth trying to keep it? If she was to stay in Covenant Falls, yes. She needed the money, but even more than that she loved the town and its people. Most of them anyway.

She politely bid June goodbye, found Nick and his grandparents and they went on to Maude's. It was a perfect day in Covenant Falls. Not a cloud in the sky. The weatherman in Denver, though, predicted a storm tonight. She only hoped it wouldn't be as powerful as the storm swirling around in her heart.

CHAPTER FIFTEEN

JOSH WAS UNUSUALLY restless Sunday. Cabin fever, he thought. Or maybe it was wanting something he couldn't have. Except he really didn't know what he wanted.

Or did he?

He woke early, and for the first time since he arrived he didn't have an immediate goal for the day. The kitchen was finished except for mostly empty cupboards.

The flooring in the living area had to wait for Monday. Nate had other obligations today. He could start painting his bedroom, but maybe he needed a day to relax.

He took Amos for a long walk. Lake Road narrowed and became a trail going up into the forest. Since he was climbing, he took his cane. Amos came reluctantly. He kept looking around, and Josh wondered whether the dog was looking for Nick. Young Nick certainly had a way with animals, and if Fancy was any example, he wondered what the other Douglas dogs were like. He smiled at the thought, and the smile grew as he thought of Eve, her head tipped upward in challenge.

He reached a good resting spot—a big rock—and looked down over Covenant Falls. Not for the first time, he wondered about the name and whether it had a meaning. Sandwiched between the plains and mountains, it looked like an oasis.

The lake shimmered in the sun, and he wondered whether the fishing was good. Whether Dave used to fish there. There had once been a dock on the lake in front of the cabin, but not much of it remained.

Sunday. It was Sunday and he'd discovered that nearly everything in Covenant Falls was closed until after church services. Maybe he would drive into Pueblo for groceries. He could look at canoes, as well.

Perhaps getting out of Covenant Falls would ease his itch for something he couldn't—shouldn't—have.

When he arrived back at the cabin, he fed Amos and debated taking him along on the expedition. But by midday it would be too hot for him to stay in the Jeep, even for a few moments. He filled Amos's water bowl, pulled out some chews and toys for him. "Guard!" he said.

Amos just looked at him. No head erect, no ears pointed straight up.

"Not yet, huh? Maybe that's a good thing. You and I are civilians now. Have to act like it."

Somehow it didn't seem as bad as it did months ago when he knew he was out of the Rangers.

He climbed into the Jeep and headed for Pueblo.

Eve drank in the smell of horse and fresh air. She was on Beast and Nick was on Beauty as they took a trail that wound up into the national forest. It was well-worn, a favorite of pleasure riders.

The horses had been more than eager after two weeks of what they probably considered abandonment. Although Jim and Abby had fed and watered them, no one had ridden them since a week before the snakebite. She'd been too busy, and Nick wasn't allowed to ride alone.

"You think Josh rides?" Nick asked.

"I don't know," she replied when they slowed to walk side by side.

Beast was difficult to handle today, but Beauty was, as usual, the perfect lady. Nick chattered on about the summer. He was now free of school, and that presented a number of new problems for Eve. How was she going to work and keep Nick away from Josh? She would have to talk to Josh, ask him to dissuade Nick from visits, but that would be insulting to him. She would have to be diplomatic, but how could you be diplomatic when you're asking someone to stay away from your son?

It was suppertime when they arrived back at the ranch. She made them both hot dogs, a treat for Nick. Just as they were finishing, the doorbell rang and she went to answer it.

Tom stood there and the dogs clamored around him, asking for attention. He gave each a scratch or a pet or a tummy rub, depending on what the dog seemed to expect. He knew them well.

"Can I get you something to eat? We had hot dogs for supper, and I have a couple left."

"No, thanks, but can we take a walk? Some city business."

She nodded. "Nick, can you take care of the dishes for me?"

"Sure," Nick said, happy after the long ride and a hot dog to boot.

"There's been a burglary, this time a home. Shep Hardy."

"He wasn't hurt?"

"He wasn't home. He was out of town being honored at a rodeo. Came back this afternoon to find his rifles and his championship buckles gone. Also his coin collection. Strange because none of it will be easy to pawn, although gold belt buckles could be melted down and fetch a fair price."

She remembered reading that Shep would be honored at a rodeo in Wyoming. In his day, he'd been a four-time world champion in bronco riding and was the town's local hero. But in so doing, his body had suffered numerous breaks, and now at sixty-five he could barely get around. He lived by himself on Lake Road, only eight houses from the Hannity cabin. She'd visited there, and the house was full of memorabilia.

Anger boiled up in her. Shep was a good guy. His wife had also been rodeo, but had ironically died of cancer. Shep had taken care of her and had never re-married. Love of his life, he'd once told her.

"It was in the paper that he would be out of town," she said. "That means it was probably local. Find anything at his house?"

"Sam was on duty. The minute I heard I went over there and took over the crime scene. We dusted for fingerprints but, hell, I don't think we will find anything."

"No witnesses?"

"We don't know when it happened. He'd been gone four days and returned about noon today. We're surveying the neighborhood but no one saw anyone around his cottage. But almost everyone who lives on the road was at the fund-raiser Saturday and church this morning."

"How is Shep?"

"Feeling down, and it's a shame. He had been excited about the honor."

He was quiet for a moment. "We still can't be sure it's not Manning," he said. "But all my instincts tell me otherwise. He's a smart guy and would know most of the stuff is worthless. Still, I want to check out his property."

Eve eyed him. "If what you thought a few days ago is true, one of the rifles might well be on Josh's property, someplace where your department can find it."

"I know. The town is going to be really angry about this. It was bad enough when Maude's was burglarized, but Shep is a beloved legend."

"And somebody knew that."

"Yes," Tom answered. "I have an idea, but I need your approval."

"I'm listening."

"I'm inclined to think it's Sam," he said, "but maybe I'm prejudiced because he was forced on me and he feels safe in being insubordinate. But I can't ask any other members of the force to spy on him. If I'm wrong, it would tear the department apart.

"We have a vacancy," he continued. "I know your budget is tight and we were going to wait, but I want to hire someone now on a short-term basis, someone I know and trust."

"Someone you obviously have in mind," she said.

"I've already contacted him to see whether it's a possibility. He served with me at the sheriff's department. He was just a rookie then but had all the right instincts. He's since been hired by investigative services with the Colorado Highway Department but he doesn't start for another month. I know the sheriff and can ask him to send him over until I can get someone full-time. I'll put him on the same shift as Sam."

"He's on days now, right?"

Tom nodded. "Manning says he's seen a police car go by his house on a regular basis at night and wondered whether it was a standard patrol. It's not, and it's not Sam's regular shift but he's volunteered for extra hours since the burglaries. It's not like him to volunteer."

"Do it," Eve said. She was fully aware she was

risking her job. And it wasn't for Josh. If there was even the slightest possibility that Sam was behind the burglaries, then he shouldn't be a member of the Covenant Falls Police Department, or any other department. She couldn't get out of her head what Russ had said about a younger Sam, that he was a bully. She'd thought that maybe he'd outgrown it when he'd finished his criminal justice program, but maybe not.

"I'll call him," Tom said. "I've already felt him out. He knows what one bad apple can do to a department, particularly a small one."

She hated the subterfuge but she couldn't find another answer to the problem. She changed the subject. "June likes Josh and is trumpeting her approval all over town. So have Abby and Jim, and you know everyone listens to them. If our thief is Sam, he might well be panicking. He might do something really stupid."

"Like rob Shep," Tom said.

"If we're wrong, then no harm done. Your guy will just come and go with no one the wiser."

"And we'll still have the problem of multiple thefts and an unhappy town."

"Part of the job," she said.

"I'll have to talk to Manning again," he warned her.

"You're surveying all the neighbors, aren't you? It's only natural to include him. Nothing more than that." She gave him a big hug. "No one will ever replace you."

He left. She watched him walk slowly to the car.

She was asking too much of him, but she didn't know what she would do without him. She would just have to find a way. He seemed to have aged several years in the past few days. First thing in the morning, she would make some calls.

JOSH PULLED INTO his driveway in the late afternoon. There was more activity on the street than he'd seen before. Small groups of neighbors chatting. They stared at his Jeep as he passed them.

His mental alarm system told him something had happened. He parked and hurried inside to check on Amos.

Amos was agitated, his ears up. He growled, but not at Josh. It was the same low, steady sound Amos had made when scenting danger.

Josh went through the cabin. His gun was still in place. The door locks did not appear to have been tampered with. Probably thanks to Amos. Few knew he had resigned from being a soldier dog, and he was formidable looking.

But something had made Amos nervous while he was gone. After the neighborhood calmed down, he would go outside and take a look around.

He put away the groceries. Staples like coffee and salt and butter, some steaks, potatoes, bread, beef jerky for Amos and charcoal for the grill. He'd also bought glasses and plates, things he had avoided before.

He had resisted buying a canoe, but he had looked

at several and planned to return later. But still, none of this had to mean he was going to stay. It just meant that he and Amos would be more comfortable while he finished with the cabin.

He sat on the sofa and thought about Covenant Falls, Eve and Nick. It was the first time in years he had thought much about the future. It had always been better to take one day at a time.

But Eve kept creeping into his mind, as did Nick. And the funny little dog named Fancy to whom Amos had taken a shine, and Mrs. Byars, who had made him brownies. Warm thoughts. God knew he hadn't had many of those.

He looked out again, and the crowd had dispersed as the afternoon turned into dusk and, he supposed, suppertime for most families. He was suddenly struck with loneliness. Lights went on in the cottages and cabins down the road and across the lake. Maybe he would take Amos out earlier than usual.

He started for the door and Amos stood and followed him. Josh went out into the yard, intending to walk around the lake. But Amos was sniffing near the house. He was following a trail. It ended where the Harley was parked under its cover, waiting to be repaired.

Amos stood next to it. Waiting. Trying to tell him something.

Josh lifted the cover and saw a rifle. It was obviously expensive. In the faltering dusk light, he could read the silver plate on the rifle: Shep Hardy, Bronco Riding Champion. 1970.

It hadn't been there a week ago. His thoughts went back to the small groups of people who had gathered on Lake Road earlier.

Maybe it had something to do with the rifle. Maybe not. But it made the hair on the back of his neck stand up.

Scenes flashed through his mind: the belligerent deputy who had confronted him at the diner and had sent him heated looks since then, the patrol car at night, some of the suspicious looks he'd received in town, a chain of petty burglaries.

He went inside the cabin, retrieved his cell phone and then took several photos of the rifle where it was nestled on the seat. Ordinarily he would have called the law, but he'd discovered some heavy currents in Covenant Falls politics and he wasn't sure where all the loyalties lay.

He searched the property with Amos. Nothing else seemed out of place.

No one was lurking around.

He returned to the cabin and found the scant list of phone numbers he kept, most of them of men he served with. He punched a number into his cell.

"Sanford Security."

"Scotty? Josh here."

A silence. Then a voice said, "Damn but it's good to hear from you. Last I heard you were in the hospital, then you just seemed to disappear."

"I'm in a small Colorado town called Covenant Falls. It probably isn't even on a map. Dave left me a cabin, and I'm not sure what in the hell I'm going to do with it."

"I'm still interested in you. Love to have you train some of my guys. Good salary. Perks."

When Scott Sanford had left the service two years ago, he'd approached both Dave and him about joining a security firm he was planning to build. Neither had been interested. "I appreciate it," Josh said, "but I haven't made any decisions yet. I do have a favor to ask."

"Name it."

"I need some small outdoor spy cameras. Battery-operated. Not top-of-the-line, just functional. Five of them, if you can manage it."

"I can do that. Nothing illegal, I assume."

"No. Just securing Dave's property."

"Where do I send them?"

Josh gave the address and directions in relation to Denver.

"When do you need them?"

"Morning, if possible."

"Can get them to you before ten. Anything else we can help you with?" There was a note of concern in Scott's voice.

"Just the cameras for now. Thanks."

"None necessary. Just remember you always have a job here."

Josh hung up. And found himself calling Eve.

After several rings, he was about to give up when she answered.

"Eve?"

A hesitation. "Josh?"

"Yes." He got right to the point. "Something happened on this street tonight. I went to Pueblo and when I returned, it seemed all the residents were outside talking. Can you tell me what happened?"

She hesitated again, then said, "Another burglary, this time a private home on your street. Shep Hardy. He's a local hero. A national rodeo champion. He was out of town for several days, being honored at Frontier Days in Laramie."

"What was taken?"

"Some rifles, gold championship belt buckles and a coin collection. The buckles would probably be worth something if melted down. The rifles were prizes and would be easily identified and hard to sell. Why?"

"Just wondering since the police chief seems to have taken a special interest in me."

"Josh…"

"Do you trust him?" he said abruptly.

"Yes."

"Completely?"

"With my life. He's one of the most honest men I've ever met."

"Thanks," he said and hung up. Cool. Real cool, but he wasn't ready to say that a stolen rifle was on his property, hidden within another piece of his personal property. Not yet. Not until he had a little protection. He wanted everything on camera, and since the cameras wouldn't be here until morning, it meant he and Amos would keep watch all night. In the meantime, he would put the rifle somewhere else.

EVE HUNG UP the phone. The joy of the day with her son was slipping away. She'd sensed a coolness Saturday, but Josh was certainly abrupt tonight. At least he had called her when he wanted information.

She realized the chill had come from Tom's visit. She couldn't say she wouldn't have felt the same way if she had been paid a visit by the law in a new town.

The town was divided. The burglaries scared them. That the latest was a private home deepened the fear. It brought back the specter of four years ago when a motorcycle gang had terrorized the town and killed her father.

People were beginning to listen to Al and Sam. Others—those who had met Josh—were defending him. If she were Josh, a man who had spent seventeen years defending his country, she would probably be angry, as well. She certainly would question a town jumping to conclusions. That thought hurt. Covenant Falls was a good town, a caring town.

Hoping she wasn't making a mistake, she called Tom, told him about the curt conversation.

"I wonder what prompted the call," he said.

"I don't know. It was short. Have you heard anything else?"

"No. I've notified the county and state police and

Julia's contacting area pawnshops. We're going to cover the state. I've also contacted Ryan Keller, the sheriff's deputy I told you about. He'll be here soon, and I'm going to pair him with Sam."

"Good."

"I'll go out and talk to Manning first thing in the morning. Maybe something prompted him to call you other than curiosity."

CHAPTER SIXTEEN

JOSH STAYED AWAKE all night. After midnight, he put on garden gloves and found a roll of oilcloth. He went to the Harley, wrapped the rifle in the oilcloth and took it to the back of the property and the path that led upward. Using a pinpoint flashlight, he went off trail and buried it under a mound of pine needles.

Then he returned to the cabin. He placed a folding chair where he had a view of the Harley. Amos stayed at his side as if he knew he was supposed to be alert.

It reminded him of all the other sleepless nights he'd spent looking for the enemy. He wasn't used to this kind of enemy. A homegrown one who, for some reason, was intent on framing him.

Wasn't going to happen.

Sometime during the night he had decided that no one was going to run him off before he himself was good and ready to get out of town.

It had nothing to do with Eve. Nothing at all. He just wasn't good at running.

Dawn seeped in the windows, and he left his perch and made breakfast. He'd already had enough coffee to sink a battleship. He took a cold shower before he remembered that Nate would be here to help replace the flooring in the living room.

He called Nate at seven and asked whether he could come at noon instead of eight. Something had come up. Nate readily agreed.

A messenger arrived at eight-thirty. Josh tipped him well, then took the package inside and opened it. There were five small state-of-the-art portable cameras, plus a small listening device. He took a ladder outside, attached cameras to two spots on the roof. Then he attached one to the back of the roof and finally two more in the front yard—one in a tree, again with a view of the Harley, and another with a view of cabin. His cell phone could display what the cameras were seeing. Technology was amazing.

He was finished by ten, just in time to see the police chief pull into his yard. He tucked the bug in his pocket and went to meet him.

"Can I come inside?" MacGuire said.

Josh led the way. Amos had seen the chief before and didn't bound for safety. But he kept his distance.

"There was a burglary on the street," MacGuire said.

"So I heard. When?"

"In the past four days. Owner was out of town. You walk your dog," he said. "I hoped you might have seen something. I'm questioning all the neighbors. Shep's a good guy. This just about broke his heart. If it had just been money, he wouldn't mind so much. But it was his championship buckles and prize rifles."

Josh heard the regret in the chief's voice.

Maybe it was time to trust someone. He had little choice. But he also had backup. He intended to keep the cameras and bug a secret for now.

"I have one of his rifles," he said flatly.

The police chief waited for him to continue.

"It appeared on the seat of my Harley yesterday. I went to Pueblo earlier in the day. Amos was agitated when I got home and when I let him out, he went straight to the Harley. I called Eve and she told me about the burglary and that the stolen items meant a lot to the owner."

"She's right."

"I did consider the fact, though, that someone obviously wanted it found on my property. Just like someone saw my Jeep in a place I didn't even know existed. So I moved it."

"Did it occur to you to call me?"

"It did. There was a question of trust."

"And?"

"Eve said I could trust you, and I trust her. And…I have a little backup."

"I don't suppose you want to tell me about that."

"Then it wouldn't be backup." He took out his cell phone and showed the photo of the rifle on the Harley. "I decided it wasn't wise to leave it there. I'll take you to it." He led the way back to where he had left the rifle, and brushed off the pine straw.

The chief took gloves from his pocket, pulled them on and lifted the cover. "It's Shep's, all right, and he'll be mighty glad to get it back. Didn't see any belt buckles, did you?"

Josh shook his head. "I'll keep my eyes open." He paused. "How do you think that rifle got there?"

"I have some ideas."

"Care to share them?"

"I appreciate your telling me about this." The chief avoided Josh's gaze as he also avoided the question.

Josh got a sick feeling in his stomach.

"Eve said I could trust you," he repeated.

The police chief looked uncomfortable. "One of my officers might come by looking around. Just let him look. Don't tell him I have it. All right?"

"You going to tell me why?"

"I think you're smart enough to guess," the sheriff said.

"I remember an unpleasant officer singling me out at Maude's."

"I think he might see you as an opportunity for promotion."

"And he's still an officer with your force?"

"I can't prove anything. On paper, he looks good, and his uncle is on the city council."

"But…"

"He's been doing a lot of mouthing off about you, and I don't believe that a professional burglar would pick the businesses that were robbed, and they *were* professional. No fingerprints. No clues. Picked places with easy locks. Not a great deal of money involved, and for a pro they just aren't worth the risk. The recent burglaries started just after you came, just as he was pushing for my job."

Josh didn't like where this was leading. "If you are saying what I think you're saying—that your officer stole and planted the rifle so he could find it later and charge what he knew was an innocent person—you have a very big problem in your department."

"More than you know. I've had several heart attacks. My wife wants me to retire. Sam's uncle is president of the city council and he has the votes to name him police chief if I retire before Eve finds a better-qualified candidate. They won't go against her as long as I hold the office. I have more friends than they do."

"You want to catch this officer with his hand in the cookie jar?"

"Something like that. I have a new officer coming in to keep an eye on him, but I think Sam is getting anxious. This burglary was just a few doors away from you."

"So you know, or think you know, and all you can do is make me bait."

The chief's pained expression told him he was right.

"It may have been more professional to consult me first," Josh said sharply.

The chief's face went red. "You're right. But after I saw your military record I knew Sam was outclassed. He was too lazy to check it, and I saw no need to share it with him. Since Sam never listens, I don't think he's aware that opinion is mostly on your side since the rattler bit Nick. He didn't consider the fact that you would make friends so quickly. I thought I would let him hang himself."

Josh raised an eyebrow. "Me? Friends?"

"You have pretty fervent admirers in the Douglas clan. The pharmacist is an influential person in a small town, and his wife, Abby, is in every women's club in town. Mrs. Byars, who is an institution in town, has been telling everyone what a nice and hardworking young man you are, and that you're a hero like her son. Word like that gets around.

"I really didn't think Sam would go this far, this fast," the police chief continued. "Try to find something against you, yes, maybe even plant evidence, but I had planned to have someone watching him, and other officers making frequent checks on businesses. I never considered the fact he—or anyone—would take Shep's trophies. I guess Sam thought everyone would be so outraged that the council would name him police chief when he solved the crime."

"That's if he's guilty," Josh said quietly. "Seems to be a lot of jumping to conclusions in this town."

"Don't get me wrong, I'm not about framing or enticing anyone. This is a guess only. Until now I thought our burglar could be a hunter. But if it was Sam, we want to be there if he walks through the door." He paused, then added, "Sam is a would-be rodeo rider. Never made any money, and his uncle cut off supporting it. Maybe Sam thought he would take trophies another way and blame it on you."

"Uncle? What about father or mother?"

"His mother, Councilman Monroe's sister, died in an accident that also killed Sam's father. Both of them had been drinking. Al Monroe didn't have any kids of his own and raised Sam."

Josh processed that information. "But why hide the rifle in the Harley?"

"My guess? It wasn't his first choice. If it was Sam, he's afraid of dogs. And I noticed you closed in the crawl space under the porch. Couldn't hide it there. You said a police car's been out here a lot. Sam probably noticed the Harley is always in the same place and assumed you didn't ride it often."

"Mayor Douglas know about all this?" Josh asked. He sensed he wouldn't like the answer. He didn't like being used.

The police chief hesitated. "She knows about Sam's ambition. I told her I was bringing in someone on a short-term basis to keep an eye on Sam."

The reply didn't exactly answer his question, which was an answer in itself. "You have the rifle now," Josh said. "Maybe there's prints on it."

"Could be, and we'll sure check it. But Sam isn't dumb. No prints in the other three crimes. But when he searches here, and I expect he will, and finds the rifle gone, he might well do something foolish."

"Like come after me?" Josh said quietly. He didn't like being a target. There was a saying in the army about plans going awry, but soldiers used much more vivid language that he'd tried to forget once he left the service. He wanted to use every one of those words now.

He felt like someone just stabbed him in the back. Or the gut. Eve had seemed to be forthright and honest. He had liked her directness. And now he wondered if she was any of those things.

"Is this ethical for you?" he asked.

The chief gave him a long, searching look. "Have you ever done something you had doubts about but couldn't figure another way of accomplishing the objective? That's where we are—Eve has done so much for this town. She doesn't do it for the money, which is a pittance of what it should be, or the power. She runs an honest administration. She does it because she loves Covenant Falls. We're a small town and don't always use the same rules as big departments do. Sometimes you have to go with what you have. I suspect you know something about that. Sam handed us an opportunity with that rifle. It may be the only one we have. Otherwise he'll keep abusing power, and God help this town if he becomes chief."

Josh shrugged off that defense. "You might think about looking in the mirror. I'm not going to stop you, but I'm not happy about it. I've already fought in a number of battlegrounds. I don't need one here in the States. I'll be out of here as soon as I finish and sell the place."

The chief sighed. "Can't say I don't understand, but I hope you reconsider. We need people like you,

nd Covenant Falls is a fine community with mostly
good-hearted people." He hesitated, then added,
"Don't blame Eve. This wasn't planned. Sam just
dropped it in on my lap."

Josh gave him a long, steady stare. "I don't like
crooked lawmen, and I didn't like your officer, so I'll
go along with you up to a point. But you *will* keep me
nformed about how you plan to prove he's the thief."

The older man nodded.

"I also want a dated letter about the rifle. I want it
o say that I found it and reported it, and you asked
ne to say nothing."

Chief MacGuire's face flushed. Then he nodded.
"You'll have it in the morning."

"I would prefer right now," Josh said. "I have a
pen and paper."

He watched as the police chief wrote a few sentences on the paper Josh handed him and returned it.
"I'll also want a more official version in the morning
with the city crest, along with the mayor's signature."

The chief gave him a wry smile. "I don't think
that will be a problem." He paused. "I do admire the
way you think."

Josh watched as the older man went out the door,
holding the rifle in gloved hands. He carried it to his
car and put it in the trunk. Then Josh closed the door.

He looked at his watch. Nate was due soon. He
sighed.

Why in the hell had Dave left this place to him?
Was it his last joke?

NATE ROWLAND APPEARED at noon, an hour after the
police chief left.

In four hours they had pulled up all the old board
and in another two had installed the subfloor. Then
came the jigsaw puzzle of joining each board, using
a nail gun to secure them and cutting pieces to fi
the odd places.

They worked through lunch, taking out only a few
moments for a sandwich and glass of milk. They fin
ished around six, then swept and cleaned the floor.
The old sofa had been shoved into the second bed
room, where it would remain for the next day.

Josh offered Nate a beer. They were both hot and
tired.

Nate accepted immediately and he and Josh took
the new folding chairs outside by the barbecue pit.
"Pretty place," Nate said. "Gonna be real nice when
you finish. You have a feel for this kind of work." He
paused. "You could be real useful Saturday."

Saturday? Then Josh remembered. Nate was going
to help put a new roof on a house for a widow. What
the hell. He wouldn't be finished with the cabin yet,
and maybe he would find out more about this town
and Clark. "What time?" he asked.

Nate grinned. "Daybreak or thereabouts. But roof-
ers come and go throughout the day. Whenever you
can get there."

"I'll be there."

"The house is easy to find. Three blocks down
Mine Street from Stephanie's clinic. You won't miss

t. There will be trucks and several big bins and lots
of cars." Nate clinked his bottle to Josh's. "Welcome
o Covenant Falls."

After he left, Josh took Amos for a walk. He no
onger felt he had to wait until dark. Amos was ad-
usting to the little traffic on Lake Road and didn't
protest. Instead, he'd started looking alert at the word
walk.

A slight breeze ruffled the pine needles and a
hawk circled above. The sun had just dropped behind a mountain and its last rays turned the sky into
a mad painter's canvas of pink, gold and crimson
shades. He couldn't remember the last time he'd
looked at a sky with pleasure instead of worrying
whether moonlight would give away his position, or
that a lack of moonlight would cover the movements
of an enemy.

Did he really want to participate in another war?

Could he run away from one?

Since his arrival here, he'd wondered why Dave
had never talked about Covenant Falls. He'd figured
that if Dave hadn't wanted him to know, then it was
none of Josh's business. But now, suddenly, it was.
He would contact the attorney in Pueblo to see if he
knew anything.

He passed Mrs. Byars's home and saw her sitting
on the porch with what looked like a cup of tea. He
gave her a brief salute, and her smile warmed him
as he moved on.

He smiled when Amos stopped and sniffed a plant
then another. Maybe Amos was feeling more at home.

Or was it a mirage? An illusion covering any number of dangers?

"WANTED TO WARN you, Eve, Josh Manning is not a
happy man." Tom paced Eve's living room. Nick had
gone to bed.

"You told him about Sam?"

"Yes."

"He didn't understand?"

"He understands."

Eve felt the floor wavering beneath her. It had been
obvious from the beginning that Josh didn't trust easily. "You explained…?"

"I tried." He sat down, looking years older than he
had yesterday. "Tell you the truth, I would be mad
as hell, too. I might well have put him in danger. I
don't know how far Sam will go, but at least Manning is aware now."

"Maybe I should go and talk to him tomorrow,"
Eve said.

"He's a quiet man, Eve. I know the type. He keeps
feelings buried deep inside, but they're potent. He's
angry now. I think he needs time to cool off."

Eve felt herself go cold. He would feel betrayed,
just as she would in his place.

"Eve…"

"You had better get someone up there to watch
Josh's cabin," she said tonelessly.

"Sam's off tonight and he can't ask for a search warrant from the county judge until he speaks to me first, and he knows he needs one to make a search tick. All the judges know I have to sign any request. called Ryan and asked if he could be here in the morning. He said he could. I'll pair him with Sam tomorrow."

"You think Josh is okay tonight?"

"Sam will want everything legal. Otherwise all his planning will be wasted."

"And if it isn't Sam?" she asked.

"I'm guessing Manning can take care of himself."

"He shouldn't have to."

"You're right."

She didn't reply. She thought about Nick. He adored Josh.

And Josh was in her mind nearly every waking hour. There was something kind and honest in the ough exterior. No pretensions. No games.

He put his arm around her. "You really like him, don't you?"

"Against my better judgment, yes."

"Why against your better judgment?"

"Because he's made it clear he's a loner and a wanderer." She was conscious of a tear forming on the edge of her eye.

"Did you ever think he might be protesting too much? Just like you're doing?"

She shrugged. "It doesn't matter. Now Josh knows

we involved him or were going to involve him. He won't trust me again."

"At least now he knows someone might be coming for him. And it isn't because of us. It was already happening." He touched her cheek. "And if it's meant to be, it will be."

"Pretty philosophical of you."

"Damn," he said. "You're like a daughter to me. would cut off a hand before hurting you."

"I know." And she did.

"I'll try to fix it," he said.

"No. I have to do it." She looked up at him. "It's insane. I've only known him a few weeks. I never believed in quick romances, and we don't have a romance anyway."

"The moment I met my wife, I knew she was the one," Tom said. "Lightning strikes sometimes."

"Not with me," she argued. "I think it takes a long time to feel…"

"Don't look now, but I think it's happened."

"That doesn't mean he returns…my feelings, or that it would work."

"I saw his face. I think that lightning hit him, as well."

"Maybe before."

"Don't give up on him, Eve. I like him. I liked the way he handled himself. He asked all the right questions. He was angry, but not enough to let the bad guy off the hook. He would make a pretty good cop."

"No," she said sharply. "I lost my dad that way. I'm not going to lose anyone else." And then she realized what she had said.

"I've got to go," he said. "Maggie has dinner waiting."

"You go," she said. "I'm fine." She wasn't, but she pasted a smile on her face.

She shut the door behind him and went to Nick's room. The night-light cast just enough glow that she could see her son curled up with three dogs on the bed and Braveheart snoring on the floor. She smiled at the scene.

They were all she needed. Nick was the heart of her heart.

Dizzy, the cat, had followed her into the room and jumped up on the bed, squeezing in between Nick and Miss Marple.

"Traitor," she whispered and closed the door.

Ten o'clock. Early for bed, and she was restless. She walked out to the barn, picking up some cubes of sugar. Beauty and Beast neighed in welcome and eagerly snatched their treats. She wondered whether Josh rode. She wondered so many things. She knew practically nothing about him except he was from Atlanta and served in the military and was good with his hands.

They had never even had an official date.

So why was she so attracted to him? Why did her heart race when she saw him and her blood run hot when he touched her? Why was his kiss pure enchantment?

Had she ruined any chance to find out?

CHAPTER SEVENTEEN

EVE NOW KNEW how a cat on a hot tin roof felt.

She suffered through Tuesday morning trying to answer constituents on why the budget didn't include a new swing, and hearing another complaint about a neighbor playing music too loud.

Even Nick didn't help. School was out and he had begged to come to the office. He read for a while, then went down to see Tom and play detective.

To her surprise, and to Tom's, Sam had not sought a search warrant Monday. Maybe they had been wrong about him.

To her relief, Tom's new officer had arrived this morning and, against Sam's wishes, was partnered with him "for training." She went down to the police department, and Tom introduced the temporary officer.

Ryan Keller had a firm grip and intelligent eyes. "Glad to have you," she said.

"Thanks. I like small departments. Tom taught a course years ago that I still remember. I saw this as an opportunity to work with the best."

Sam stood by with a sour expression. He obviously

thought the newcomer beneath him, or worse, a possible candidate for police chief.

"Good to see you, too, Sam," she lied, then left before she said something she shouldn't.

An hour later Al Monroe charged into her office without knocking, and she knew Sam had called him. "Any news on the robberies?" he asked, although he obviously knew the answer.

"Sam hasn't found anything yet," she said sweetly. "But we have a new man on patrol and maybe between the two they can come up with something."

"I didn't think we had money for more officers."

"We had one vacant position and, like you said, Tom will probably retire soon."

"You know the council will never approve an outsider, particularly a young one, as chief."

"Did I say he was being considered for the chief's job? He's just here temporarily. Perhaps new eyes will see something we didn't."

"Sam hasn't been able to investigate," Al said. "Tom keeps stepping in his way. He's pretty sure that guy in the Hannity cabin—Manning—is guilty, but Tom won't okay a search warrant. Says there's not enough evidence. Hell, the thefts didn't start until he came."

"Now, that's certainly condemning," she said. "But no judge would approve a warrant on that."

"Maybe not, but he's been spending a lot of money lately."

And how would he know? "It's up to Sam to get the

evidence, and right now I'd say we don't have any," she said, then added brightly, "Thanks for your donation to the community center."

He had sent fifty dollars. He could have sent much more, but then he might have sent nothing, so she wasn't going to complain. He hadn't attended the fund-raiser, although the other council members had. Not wise if he really intended to run for mayor.

Al continued, "I have to get back to my office, but I wanted to check with you on the investigation. Tom doesn't look good. He might not be up for something like this."

"He'll thank you for caring, and I'll keep you and the other members of the council posted as soon as there are any developments," she said carefully.

Al had no choice but to retreat, but she saw the veins in his neck contract.

Merry came in. "I have a contract for you to sign." The rest of the morning went fast, and she was grateful. It kept her from thinking about Josh, from running over there to explain why she'd agreed to Tom's plan. She longed to be with him.

The fierceness of that desire was exactly why she shouldn't go. She wasn't ready. She had been so angry when Russ died. She'd screamed at him in the silence of their bedroom when Nick was with his grandparents. She'd packed up all his belongings and taken them to the Presbyterian church's clothes closet for the needy, only to return later to take his team jacket back. She'd never understood why he died when he was so healthy, took such good care of himself. How could he leave her and Nick?

Her fury hadn't been logical. She'd known that, but it hadn't relieved the anger or pain. Then her father was shot down in cold blood, and she didn't know whether she—or Nick—could survive another loss. She'd decided then she would never open herself to that kind of pain again. For her sake. For her son's sake. She'd never even been tempted.

Not until Josh came to town and turned her world upside down.

He ignited fires she hadn't felt with Russ.

At noon, she was ready to jump out of her skin. When would something happen? When would Sam go to Josh's cabin to find the rifle? Maybe it wasn't Sam who planted it. Maybe it was someone else.

She took Nick to Maude's for lunch, but only picked at her food.

Why did she keep thinking about Josh Manning? *Fool!*

At three, she realized she was accomplishing nothing. The roof was getting hotter, and there was a magnet named Josh to whom she owed an explanation. Where had her conscience been when she'd okayed Tom's plan? No matter how she justified it to herself, she didn't feel one bit better. Worse yet, she had allowed Tom to do the explaining.

She didn't want to take Nick with her. Too much needed to be said. She called Abby and asked if it would be okay if Nick spent the rest of the day with her.

Abby was delighted, and Eve went downstairs to send Nick across the street to his grandparents' house.

She watched from the window as he walked across the street and reached Jim and Abby's, then told Merry she was leaving for the day on personal business.

She went by Maude's and bought three heaping ham sandwiches and two iced teas. Then she drove home and was letting the motley crew out when her cell phone rang.

"Hey, Mrs. Mayor."

She recognized the voice immediately. Nate Rowland.

"Hi, Nate."

"I have another volunteer for the roofing party this weekend."

Good news at last. "Who?"

"Our newest resident, Josh Manning. He's pretty good with a nail gun."

She was stunned. She hadn't mentioned the roofing party to Josh, never expected he would agree.

Did he agree to join the roofing party before or after he learned that he was being…used?

"He seems like a good guy," Nate said. "He hired me to help with the flooring at his cabin. Worked as hard as I did and paid me well. Said he might need me again."

Nate had been on the high school football team

with Russ and was one of his best friends until he'd moved to Denver and married.

"Good," she said. "And thanks for enlisting him. Oh, and Nate, when did he volunteer?"

"Over a cold beer last night. And just to let you know, we only had one before I left."

"Thanks, Nate."

She hung up and swallowed hard. So he wasn't running for the hills. He was going to stay, at least through the next weekend. But why help with the roof?

Because he *was* a good guy. But that didn't mean he was going to stay or that he enjoyed being in the position in which she and Tom put him.

By the time she reached Josh's cabin it was 4:00 p.m.

She knocked on the door and when he opened it, she was at a loss for words. "Hi," she said. A weak beginning.

"Hi," he echoed, a question in his eyes.

"I'm just taking a break and hoped you wanted one, too." She hoped she sounded casual as she looked up at him. He was wearing his usual jeans with a paint-splattered T-shirt. It was loose but still outlined every muscle when he moved. "I wanted to thank you," she said.

"If it's about the rifle, no need. I don't like bullies." His voice was cool and his expression unreadable.

"That, and Nate said you volunteered for the roofing party."

"I need Nate to finish the porch," he said. "If I help him on Saturday, maybe we can get started on it sooner."

She raised an eyebrow. "Is it so hard to just admit you're willing to help a stranger?"

He shrugged, but there was a slight twitch to his lips as if he was a small boy caught in a white lie. "Or maybe it's because I've spent half my life blowing things up. I kinda like the idea of putting something back together."

"Is that why you're working so hard on the cabin?"

"Haven't thought about it that way, but maybe," he admitted with a rueful look.

"Can I see the inside?" she asked.

He opened the door. The large room with the fireplace cleaned and stocked with wood, new hardwood floor and sand-colored walls looked warm and inviting. She couldn't believe the transformation. But except for the old sofa and some dog toys, it was bare. No sign of permanence. Her heart jerked.

"I'm impressed," she said and tried to keep her voice neutral. "It's amazing what you've done. Have you thought about starting a contracting business?"

"I'm not ready to start anything," he said.

"You like being busy, that's obvious."

"Maybe I just want to get it ready for sale."

She wanted more than a curt answer. She wanted trust, and she feared she had ruined that. "I brought a late lunch. Or an early supper. I want to show you our falls."

"So there really are falls?"

"Yes. Really. Maybe seeing them will explain a lot."

He studied her for a moment, then nodded. "You sure you want to be seen with me?"

She shrugged. "Miss Mollie is sitting in front of your cabin."

"True," he said.

She knew if she waited until the thefts were solved, it would be too late. Too late to be his friend. To be anything to him. She changed the subject. "What are you going to do with the porch?"

"Ah, the building permit," he said. "I wanted to expand it to the length of the cabin, make it a rocking-chair porch."

She noted the word *wanted*. She didn't say anything.

"I've wondered why Covenant Falls doesn't attract more visitors," he said, "but I'm beginning to learn. You don't really want newcomers, do you?"

"The president of the council doesn't," she said. "I do."

"Is he God here?"

"Pretty close. If his nephew becomes police chief, I'm afraid he *will* be God."

"You're mayor. I take it you were elected by the majority of the town."

She met his gaze. "Mainly because he didn't oppose me. He thought I would go along with whatever he wanted." She watched his face as he digested the information. "I had been city clerk before the election and I knew everything there was to know about the finances. The former mayor didn't. He just liked the title. I basically did his job, so Tom urged me to run. I think Al thought he could run over me as he did my predecessor."

"And he can't?"

"No, and it wasn't for lack of trying. But my dad was police chief before Tom. He was a good man, and he taught me to stick up for myself."

"What happened to him?" Josh asked, and she realized something in her voice must have told him something had.

"He tried to stop a motorcycle gang from robbing the Rusty Nail and probably killing a few patrons. He was killed instead."

"Did they catch the killers?" His voice was neutral.

"No. Nick worries about that to this day. He's much too interested in cop shows, and he adores Tom. I'm afraid he'll want to be a cop, too."

Josh's eyes softened. "That's tough on a kid. Losing both a father and grandfather. Especially like that."

He spoke as if he knew loss. There was a lot of pain in him, and she longed to take some of it away. And she wanted him to say he wasn't going to leave because of some half-baked scheme she and Tom had conjured.

"I'm sorry," she said. "We should never have involved you in this. Tom can say we found the rifle."

"And where might he have found it?" Josh asked rhetorically. "And how? Seems your Sam Clark would want to know. There wouldn't be any proof as to who put it there. Could have been me as far as the town's concerned." He paused, then added, "Seems to me it was Sam Clark who involved me. You're just taking advantage of that. Problem is, nothing ever goes as planned."

"My father would turn over in his grave if he knew that someone like Sam is wearing a badge. I should have done something earlier. It isn't right putting you in danger."

"I've been in danger since the moment I was born."

It was a loaded statement that begged explanation. But she suspected she would need more trust before he expanded upon it.

She stood on tiptoe and her lips brushed his, and all her senses went into overdrive. He touched her hair, ran his fingers through it then drew her closer and the kiss deepened. He was the one who backed away, but she knew from his eyes it wasn't what he wanted to do.

Eve bit her lip against tears suddenly hovering in her eyes as his fists clenched so tight the knuckles were white. She knew, and knew that he did, that they were both trying to protect parts of themselves. She saw a haunted look cross his face. *I've been in danger since the day I was born.* She had seen the caring parts of him in the way he interacted with his dog and her son, but now she saw the depth of emotion in his impossibly deep green eyes.

He took her hand in his. Heat ran up through her arm and spiraled through her body. The electricity was there, more intense than before, but there was something else, as well. Another kind of warmth. The kind that wrapped around you and made your soul sing.

She treasured that feeling. His arms went around her, and she didn't want to move, didn't want to break the magic. She rested her head against his heart and thought she never wanted to leave his embrace, his warmth, the passion that danced between them like dueling strikes of lightning.

His lips touched hers, featherlight at first, then more firmly, and her arms went around his neck.

"Mmm," he whispered. "You taste good."

"So do you," she answered, but she feared the sound of her voice was more a moan. She didn't want the kiss to stop, but she knew it should. In a few more seconds they would be in bed. But she wasn't ready for that commitment yet because, to her, that was what it would be.

And she had a mission. She wanted to show him Covenant Falls was worth saving.

She leaned back in his arms, her fingers tracing the lines of his face, lingering at the scar, then moving on. "I like your face," she said. "It has...strength. And integrity."

When he didn't reply, she clasped his hand. "I

brought a picnic. I want you to see what Covenant Falls is all about."

"I can't leave Amos alone, not with what is happening."

"He's invited, as well."

"I'm expecting a visit from the police."

"Tom will call me if Sam makes a move. Sam has a shadow now who will stick to him like they're Siamese twins."

He studied with those remarkable emerald eyes, then nodded. He went inside and called Amos, and they both came out. He locked the door behind him. As he turned, she saw the holster on his belt. She didn't blame him. A police officer was trying to frame him, and there was no telling how far he would go. But then she didn't know how far Josh would go, either.

"This really isn't the Wild West."

He ignored the comment and looked at the truck. "Is there room for both Amos and me?"

"There's space behind the seats. Nick's dogs travel back there."

Josh opened the passenger-side door. Amos hesitated for a moment. "It's okay," Josh said.

Amos jumped in. Eve saw Josh's mouth bend into a smile as his dog sniffed the nest of blankets he found. Amos had obviously started to trust him, and her heart hurt to see how much that meant to Josh. He ruffled the fur along Amos's back as Eve started the car.

He didn't say anything as Eve drove out onto Lake Road and then Mine Street. They rode past the Rusty Nail, then she turned onto an unmarked narrow road that wound through a forest of pines.

Twenty minutes later, she took another turn onto a gravel road that led upward and quickly became enclosed by pines on both sides. Another two miles and she pulled into a clearing.

She didn't wait for him to get out, but stepped out herself and went to the bed of the truck. She grabbed the picnic basket and headed for a well-worn trail that overlooked a ravine and a river below. The trail was protected from the edge by a rustic wood fence, a safety measure her father had worked hard to obtain.

A short, curving walk led to a viewing area with picnic tables. The falls were suddenly in sight. Sixty feet of foaming water tumbling over rocks into the fast-running river below. A rainbow curved into the heart of the falls.

She was awed as she always was when she saw it. The rainbow wasn't always there, but frequent enough to be a reason for a visit.

She turned to look at Josh, and even he looked affected. Amos, obviously unimpressed, stayed by his side.

"There's an old path that goes to the top and over the mountains to a mining town. It's a ghost town now. The town of Covenant Falls was originally Monroe Lake. Its history goes back to 1863, when Angus Monroe found a natural lake fed by melting snow and the falls and started a trading post. Gold seek-ers, mountain men and pioneers stopped for supplies. Some stayed after the mines played out. Monroe cam-paigned for statehood and made important friends in doing so, and Covenant Falls eventually gained city status.

"Family members and friends of the family have pretty much run everything since then. It was pretty much benevolent until Al became heir and started throwing his weight around. Neither he nor his father had the magic touch in business that their ancestors had, and I think he's terrified of losing everything they built. He's the last of the line with the Monroe name. He and his wife don't have children. They tried but his wife never could bring one to term. I'll give him one thing. He didn't try to divorce Lily. He re-ally loves her."

"Al doesn't sound Scottish."

"It's really Alistair. Alistair and Angus and Jaime all pop up on the family tree. But Al hated that name."

"And the police officer? Your police chief said he's the nephew."

"Sam is Al's only sister's son, the only heir. His parents died when he was ten. That's why the name is different. Al tried to bring him into his business but he had no interest in the insurance and realty busi-ness. He received a degree in criminal justice, which, in Al's point of view, makes him qualified to be po-lice chief. It doesn't. He's not stupid, but he's always been spoiled. Always got a free pass when he got in trouble. What Sam wants, Al wants for him. Especially when it benefits him, as well."

"How?"

"Al lost the family ranch, but he has a stake in the county bank and owns the only insurance firm in town. The town does business with both."

"Is that legal?"

"He abstains from decisions affecting the bank and insurance company, but the other council members pretty much do whatever he wants. I shudder to think what would happen to this town if Al was mayor and Sam police chief." She hesitated, then continued, "Tell you the truth, I don't think Al is aware of what we suspect. I think Sam thought this up on his own. He thinks being the Monroe heir makes him something akin to God. He resents the fact people don't recognize that. When you came to town, I think he saw it as an opportunity to become a hero. Prove he's a competent officer."

She paused, then added, "Don't underestimate him. If he's thwarted, I think he can be dangerous. He doesn't have limits. I can't tell you how much I want him out of the department."

Josh looked thoughtful. After a moment, he asked, "What powers do you have?"

"I hire staff. That includes the police department and the chief. But while I prepare a budget, the council has to approve it. The council refused to fund the community center, which is why we have fund-raisers to finance it and volunteers to run it. If the council doesn't approve of my police chief, they can eliminate the police force."

"What happens then to law enforcement?"

"It goes to the county to take over. But the sheriff's office is understaffed. There wouldn't be anyone here permanently."

"There's no one on the council who supports you?"

"One wholeheartedly, one halfheartedly."

"That comes back to the question of why me? Why did Clark pick on me to be the criminal mastermind?"

"You're new. No connections in the community. No one to defend you. When you first arrived, neighbors saw you and Amos walking late at night and feared you were up to no good. But he made a mistake. The burglaries had to be committed by someone who knows which businesses have weak spots and something worthwhile to steal. That eliminated you in Tom's mind."

She studied him. His green eyes were penetrating, his expression appraising. He was assessing every word, withholding judgment, asking all the right questions.

"I don't want you to think ill of us," she added. "This place is steeped in history. Most of the people here have roots going back as far as five and even six generations, including Al Monroe."

His green eyes were bright with interest. "Was your family one of the early ones?"

"On my father's side. His father had been foreman of one of the large ranches, and my dad grew up a ranch hand. Then he was drafted and served in Vietnam and he received a bunch of medals. He came back and joined the county's sheriff's department. He helped capture a murder suspect from Philadelphia and met my mother when he was up there helping with the case. But Colorado and the mountains were in his blood. They moved here, and Dad became police chief."

"Where's your mother now?"

"She hated Covenant Falls," Eve said stiffly. "Didn't like it from the day she saw it. Too small. Too provincial. Not enough 'right' people. But Dad wanted me raised here. It was a battle between them all my life. She stuck it out because that was the proper thing to do.

"And she loved him. But the day after Dad's funeral she went back to Philly. I was married then and had Nick, and there was no question about staying or not staying. I agreed with my dad. I wanted my son to grow up in open spaces, clear skies and fresh air."

"Do you see her?"

"I take Nick once a year for a week."

"So Covenant Falls is in your blood, too," he said. It wasn't a question, more a statement.

"Yes."

"How did the Hannitys come here, then? From what I understand, the cabin was mostly a vacation place."

"Summer visitors were welcome then," she said. "Al's father, Jaime, thought growth was a good thing, especially those from out of town who owned property and paid taxes without using much of the services. The land on your side of the lake was advertised as mountain retreats. The Hannitys were one of the first families to build a cabin they used in the summer. They were followed by others. Then Mr. and Mrs. Hannity were killed in a private plane crash. The next year David returned with his uncle, who I understood was his guardian. His uncle drowned in the lake a year later. David left and never returned."

"And the others?"

"After the drowning and all the talk, out-of-towners stopped coming. A recession sped up the process. Home prices fell so low that people in town could afford to buy them. Shep was one of them."

"What talk?" She should have known he would zero in on that comment.

"I would rather not repeat rumors," she said. "My husband knew and liked David and I did, too." She turned toward the falls. "Like most places, Covenant Falls has its secrets and tragedies, its good people and those few not so good. No worse and probably better than many towns. With the lake and mountains, it's a great place to raise kids."

"Except when they get older and can't find jobs," he said skeptically.

"A lot of us want to change that," she said.

She looked up and wished he wasn't so difficult to read. "I understand why you wouldn't want to be involved," she said.

"Sam Clark *has* involved me," he said.

"You'll stay, then?" she said. Her heart pounded so loud she was sure he must hear it.

He took her hand, holding it loosely in his. "For a while. You know, you're very pretty when you get impassioned."

She felt her cheeks growing warm. He looked pretty darn good himself, with a shock of sandy hair pasted against his face by the mist. She found herself leaning against him.

The rainbow looked close enough to touch, and a breeze seemed to caress them. The moment was magical.

Amos barked then and, startled, they both looked down at him.

"I think he likes the falls, too," she said, leaning down to scratch his ears. "I have a treat for him if that's okay?"

"It's good with me if it's good with him," he said.

She went to the picnic basket and took her time finding a strip of chicken jerky. She needed a moment to steady her emotions. She was quaking inside.

She held the piece of jerky to Amos, who sniffed it and looked at Josh. "Yes," he told the dog.

Amos took it in his mouth and sat, still looking at Josh. Half of the jerky hung out of one side of his mouth like a cigar.

Eve laughed. "I would like a photo of that. He looks like a thin Churchill."

A slow smile spread across Josh's face and eased

the harsh lines around his eyes and mouth. There was something incredibly appealing about him with his barriers down. He leaned down and his lips touched hers. Gently at first. Her heart caught at the tenderness. Then the heat came, and the kiss turned urgent. A melting sensation settled in the pit of her stomach, and her arms went around his neck. The air between them was combustible, churning with winds of temptation.

Then her world exploded, and all her reason with it.

CHAPTER EIGHTEEN

JOSH'S LAST THOUGHT before prolonging the kiss was that it was the worst idea ever. And the most irresistible.

She'd looked so appealing with the breeze and mist coloring her cheeks and her dark hair framing her face. He was charmed by the passionate way she talked about the town and her obvious fascination with history, an interest he shared.

Her hazel eyes sparkled as she talked, and he'd wanted to bottle that delighted laugh when Amos had taken the jerky.

When their lips met, he felt a warmth he'd never experienced before. It flowed through his body like warm honey. He felt her tremble as they pressed together like magnets, both helpless to resist the pull of the other.

Tension coiled in his stomach as the kiss deepened. Her arms went around his neck, her fingers sending sensations reeling throughout his body. Heat erupted wherever she touched him as their lips played with each other, tasting, exploring. She seemed to melt into him as if she was made for him and he for her.

He took in a shaky breath. He wanted to draw her

to the ground and make love to her that minute. He fought that urge with every ounce of willpower he had.

If he continued, they wouldn't be able to stop. He knew that.

Emotionally, everything was right with this. God, how he wanted it. Her kisses told him she wanted it. But everything else was wrong. She was not the kind of woman he'd slept with before. She was not the type you bed and leave. He pulled back. But she was still too close, too pretty, too ready for more. He knew a dozen reasons why he should stop, but none of them seemed imperative.

"Don't go away," she whispered. He knew she meant more than a kiss.

Good intentions went to hell in a basket. His arms went around her again, and he wasn't sure whether the sound he heard was the thunder of the falls or his heart. He kissed her forehead and worked his way down to her mouth. The meeting of lips this time was explosive. It was not lust that was so powerful, although it was certainly there. The problem rested in the fact that lust was only a small part of what he felt. He didn't just want her in bed, he wanted her with him in the morning, and the next day and the next.

He didn't believe in love.

He kissed her again, slow and sensual. Her mouth opened to his, and his hands climbed to the back of her neck. If they had been anywhere but the falls, he wouldn't have stopped. He wanted so much more than a kiss. He wanted the potent mixture of tenderness and fire he'd just barely tasted. He wanted to learn her every mood. He wanted to hear her laugh again. Hell, he wanted *her*.

But this wasn't the time or place. Anyone could be driving up here, even on a workday. She could be destroyed in the town she loved.

He stepped back and it was one of the hardest things he'd ever done. "We should go," he said.

She looked dazed. Well, he was a little dazed himself. Make that a lot. "Wow," she whispered. "What just happened?"

"Damned if I know," he replied. Not very eloquent, but it was honest.

He looked down. Amos was looking from Josh to Eve and back again. "It's okay," he said softly. Amos whined, apparently feeling the tension in the air. "It's okay," he said again.

He turned back to Eve. Mist had dampened her hair, and a curl clung to her cheek. He pushed it back and caressed the smoothness of her cheeks.

"I like your falls," he finally said. He was too shaken by the intensity. "Is it always this empty here?"

Her voice was none too steady when she answered. "It's pretty busy on the weekends. Families bring picnics. But during the week, most people work, and if they don't, they go fishing in the lake. We get a few tourists during the summer, but mostly they have to stumble on us. We're out of the way, and there are no other attractions around." She paused, then grinned. "We do have a legend, though."

"Let me guess," Josh said. "Two forbidden lovers jumping together?"

"We're not nearly that predictable," she teased, her eyes full of mischief. He had never seen her like this before. Fanciful and easy and ever so irresistible.

"A happy legend, then?" he asked.

"Yes, and it's why the town is named Covenant Falls. Angus Monroe found the lake when he was almost dead from thirst. He had emigrated from Scotland with his brother to look for gold. His brother didn't make it that far. He'd drowned while crossing a river.

"Gold," she continued with a beguiling smile, "had been his brother's dream, not his. He was a trader by instinct, and he decided there were better ways to get gold than digging for it. He built a small cabin and hunted beaver that he sold. He saw settlements springing up throughout Colorado, and he envisioned a town built around this lake. Gold had been found, though, and it had a stronger call for others. It also stirred the Native tribes that were being pushed from their ancestral lands. Attacks became more frequent and no man was willing to bring his family to an unprotected new settlement." Eve paused and looked back at the falls.

"One day while returning from trapping, he found a badly injured Ute man at the foot of the falls. He had been shot by miners while hunting and had made it to the falls before collapsing.

"Angus had learned a little about medicine, and he doctored the brave back to health. His patient turned out to be very important member of the Utes and when he survived, the Utes rewarded Angus with a covenant of protection.

"They kept that promise and when other settlements were threatened by Native raids, Covenant Falls became a haven. Angus filed a squatter's claim and lured other settlers to his new town. It grew slowly. Angus wanted a village like those he'd known in Scotland, with a kirk and school. Since it was the falls that created the lake, he decided to name his town Covenant Falls.

"There's something else," she said. "Angus was rewarded with the Ute's sister for a wife. From all the tales, he really loved her and treated her well. She died giving birth to their third child. Nothing he could do saved her. He never married again."

It was a good story. Being a natural skeptic, Josh wondered how much of it was true and how much was romanticized.

"Angus's Bible is in our church," she said as if she knew exactly what he was thinking. "He recorded the day they married, first in the Ute village, then later in the church he built, along with the births of their children, two girls and a boy. Al is descended from that marriage and that son."

He felt, and saw, her emotion in telling the story.

Two people from radically different lives. A Scottish trader and a Ute woman, but love apparently made it work. Eve's eyes glistened as she looked up at him. The no-nonsense mayor had disappeared. He wanted to touch her again. Hell, he wanted to throw her down on the ground and make mad, passionate love.

A comparison between her life and his flashed through his mind. He really didn't know what love was.

She touched his face. It was an infinitely gentle and wishful gesture.

"What are you thinking?" she asked.

"I've never met anyone like you," he admitted.

"I'm not sure whether that's good or bad."

"I'm not, either," he said. "You don't know much about me."

"I know what I need to know," she said. "I know you care about kids and dogs and you're loyal to your friends. Dave was lucky to have you. I know you're a craftsman in whatever you do. I know that you don't trust easily. I know I like you more than I should. I never wanted to…get romantically involved again. I'm cautious, too. I don't want the pain of loving and losing someone again, and even more I don't want Nick to go through that darkness. But I…can't seem to convince myself to stay away."

Her honesty touched him. He closed his eyes, tried to think of reasons he should run, like he always had when confronted by anything that intruded on his self-imposed discipline.

That wall was falling in pieces around him. Amos had punctured it first, then Nick and his mother.

It's that damned rainbow.

The rainbow was as good as anything to blame. He'd never seen one that was so perfect.

"Josh?"

Her voice startled him back into the real world. His name on her lips sounded different.

They were both on guard now. Her voice was unsteady, and he knew his was hoarse with want.

"Hungry?" she asked in an obvious attempt to defuse the tension. "I did bring more than chicken jerky."

He nodded and she took some sandwiches from the picnic basket, along with drinks.

"There's a sandwich for Amos," she said.

"You're trying to steal my dog's affections," he said.

"You can have one of my dogs in trade," she retorted with a grin. "Take your pick."

"I think Nick would object."

"Yes," she said. "He probably would."

He took a bite from one sandwich and shared the second with Amos. To his surprise, Amos gobbled it down.

Then they started cleaning off the table, and just as they had at their first meeting their hands brushed, this time on purpose. If there had been a spark then, now it was a forest fire.

He saw her swallow hard. He did the same.

"Why did you join the army?" she asked.

"I wanted a home," he said simply. "I never really had one. A coach at the high school I attended was a former Ranger. Said the service had paid for college, that it had given him a sense of belonging. Sounded good to me." He shrugged. He hadn't meant to say that, but then he hadn't planned to do any of this, including kissing her. There was something about her that drew out words and emotions he'd always kept hidden somewhere inside.

"You miss it?"

"Parts of it," he said.

Her hand reached for his free one and tightened around it as if she sensed the other part. The loss part. It was as if she sensed the pain that lived in him.

It wasn't pity. He couldn't stand that. Rather, it was a balm to the pain he felt, and always would, when he thought about how Dave had traded his life for his. Survivor's guilt, the shrink had called it. Common in vets.

It was not common to him. It was like a red-hot pitchfork impaling his heart.

She must have felt the sudden agony surging through him. A tear from her eye dampened his cheek. It took every bit of strength in him to keep his own tears at bay. He couldn't remember ever crying before. Not when he'd awoken and learned Dave was dead along with most of the rest of his team. Not when he'd been told his army career was over. Not when his mother had died of an overdose.

Men don't cry. Rangers don't cry. Not even for each other. Yet the tears were like an expanding substance in a bottle, ready to explode through. She must have felt him pull back because she took a step backward herself, though still clung to his hand. "Tell me about David," she said softly. "And Amos."

He was ready. He was finally ready. Maybe because it was time, or maybe because it was Eve asking. "Dave and I were in the same outfit for ten years," he said slowly, painfully. He had given Nate the short version, the unemotional version, but now the whole story was being wrenched from his heart. "We trained together, fought together." His voice grew hoarse. "He died saving my life. Six others died as well because we were given the wrong information."

He paused as he relived that battle, just as he had so many times. "I was hit several times, and Dave covered my body with his as our copters were coming in. He received the Silver Star posthumously, little good that it did him."

He didn't know why he was telling her about the last battle except it had haunted him, was still haunting him, and she needed to know that it might always haunt him.

It came flooding out now. "I woke up days later in Germany. I was told by a surviving member of my team that when he didn't come back, Amos kept looking for Dave. Amos hadn't been with us on that last mission because he'd cut his paw badly the week earlier. I'd promised Dave that I would look after Amos if anything happened to him. He loved that dog, and Amos loved him." His voice was raw. "But I couldn't look after him, not for months." His fingers knotted into fists.

If she noticed, she didn't say anything. Her eyes hadn't left his, and he saw another tear roll down her cheek. "I'm so sorry," she said. "I shouldn't have asked."

"People here should know what kind of a man Dave was," Josh said, "and they should know about Amos. He waited and waited for Dave to return. He wouldn't obey any other handler. Finally, he was sent back to Lackland Air Force Base to be retrained. He refused, just huddled in the back of his kennel. Waiting. Waiting for Dave."

"Until you found him," she prompted when he hesitated.

"He recognized me, but he still wouldn't obey or react to me. I could barely get him to eat. He let me take him to my car, but he was a frail shadow of himself. He used to chase balls and KONGs with such joy. Because Dave was throwing them. I can't get him to chase anything."

She let go of his hand and stooped down to pet Amos, running her hand through his fur from his neck to his tail. When she finished, she dropped her hand to his nose and let him sniff. He gave her a lick and gazed up into her eyes. "Good, loyal Amos," she said. Josh saw her bite her lip and knew she was holding back tears.

Shared grief. He knew she had suffered, too, that she understood loss, and she realized dogs felt it just as strongly as humans. Maybe that was why he could talk about David and that day. For the first time since that firefight, he didn't feel alone.

She stood. "I have to go," she said. "I don't want to, but I have to be at the rehearsal for the high school graduation." She hesitated, then said, "Come with me tonight."

He shook his head. "I have work to do."

But he touched her chin and lifted it so their eyes met. "Thank you for bringing me here."

Her eyes were soft, damp, and he crushed her to his chest for a moment, just holding her.

"Did he ever marry?" she asked suddenly.

"Dave?" he asked, surprised at the question.

She nodded.

"For a very short time. When we were overseas, she drained his bank account and divorced him."

"I'm sorry to hear that."

"He was more careful after that."

"And so were you." She said the words with a small, wistful smile.

"I've always been careful."

She hesitated, then said, "I didn't know David well, but what I did know I liked. So did Russ. One time they raced across the lake on a dare."

"Russ?"

"My husband."

"Stephanie told me he died suddenly." Words also carefully said.

She nodded.

"I'm sorry," he said, not knowing what else to say or even why he'd mentioned it. Maybe because he wanted to know so much more about her.

"Nick's just now coming out of his shell. The dogs helped."

Like maybe Amos was helping him. She didn't say that, but he knew it might be true. He was slowly loosening up. To Nate. To Stephanie, certainly to Eve. He was allowing others into his life. People who were not military.

He didn't know what to say then. Emotions were running strong in both of them, and he sensed she was just as reluctant to talk about her husband as he was about Dave. It hurt too damn much.

"We had better go," he said. He offered her his hand. She took it, and it felt warm and welcoming.

She nodded. "Thank you for coming."

They looked at each other. Didn't move. Knowing if they did they would fall into each other's arms again. And there was still too much separating them. He knew that. He saw that she did, too.

But still they held hands as they walked back to her truck. To Miss Mollie, as she called it. It had always seemed a whimsical name for the truck of a businesslike mayor. Now he realized it reflected one of the many facets of her.

He looked back at the falls as they turned away from them, and he noticed that she did, too. The rainbow was fading as the day faded. Yet its glow stayed with him.

CHAPTER NINETEEN

THE FLASHBACK CAME back that night with a fury. Josh woke in the middle of the night, thrashing around until the sweat-soaked sheets knotted around him, trapping him. His heart raced as he struggled against them, frantic to find his rifle.

Amos whined, nudged him. He took the dog's head in his arms and held tight as the images slowly faded away. "Thank you, Amos," he said.

Amos licked his face.

He moved over and Amos crawled up on the narrow bed with him, just as he had with Dave. Josh slowly relaxed as the first light of dawn seeped in.

He thought of Eve. What if the flashbacks occurred while they were in bed together? He could hurt her.

He knew he wouldn't get more sleep, although he had worked until late into the night. He'd painted the second bedroom after moving the new furniture into the living area. The afternoon he'd spent with Eve made relaxing impossible. Too many feelings intruded.

She had just dropped off him and Amos yesterday afternoon. She hadn't come inside. Both of them knew that wouldn't have been a very good idea. He'd taken a cold shower, a very cold shower, then started to work. Exhaustion had done nothing to quiet his emotions.

He couldn't stop thinking about Eve and what had happened earlier and what it meant. Or didn't mean. There was no question that the attraction was explosive and mutual, but that didn't make it right for them. They were different in every way: backgrounds, goals, lifestyles, hopes and dreams. She had a lot of them. He didn't have any.

Just keep busy. Maybe the best thing for them both was for him to finish the cabin and leave. He stood painfully. Standing on his feet, painting, was more difficult than walking. He wondered whether the pain would ever go away. The doctors said yes, with exercise and the strengthening of muscles, but his leg was never going to be what it once was. In the beginning, one step was progress. Now progress was measured by climbing a few steps of a ladder, catching himself from falling when his leg started to buckle and standing for longer periods of time. But he was damned if he was going to let it get the better of him. Not when so many other vets were fighting much harder battles.

He was confident no one would serve a search warrant at six in the morning. At least not in Covenant Falls. It galled him that he had no control over that, either, that he had to depend on a police chief he really didn't know and a woman with mixed loyalties.

He made coffee and waited for it to percolate as he refilled Amos's water dish and tried uselessly to tempt him with one of several KONG toys he'd filled with peanut butter. That would be the true test that Dave's dog was recovering.

Dave's dog? He looked down at Amos. He'd thought of Amos in that context. But now he suddenly realized that was no longer true. Amos was *his* dog now, whether or not Amos realized it yet.

When the coffee was ready, he filled a large insulated cup. "Come, Amos." Amos followed Josh outside. The air was fragrant from the pines, and a parchment moon was still visible in a pure blue sky even as the sun rose in the east.

He thought of the sheer beauty and power of the waterfall he'd visited yesterday. And he thought about the first Monroe, who had been almost dead from thirst when he found the lake. He had to admit both the reality and the story behind it were compelling.

He also had to admit that Covenant Falls, with its forest and lake and falls, was growing on him. There was a peace in these mountains, a pristine beauty that was a salve for his memories. Afghanistan had been mountainous, too, but it had a harshness that was more threatening than tranquil.

Dave had obviously cared for these mountains as well, since he'd hung on to the cabin for so long. That brought up the persistent question: Why hadn't Dave mentioned Covenant Falls? Why hadn't he sold the cabin years ago? He had even managed to protect it from Claire, his ex-wife. It had obviously been important to him.

He would have to ask Laine Mabry, the attorney who drew up the will. But Mabry's office was in the county seat, and this was not something Josh wanted to do by phone. He heard a rustling in the woods. Probably a rabbit. Amos looked alert but made no move to go after it. Josh wondered whether the dog stayed next to him because he wanted to, or out of simple disinterest.

Either way, Amos wasn't hiding or shivering. He had started to eat. He had friends in Nick, Stephanie and Eve. Covenant Falls had been good for Amos.

Josh hoped Amos was beginning to think of him as the alpha of his pack, but he wasn't there yet. Dave had explained the "pack" concept to him when he first became Amos's handler. The alpha was the leader of the pack, and in Amos's world Dave had been the alpha. The other soldiers were also members of his pack but they were not alphas. Josh knew he had to earn the position.

He sat on a rock and talked to Amos as Dave had done. Amos sat and looked at him through big brown canine eyes. "Stay or leave Covenant Falls, Amos?" he asked the dog. "What should we do?"

Amos didn't blink. No answer there.

SAM CLARK STRUCK at midmorning. He brought a search warrant to Tom's office with the signature of a county judge.

Cited reasons included the contentions that burglaries began at the same time Josh Manning came to town, that his vehicle was recognized at one of the crime scenes and that a witness had seen him prowling around Shep's home.

Tom shook his head. "He lives in the neighborhood. He walks his dog. And the so-called witness to the burglary of the saloon who said he saw a Jeep that looked like Manning's? That particular individual does not have a sterling record of veracity."

"The judge thought it was enough," Sam retorted.

Tom gave it one last try. He would see this farce to the end, but he knew it would cause havoc in town. "I've talked to Josh Manning, looked around his property. Didn't find anything unusual."

"But you didn't question him officially."

"How do you know?"

Sam flushed. "He wasn't in this office."

"Sam, as long as I am chief, I will question people my way, not yours. Is that understood?"

"People are wondering why we're not doing anything."

"I don't know why Judge Henley signed it, but Officer Keller and I will go with you. I want this by the book. You will be polite. You will search only those areas included in the search warrant."

"The entire property," Sam said. "Inside and out."

"I'll take the interior. He has a dog. It's an ex-military dog, and I want you to be damned careful. Anything happens to that dog, and there's going to be a lot of hell raised around town."

"It's just a dog," Sam said. "It's trained to kill. I have the right to shoot if it attacks me."

"I'm going to make sure it doesn't. Don't test me on this," Tom warned. "You may think your uncle is the most important person in town, but I know a lot of people in law enforcement. I can make sure you never wear a badge again. Even here."

"And if we find something?"

"I'll say, 'Good police work.'"

Sam nodded reluctantly. "When do we leave?"

"When Officer Keller gets through with some paperwork. I have a few calls to make."

Tom wondered what Al had on Judge Henley, who had promised him a year ago he wouldn't sign a warrant without Tom's approval. Then he went to see Eve, closed the door and told her what had happened. "Is Manning at home today?"

"I don't know."

"Henley signed the search warrant. I plan to have some words with him later this week because of the principle involved. Both Ryan and I are going with Sam. I don't want to give him a chance to plant anything else."

"Maybe he already has."

"I doubt it," he said. He didn't add that he'd noticed that Manning had mounted several cameras around the cabin. He noticed them only because he'd been planning to do the same thing, and Manning's cameras were in exactly the same places he'd considered.

If Sam had second thoughts and tried to move the rifle, it would be on film.

"Don't call him," he warned Eve.

"I won't."

He turned and left, closing the door softly behind him.

JOSH HAD JUST finished painting his bedroom when he heard cars pulling into the driveway. He closed Amos in the second bedroom and opened the door before anyone pounded on it. Three officers, including the police chief and the arrogant officer he'd met at Maude's, stood there.

The chief handed him a piece of paper. "We have a search warrant," he said.

"Who did you bribe to get it?" Josh asked casually.

The chief shrugged, but Josh saw the officer named Clark smirk.

The chief turned back to Josh. "I think you know Officer Clark. And this is Officer Ryan Keller. I'll take the interior. The two officers will search the property outside." He waited until Clark and Keller turned around, then followed Josh inside the cabin.

Josh went over to the window.

The chief joined him.

"Have to ask," he said. "Have any stolen property?" he asked.

"Not to my knowledge," Josh said.

"No weapons other than your handgun?"

"Not unless you include a nail gun."

The chief's attention turned back to Josh. "I really didn't think he could get that warrant."

"Maybe he's not the one who put the rifle there."

"We'll know soon. Sam isn't good at hiding anger or frustration. The whole point of this exercise is to satisfy Ryan and me that Sam is the one who placed that rifle on the bike before we go any further. It won't prove anything we can use in court, but it does give me ammunition to take to the Colorado Investigative Branch. It's not something I should handle on my own. My bias is already clear. I've tried to fire him before, only to see him reinstated by the council." He turned to the window.

Sam, with Ryan Keller at his side, started the search at the opposite end of the property from where the Harley was parked. The two worked their way around to the back until they appeared again near the porch. The chief backed away from the window as Clark, followed closely by the other officer, approached the porch and looked at the new boards that covered what had been the space where the rattler had taken up residence. They then headed for the Jeep.

It was locked, and the two officers returned to the cabin. When Josh opened the door, Sam demanded the keys. Chief MacGuire looked pained but said nothing as Josh handed them over.

The two officers searched the Jeep. They started back to the cabin, and Josh wondered whether the sheriff, Eve and he had been wrong, or that Clark suspected a trap. But then the officer stopped, took a long look over the property and then headed toward the covered Harley. Ryan said something to him, then shrugged and followed.

Josh watched intently as Clark uncovered the Harley. He couldn't see the officer's face but the man's body language radiated confidence. Even from where Josh stood, he noticed the stiffening of Clark's body as he saw the rifle was no longer there. He glanced around wildly.

The officer with him had his phone out, and Josh hoped he was taking photos.

"You were right," Josh said to the police chief.

"Unfortunately. I hate a crooked cop. I didn't have respect for Clark, but now I know what he is, and I have to prove it."

"He can't let this go," Josh said. "He'll have to know what happened to that rifle."

"I can go to the state now and get help. Hopefully keep Ryan around longer. But Sam might come after you now."

"I don't think there's any question about that. He has to think I found it, and now he'll want to know what I did with it. But you knew that from the beginning."

"I thought it a possibility. After seeing his face, I know it's a certainty. This was probably a bad idea."

"And kinda questionable legally. Isn't there something called entrapment?"

"We do things differently in a small town," the chief said. "And anyway, I'm on my way out. Bad heart. But I'm not going to leave that…thief in a uniform, much less mine." He looked at Josh. "You can stop this now. Just report having found the rifle, and that you gave it to me. You'll have my dated letter as proof."

He was giving Josh an out. One last chance.

And he did think about it, but not for long. "As you said, there's no proof other than the fact he was angry. He could just be angry because he couldn't find evidence."

"True."

"You need my help."

"I shouldn't be asking you. You're a civilian now. You did your part, and more."

"It means staying here longer," Josh said slowly and, to his surprise, that didn't sound like such a bad idea.

The chief nodded. "And you could be in danger, although I doubt he has the nerve to go after you directly. He'll probably try to plant other evidence. But I notice you have cameras installed around here, and Ryan will keep a close eye on him."

"You noticed, huh?"

"I was going to do the same thing. You saved the city some money."

"There was a saying we lived by in the Rangers. 'If anything can go wrong, it will.' Thought it would be good to have a record."

"Can't say something won't go wrong," the chief

said. "Sam can be unpredictable, but I never thought he would go this far."

"I would like that official letter," Josh said.

Tom took an envelope out of his pocket and handed it to Josh, who opened it and scanned the contents. It outlined everything he'd requested.

"We have a witness now, and Ryan will make a fine one. He'll know all about this conversation."

"I'm in," Josh said simply.

"I want to hire you," Tom said.

"Can you?"

"Other than Sam, I can hire whoever I want if it's within my budget. Would a dollar a year be okay?"

"Eve told me the city had a small budget. Didn't know it was that small. But are you sure about this? It's a lot of trust on your part."

"I've read your service record."

Josh raised an eyebrow. "I thought that was confidential."

He looked at Josh. "No one will know about this arrangement but the four of us. You, me, Eve and Ryan."

Just then Clark and the other officer came inside without knocking. Sam looked as if he was about to have a heart attack. His face was red and he was breathing hard. "Where is it?" Sam asked.

"Where is what?" Josh replied.

"I know you burglarized the house down the street."

"And how do you know that?"

Officer Sam Clark glared at him. He turned to the police chief. "Did you find anything?"

"No. Just a Glock, and he has a permit. No rifles. No belt buckles. You were just plain wrong, Sam, and I'm going to have a little talk with Judge Henley."

"I say we search longer." Clark's face was even redder.

Keller interjected, "We've already searched everywhere."

Chief MacGuire said, "We're going, unless you give me a solid reason why we shouldn't."

"I just know..." Sam's voice trailed off.

"That's it." The chief turned to Josh. "Sorry to have bothered you, Mr. Manning." He led the way out, and Clark didn't have a choice but to follow. Clark turned around and shot Josh a poisonous look. Josh would have pitied him if he wasn't dangerous. Any bad cop with a uniform and gun was dangerous. The officer had to know the rifle had been found, but he couldn't ask questions without revealing guilt.

Josh knew the police chief intended to keep him wondering.

EVE SUFFERED THROUGH most of the morning working on her comments for the graduation tonight, but her concentration was in tatters.

She'd watched as two police cars pulled out of the lot. Nick was staying with his grandparents again.

She hated the cloak-and-dagger stuff. It cheapened her job. She didn't like subterfuge or secretive conversations in her office. But the fact that Sam had gotten a warrant without Tom's approval and felt he could plant evidence told her exactly what he would do if he had more power.

She was to give out the awards for scholarship at the graduation tonight. She reworked her comments, wanting to make them personalized to each recipient. Sandy Evans, English prize, had babysat her son and was a tutor for younger kids. She also worked with the animal rescue group and was constantly harassing people to adopt rescues. Kaylee Bradley, math prize, had the voice of an angel and sang in the choir and community chorus as well as being a math whiz. And then there was Ken Barrett, science prize, who was the son of the Presbyterian minister. Russ had coached him in youth football and had said the wiry young man was the most determined, if not the most athletic, player he'd coached.

The ceremony itself would be held in the school auditorium with a reception later in the gym. She had convinced the grocer to donate ingredients for a punch, and the PTA was providing food. She figured they wouldn't need much. The kids were bound to leave early for their own parties at the lake beach.

She usually loved the graduation ceremonies and had attended nearly every one since she and Russ graduated, even when she wasn't mayor, because she'd known someone who was graduating. Too many would leave Covenant Falls and she would only hear of them through their families.

She looked at her notes again. They sounded trite, but she couldn't concentrate. She wished Tom would call or come sauntering in. She looked at her watch. 1:00 p.m.

Her heart was about ready to jump through her body. Why had she ever given Tom the go-ahead for the plan?

CHAPTER TWENTY

THE QUESTION NOW was what would Clark do to save himself?

Josh mulled over the question later that afternoon as he pulled up to the hardware store in the Jeep. Amos sat in the passenger seat. Josh was not going to leave Amos alone with Officer Clark on the loose. He'd told Amos to stay, and to be sure, he'd tied the leash to the door.

As he entered Wilson's hardware store, Calvin Wilson greeted him as if he was an old friend.

"Heard you're joining our roofing party."

"Is everyone in town going to be there?" It felt as though half the town had made the same comment.

"Quite a few. The ladies serve refreshments. I'm too old to get on the roof, but I'm donating the nails. Right now we have twelve men and one woman who have volunteered to work on the roof. I expect there will be others now that they know you're coming."

"Why is that?" Josh asked with real puzzlement.

"Well, word is you're army. We're real pro military here. Don't know if you've seen it yet, but we all contributed for a memorial to honor our fallen heroes. It's in the park near the community center. We're real proud of it."

"Lose a lot of guys?"

"And one woman. Five so far in the Middle East, nineteen in Vietnam and two in Korea. There were forty-two during WWII. Most in the same outfit on Omaha Beach."

"That's a lot for a small town."

"Most of us have roots that go back to the 1800s. Real strong on patriotism. I was in the infantry during Korea. Didn't have the choice then, what with the draft. I appreciate those who volunteer today. All of us do," he added, then mumbled, "except a few." He paused, then said, "We're also mighty appreciative of what you did for the Douglas boy. Eve's had too much pain already.

"And she's been a good mayor," Calvin Wilson continued. "Best we've had in my memory."

"How do people feel about the rest of the council?"

He shrugged. "Different opinions." He changed the subject. "What can I get you, Mr. Manning? Seems you've been doing a lot of work on the cabin."

"I'm enlarging the porch. I have a list of materials here." Josh handed it to him.

"Big porch, huh?" Wilson commented.

"The cabin deserves one," he replied, then was suddenly struck by what he had said. The cabin was becoming personal. Now, *that* was worrying.

"I have most of the hardware," Wilson said. "I'll have to order the lumber, if that's okay."

"How long?"

"Five days to be safe unless you want to pay extra for rushing it."

He wasn't going anywhere in the next few days. He was going to see the Sam Clark matter to its end now. He was committed, whether or not he liked it. "Five days will be fine. Might do some fishing in the meantime."

"Good bream and trout. The lake was stocked years ago and the fish really like the cold water coming down from the peak. They multiply faster than we take them. You need any fishing equipment?"

"I have a rod. What do you use as bait around here?"

He was *chatting,* for God's sake. Was Covenant Falls beginning to get to him?

When Josh left, he had several new lures and had arranged for the screening and lumber. He could have gone to Pueblo as he had for the flooring, but he might as well patronize the local businesses even if it did cost a bit more. Eve had said the merchants were having hard times.

He thought about the shortsightedness of Al Monroe. This could be a thriving community. There was certainly enough scenery to go around.

There were good people here, too.

He couldn't help but admire a town where people had parties to roof the homes of residents who couldn't afford repairs. Who raised funds for a library and community center staffed by volunteers.

It was sad that so many of the young people had to leave to find jobs.

Tourists and more residents would bring more services and more opportunities.

He didn't know why his brain was popping with ideas. Maybe it was just his training. See a problem; find solutions.

But it was more than that. He found himself growing indignant on the town's behalf. That was even more worrying.

He took Amos from the car and walked him down to Stephanie's clinic.

She was tending to a Chihuahua, according to Lisa, Stephanie's vet tech. He looked at the bulletin board as he waited for her to finish.

Amos sat quietly. Stephanie came out with a middle-aged woman holding a teacup Chihuahua tightly in her grip. Amos looked up but ignored the frantic barking of the tiny dog. The woman stopped. "You must be Mr. Manning," she said. "Welcome to Covenant Falls."

He nodded in acknowledgment. She looked down at Amos. "And this must be Amos. Can I pet him?"

Josh wasn't sure whether Amos would welcome it or not. But he nodded. "He might be a little…"

"Would you mind holding Giselle?" The woman didn't wait for an answer but plopped the tiny dog into his arms. She let Amos sniff her hand, then scratched his ears. "Such a handsome fellow." Amos allowed her to pet him without flinching. "I'm Agnes Murray. I am, or was, Nick's teacher. He just graduated from my class. He talked and talked about Amos."

Josh found himself hanging on to the squirming yappy dog with all his strength, then it bit him.

"Oh, my." Mrs. Murray grabbed the Chihuahua. "I'm so sorry. It's not that she doesn't like you. She even bites my husband from time to time. It's her way of showing affection."

He sighed inwardly as a few drops of blood dribbled down his arm. Mrs. Murray hurried outside. He saw Stephanie grinning as she stood in the doorway.

He had a sudden suspicion. "You didn't suggest I hold…Gidget?"

"Giselle," she corrected. "And no, I didn't. I have a few scars from her myself. I'm afraid that some Chihuahuas feel they have to prove size doesn't matter." Then the grin grew into a chuckle. "I'll try not to tell anyone. But the picture of you holding little Giselle, and…" The chuckle grew into laughter.

"Will you stop laughing and give me first aid?"

She left and returned with Sherry at her side and a first-aid kit in her hands. Sherry and Amos touched noses and wagged tails. It was more emotion than Amos had shown since he'd alerted Nick about the rattler. Josh savored the moment.

"They really like each other," Stephanie said, the laughter gone. "I thought they would. Sherry is a born caretaker. She loves finding lost people, particularly kids, and it breaks her heart when she finds a body instead. She's inconsolable for weeks. Other animals seem to sense she's a gentle soul."

She paused, then said, "There's a training session next week for search-and-rescue dogs. I think Amos would be a natural."

"He's trained to find explosives," Josh said. "And to protect against enemies."

"But he has endurance, discipline and a trained sense of smell. And he's improving every time I see him," Stephanie said. "If you had told me he would just walk in here and regard everyone as his subjects a few weeks back, I would say you were crazy."

A sense of pride flowed through him.

"Okay," she said dramatically. "Stop avoiding medical aid." She brushed the small bite with an antiseptic pad, then applied a Band-Aid with a flourish. "My diagnosis? You will live."

"I'm glad to hear that," he said.

"And what are you doing in town today?" she asked.

He gave her an incredulous look. "You don't already know? I thought by now the grapevine would have it in big letters."

"Nope. Haven't heard anything about you in the past few hours."

"I'm buying supplies for a porch."

"You've decided to stay, then?"

"I'm rehabbing the cabin. Beyond that..."

"It's getting to you, though," she said slyly. "If you don't inoculate yourself, you'll catch the bug."

"What bug?"

"The Covenant Falls bug. It's deadly. Makes you want to stay."

"What about you? Have you caught it?"

"I'm in the petri-dish stage."

He laughed. "And how long did it take you to get to that stage?"

"Two and a half years. It was culture shock at first, but then I would take a walk or ride my horse in the morning. I can hear the birds sing, watch eagles glide overhead and smell the pines without car fumes, and everything seems right with the world."

He digested that statement.

"You doubt me?" she challenged.

He changed the subject. "Are you going to be at the roofing event on Saturday?" he asked.

"No. I'm working. I heard you're going to be there."

"Apparently so has everyone else."

"That's one of the disadvantages of a small town," she admitted cheerfully.

"Mr. Wilson said a woman was going to work on the roof. I thought it might be you."

"Nope. It's Eve. Her father started the roofing parties twenty years ago. She started working on them when she was fourteen and hasn't missed one in all those years except when she was in college."

He recalled their conversation at the waterfall. She'd told him about her father, but she'd omitted the part about repairing houses. Actually, she'd said very little about herself. She mostly talked about Covenant Falls.

She had walls, too.

He asked the question that brought him here. "Then could you keep Amos Saturday? If you're going to be here?"

"Sure. Sherry and I will be glad for the company."

"Thanks," he said.

He was not going to leave Amos anyplace where Sam Clark could get to him. Better safe than sorry.

He looked at his watch, then at the city building across the street, wondering whether he should call Eve. He wanted to see her. Wanted to know whether the police chief had any thoughts about what happened today and how he planned to proceed.

At least that was his excuse.

"She's probably getting ready for the graduation ceremony," Stephanie said as if she'd read his mind. "She's giving out the academic awards."

He hated being that obvious. "Does she ever stay still?"

"Not since I came here."

"I haven't had lunch yet," he said, "and it's late. What about you?"

"Already had it," she said regretfully, "and I have an appointment due here any minute. But I'm sure Maude would love your business, and you can take Amos."

"Maybe I'll do that," he said. There *were* some things about the town he liked, including Maude's steaks, her good nature. He would have liked company, but...

"It shouldn't be busy," Stephanie added as she walked him to the door. "It's graduation night. The girls are getting their hair done, and the boys are already partying."

She was right. Maude's was empty except for Maude herself, who was sitting behind the cash register.

"Okay to bring Amos in?" he asked.

"Sure. Service dogs are allowed. I consider Amos a service dog. A retired service dog. What can I get you?"

So she knew all about Amos, too.

"I'll have one of your steaks," he said.

"Medium rare, right?"

"Do you remember everyone's preferences?" he asked.

"Just my favorite ones," she said. "You just make yourself comfortable and I'll have a salad for you in a jiff."

He looked around the café, or diner, or whatever it was. There was a Lions Club sign, and a bulletin board with announcements of upcoming events.

"Heard you were going to help at the roofing," Maude said, coming back from the kitchen and placing the large salad in front of him.

"So everyone says,'" he said testily.

Maude smiled. "Makes you uncomfortable, does

it? You're somewhat of a celebrity around here," she said with a twinkle in her eyes.

"Like every newcomer?" he asked.

"Just those who save the life of the son of our leading citizen."

"I thought Al Monroe was the leading citizen."

"Maybe in his own mind," Maude said. "Don't be embarrassed. It's just that you made a grand entrance by helping Eve and Nick when he was bitten by that snake. And people who have met you like you. Me included."

He found himself turning red. He remembered those first few days when he'd offended everyone. "Not everyone," he corrected.

"*Almost* everyone," she amended.

He shrugged. "I was hurting like hell." *Now, why did he say that?*

"You still are," she said. "I can tell by your walk."

For some reason her comment didn't bother him. Maybe it was the way she'd said it, as if it was nothing at all.

"I just hope you and this fine dog are here to stay," she said, then retreated back into the kitchen.

Amos lay down next to him and put his chin on his shoe.

He was still mulling over the conversation when the door opened and Eve came to his the table. "Hi," she said softly, even a little shyly. She stooped down and said hello to Amos, whose tail thumped up and down.

"I heard you were busy preparing for graduation

tonight," he said. Damn, but the hotline in Covenant Falls had infected him, as well.

"Stephanie told me you were coming here. I hoped you wouldn't mind company." Her lips played with each other nervously.

"No," he said. "I don't mind it at all." He hesitated. "And how is Officer Clark?"

"Confused, according to Tom. Confused and angry and maybe a little scared. He's stuck in the office now, doing paperwork about the results of the search, probably until midnight if Tom can arrange it."

"And if he sees us together?"

She shrugged. "That might give him a little more to think about. I'm sure he'll hear about it."

"What about yesterday?"

"You mean our trip to the falls? Haven't had any calls today. It means we went unnoticed, which is, in itself, a miracle."

"I imagine the police chief filled you in about this morning." Although no one was around, he lowered his voice.

She simply nodded.

Maude appeared with his delicious-smelling steak and a second plate with pieces of hamburger on it. "For Amos," she said, "if that's okay?"

Amos was already sniffing the air. Josh nodded. He was trying to get Amos on a mostly dry dog-food diet, except for the occasional egg, but he saw no harm in an occasional treat.

"Go ahead and eat," Eve said and ordered coffee. "I had lunch," she explained.

The coffee came immediately and Eve looked amused as he dug into the steak and Amos into the hamburger. "Amos seems to be adjusting," she said.

Josh finished the bite and nodded. "He's still not the dog I knew before, but his interest in food is coming back. Not in toys yet."

"Nick would like to bring Braveheart over," she said tentatively.

He looked back quizzically.

"Braveheart was pretty badly treated," she said. "We think he was used for dog fighting. I found him nearly half-dead, probably because he refused to fight. He's very timid, but also very sweet." She paused. "Nick thinks Amos can help him. I don't know why."

"Nick named him?"

"How did you guess?"

"It sounds like him." He took another bite of steak. His hunger had faded with Eve across from him, but eating was a defense against her appeal. Her dark hair was pulled back by gold clips, and those eyes of hers... God, he could drown in them.

"You didn't tell me you were going to work on the roof." Josh watched her face and saw that familiar flash of mischief.

"Stephanie told you? I thought to surprise you."

"I gather there are few surprises in this town," he said.

"I was a daddy's girl," she said. "I wanted to do everything he did. So he taught me to fish, taught me how to fix a car and how to bait my own hook when we went fishing. It drove my mother crazy."

He shook his head. "You keep surprising me."

"You do the same to me. I never thought you would have volunteered to build a roof for someone else. I thought you didn't want to get involved.

"I didn't," he said.

"What about your leg? Won't it be dangerous up there?"

"I'm learning to cope."

"Back to Nick," she said. "Can I bring him and Braveheart Friday? He has a scouting meeting tomorrow."

"Sure. He's always welcome, but there will be…"

"Talk. I don't care. It's no one's business."

"What about Nick's grandparents?"

"They like you."

They liked him when he helped Nick, but he wondered whether they would be happy about a stronger relationship. Most of his life had involved violence of one kind or another. His background was no indication of lasting commitments. But then she wasn't asking about that. Just a mere visit. He could handle that.

She looked at her watch. "I have to go."

"Yeah. Good luck with the ceremony tonight."

"Why don't you come?"

That was a mile too far. He hadn't even gone to his own graduation.

"Still have a lot to do on the cabin," he said, "and don't want to leave Amos alone."

She nodded. "Friday, then. Maybe about four?"

He nodded, and she quickly left, stopping only before opening the door to look back.

And he watched until she crossed the street and disappeared back into the city building.

CHAPTER TWENTY-ONE

JOSH RETURNED TO the cabin after his early supper. For the first time, he thought of it as coming home.

It was only four-thirty in the afternoon, and he didn't know what to do with himself. He was unaccountably restless.

Damn, admit it. He was lonely. It seemed every day he became more connected to Eve and her son. Settle down? Josh Manning?

Just adopting Amos had seemed an infringement on his life. Now it didn't seem so much of one. In just a matter of weeks, Amos had wriggled himself into Josh's heart even if *he* hadn't wriggled himself into Amos's heart. Yet.

He opened his laptop and studied the plans for the porch again. The directions said the job would take three weeks, but that was assuming one person was involved. He had Nate. He was reminded of what he'd said recently about the satisfaction of building instead of destroying. He had just blurted that out, but now he knew there was a hell of a lot of truth in it.

When he finished, he filled Amos's water and food dishes, then spent thirty minutes doing the leg exercises he'd neglected. Then he turned on the stereo and grabbed the biography he'd been reading. Fifteen minutes later, he realized he was reading the same page over and over again. He stood and walked through the cabin, mentally listing everything he still had to do on the interior and sketching out a timetable. While waiting for the porch materials, he would scrape the old wallpaper from the bathroom and apply the new rolls he'd bought in Pueblo. It had a Native American pattern in browns and tans and orange that he'd really liked. Maybe later he would match it with ceramic tiles.

The interior was slowly taking on a personality— the one of the home he dreamed about as a kid. A big rocking-chair porch had been part of that dream.

He was turning it into the picture he'd carried around in his wallet for years. When he and his mother moved from one rented room to another and when she'd died of an overdose and he had no home at all, he would pretend he lived in that house.

One time when he and Dave had gotten particularly drunk after a mission that had resulted in multiple deaths, including two members of their team and an Iraqi child who had blown himself up killing them, he'd told Dave about some of his childhood and that picture.

Dave hadn't said anything about the cabin then, but he must have remembered his words.

He tried to shut down those memories. Amos, who had climbed up on the sofa, moved closer to him. A warm, wet tongue reached out and licked his hand. Josh leaned down and buried his face in Amos's fur.

He didn't know what to do with the emotions rocking him. He'd denied them for a long time, putting them in a box, according to the hospital shrink who warned him that someday that box would explode. It hadn't yet, but maybe it was leaking.

Not Now. Not today. He leaned down and ruffled Amos's fur. "Thank you," he whispered and stood. He went into the bathroom, washed his face with cold water and stared at his reflection. He wasn't sure he knew the man who stared back at him.

The cabin was getting to him. Or was it Eve?

He was playing with fire. So was she, but she didn't know it.

He took a cold shower, but it didn't cure the restlessness. The sun was just beginning to drop. He thought about the Harley. He had put off tuning it. It hadn't been ridden in more than a year, but the repair had been relegated to last place once he'd started restoring the cabin. Once it had represented a kind of freedom. Now that freedom didn't seem so important.

"Come on, Amos. Let's go for a walk." Amos followed him outside. As they reached Lake Road, he noticed cars turning out of the driveways of his neighbors, including Mrs. Byars's Buick. She waved at him. He waved back.

They were all probably on their way to the graduation. That would be a big event in a town this size.

He turned down the road toward the mountain,

passed the turnabout and started climbing the path. He reached the lookout and sat on the rock to watch the sunset. He noticed a couple of beer cans that hadn't been there on earlier walks. Kids celebrating the end of school, no doubt. Next time he would bring a bag and pick them up.

The sky was made up of vivid bands of scarlet and orange fighting for supremacy, then diffusing as they turned into a golden glow that reflected in the deep blue of the lake. Lights started to go on in the town below.

He should leave while he could still see the path. The last thing he needed was to fall. And yet he was paralyzed by the sheer beauty of the sunset. He wondered why he had never really looked at one before he came here.

He started down the path. He slowly made the fifteen-minute trip down the path and walked to the dock. He didn't dare go to the end. The supports were rotten. Another item for his to-do list.

At this rate, he might never leave Covenant Falls.

THE HIGH SCHOOL auditorium was filled to overflowing.

Eve glanced at her notes as the principal congratulated the students. The valedictorian and salutatorian delivered their speeches. It just so happened—not strangely—that two of her three award winners took those honors. This was the best part of Covenant Falls, the hopeful part.

She listened intently, even as she scoured the crowd for familiar faces.

Faces? One face. She'd hoped against hope that Josh would materialize. But he didn't. Instead, there were the faces of people she'd known her entire life. Friends.

Then it was time for her to present the awards before the formal presentation of diplomas.

She placed the notes in her jacket pocket. She shouldn't need them. She'd known these kids since they were born. She looked for Al, but he wasn't there, either. Nor was his nephew, who was on duty answering calls tonight since the regular dispatcher's son was graduating. She made her remarks short. "We at city hall are so proud of everyone on the stage tonight. You've worked hard to get here, and every one of you is a star tonight. Build on those diplomas and never stop learning. Tonight, I have the very great pleasure to recognize three particularly outstanding seniors for their achievements in English, math and science."

She then presented the awards in no particular order. Each received a two-hundred-dollar check from the civic clubs in town, as well as a trophy and certificate that gave them bragging rights on college and job applications.

Then her part was over, and the parade of graduates accepted their diplomas, some with great solemnity and others making faces and clowning. When the last name was called, the principal said, "I give you the graduating class," and the graduates threw their hats in the air to the sound of thunderous applause.

Eve felt a tremendous sense of pride in her town, in these students and the families that had such high hopes for them.

It took a while, but eventually everyone found their way into the lunchroom for the reception, but as she expected, they were all gone within an hour, most within thirty minutes.

Tom had assigned their youngest officers to be at the two sites most commonly used for partying— Covenant Falls and the picnic area bordering the lake. Tom and Eve both wanted minimal visibility, but the officers had their orders. No drinking.

When she had said her goodbyes, Eve made her way to Abby and Jim's house, where Nick was staying. When she entered the living room, Nick was curled up asleep with his head on his grandfather's lap, a big bowl of popcorn on the coffee table in front of them.

"Sorry I'm late," she said.

"It's never too late," Abby replied. "He's a delight. Nick is a joy and no trouble. But we're having a hard time keeping up with him. He can do more on a computer than we can. He's been teaching us. That young man has so much curiosity."

"Tell me about it," Eve said.

"I'm so glad you stayed here instead of moving East with your mother."

"This is home, Abby. I can't imagine leaving," Eve said.

Abby's face creased into a warm smile. "I know you loved Russ, but he would want you to be happy, wherever that takes you. One of these days you may find someone else to love. In the meantime, I want as much of this young scamp as I can have."

Eve wondered if Abby had heard anything about Josh. They had, for the most part, been careful except for that late meeting at the diner today. But then it was not that unusual for two people in this town to run into each other at Maude's. "I treasure what you have with Nick," she said softly. "I couldn't take him away from you."

She saw Abby and Jim visibly relax, and she wondered again whether there was speculation about Josh.

"And now I had better get him home. I have to look in on the horses and let the dogs out."

"Do you want us to keep him tomorrow?" Abby asked hopefully.

"I think I've imposed on you enough," she said. "I promised him he could go to the office tomorrow and then he has Scouts. It's time for us to have supper together."

Abby smiled. "I couldn't ask for a better mother for him," she said. "I'm so glad Russ picked…" Her voice broke. "Now get along with you."

Nick was beginning to wake.

"Hey, guy," she said softly. "Time to go home."

He rubbed his eyes and looked around and gave

them all that sweet, sleepy smile that always went straight to her heart.

"I suspect the crew is waiting for you."

At that he stumbled to his feet. He slipped into his shoes and laced them. "We had chicken 'n' dumplings," he said.

"And popcorn, I see." Her stomach twitched at the mention of chicken and dumplings. Abby was a great cook, and chicken and dumplings was one of her best dishes.

As if she knew exactly what she was thinking Abby gave her a worried look. "Did you have supper?"

Eve started to say yes, but Abby interrupted. "Of course you didn't. You just wait here. I have more than enough for you and us tomorrow."

Abby disappeared into the kitchen and returned nearly immediately, a plastic dish in her hands.

"I thank you and my stomach thanks you," Eve said.

Jim opened the door and followed Eve and Nick to the car, holding the dish until she stepped into Miss Mollie, then he handed it to her. "Come over for supper on Sunday," he said.

"I'll try," she replied. "It depends on how quickly we finish Mrs. Crockett's house."

"I think Abby's planning to take some sandwiches over there Saturday."

"I was hoping she could look after Nick."

"She can take him along when she takes the sandwiches. Don't worry, we'll take care of it." He paused, then said, "I hear that Josh Manning will be there."

"That's the word," she replied.

"You think he's going to stay in town?"

"I don't know," she answered honestly.

"Heard any more about that robbery at Shep's place?"

"No." She hated lying, but she and Tom had agreed that no one other than the two of them and Ryan could know their plan.

"Well, then, have a good night, Eve."

"Thanks, you have a good one, too. And thanks again for taking care of Nick."

"Anytime, you know that."

She started Miss Mollie and headed home.

CHAPTER TWENTY-TWO

EVE SPENT THURSDAY catching up on city business and resisting temptation.

She needed to spend time with Nick, including supper, something she'd neglected since meeting Josh Manning. She could certainly wait one day to see him again.

Couldn't she?

She took Nick to work with her, planning to treat him to lunch and then take him to the Scout meeting. Maybe they would even take the horses for a sunset ride.

Nick brought his book on military dogs. His nose was buried in it.

"There are about twenty-five hundred working dogs on active duty," he said, lifting his head from the text. "And they're training five hundred each year. This says about five percent of dogs on active duty get PTSD. I don't think that's fair—making dogs go to war."

"They've saved lots of lives," she said.

"Well, I'm glad Amos is home."

"Me, too," she said.

"Can I take Braveheart today to meet him?"

She was ready for him. "Friday," she said. "I already talked to Mr. Manning about it. I thought we would go riding this evening after the Scout meeting."

The promise to ride and a visit soon mollified him. His eyes went back to the book.

"I have some work to do first and I have to talk to Chief MacGuire. You can stay in my office and read your book, okay? If you want, you can also watch the television." She kept one in her office in case of breaking news that might affect her town.

"I want to see Uncle Tom, too," he complained.

"I promise you will," she said, "but this is official stuff. I'll bet, though, he'll have time to take you for an ice cream later if you're real good."

"Okay," he said, "but we can take Braveheart Friday?"

She nodded. Warmth flooded her as she thought about seeing Josh again. In truth, she'd thought about little else since the kiss. She had tossed and turned all night, her body aching for his touch. If it was just physical need, she could stay away. But it wasn't. She liked him. She more than liked him. She was intrigued by all his contradictions. There was an innate honesty and integrity and kindness in him that he tried hard to conceal, but it came out when he thought no one was looking. He must have spent a lifetime honing that tough-guy, loner image.

"Mom?"

She suddenly realized she'd just been standing

there, staring at her son. "Sorry, kiddo. I just remembered something I had to do." She gave him a big hug. "You know how much I love you?" she asked, hurting with the idea that he may not. Was that because she sensed Josh had not felt that kind of love?

"A bushel and a peck full," Nick answered, grinning. It was the game they'd played when he was younger, each trying to outdo the other.

"And all the stars in the sky," she replied.

"And all the dog kisses everywhere." Only her kid would come up with that one.

"Hmm, I think you win this time," she said and hugged him again. "And now I do have to go. See you shortly."

She left before she broke down. Drat it, she'd turned into a mushmelon of emotions lately.

The police department was housed in the other half of the city hall. There was a big bullpen area, where the officers had their desks and the dispatchers had their work area. The chief's glassed-in office was in the corner. To the left of his office was a small corridor leading to two jail cells and an interview room.

Today, after a busy night, the office space was empty except for one dispatcher and one duty officer to catch any walk-in complaints. There was one unit out on patrol.

She knocked on the window outside Tom's desk and he motioned her in.

"Any incidents last night?" she asked.

"Nope. If there was drinking, they did it off city

property," he said. "No accidents. No fights. A good night. Gary and Suzanne are patrolling the roads now. Everyone else has the day off after working last night."

"Including Sam?"

"Yep, had to do it. Couldn't keep him here more than twenty-four hours without a better explanation. Right now I'd guess he'll be sleeping for the next eight to twelve hours."

"He must be going crazy trying to figure out who has the rifle."

"He is. I had him do paperwork yesterday and I thought he would explode. He won't have to worry long. I plan to give the rifle to Shep this afternoon. Tell him some kids found it in the woods."

"Sam has to think Josh had something to do with it."

Tom stared back at her. "Josh knows that. He'll be careful."

"What about the roofing party Saturday? He'll be away from his cabin all day."

"There are small cameras all over Manning's place, and I'll be checking on it," he said. "My wife would kill me if I tried to go up on that roof."

"Can I tell Josh about the cameras? I promised Nick he could take Braveheart over there tomorrow. He seems to think Braveheart and Amos will reenforce each other's courage. Sort like the Lion and Scarecrow in *The Wizard of Oz*." She grinned. "I also promised him you will take him for ice cream."

He laughed at that. "I would be honored," he said. "And you don't have to tell Manning about the cameras. They belong to him. He beat me to it, but he's giving me access to them."

She looked at him quizzically.

"He's no one's fool. They're state-of-the-art. Much better than the ones we have," Tom said with a smile. "He's also smart enough to like you. A lot."

She felt her face flame.

"I sense it's mutual," he said.

"It's impractical," she stated firmly.

"Why?"

"He doesn't plan to stay."

"No? He keeps finding more and more projects for the cabin."

"He wants to sell it."

"He's done enough to sell it. And if he's leaving, why is he going to the roofing party?"

"He says he needs Nate's help, and Nate is one of the leaders of the project."

Tom raised an eyebrow. "Afraid?" he asked.

"Me? Or him?"

"Both," he said. "I don't know what his problem is, but I think I know yours. You lost one husband. You don't want to lose another, but in being afraid, you're cheating yourself out of the here and now… and a happy future. I'm not saying that he's the one. What I am saying is open your mind to possibilities. Your face lights up when his name is mentioned. I've not seen you do that since Russ died. Now I've had my say and I won't mention it again."

She just stared at him. He had urged her to run for office and he had always been there for advice and support. But he had never before said anything about her personal life.

"Sit down," he said, changing the subject. "How was the graduation ceremony last night?"

"It went well. No big bumps. No one forgot their speeches or fell on the steps. All the parents behaved themselves. Seven of the kids got scholarships, three for a full ride."

He nodded. "Too bad there weren't more."

"I know. I wish we could do more for those who really want to go to college but can't afford it. Several are thinking about going into the service instead. They hope to save their pay and use educational credits for college. But that's a rough way of doing it."

"Why don't you suggest they talk to Manning? He can tell them if it's the right move or not."

"You think he would?"

"I think you know him better than I do," he said with a twinkle in his eyes.

"I don't think anyone really knows him," she said.

He shrugged. "Maybe it's time that someone did."

She left on that note. She had let her work slide in the past week.

Nick was still reading. "Why don't you go down and say hello to Uncle Tom," she said. "He likes the idea of ice cream midmorning. You can take your book down there."

She didn't have to ask twice. He was off practically before she finished the sentence.

She buried herself in work for the next two hours, then Tom called and said he and Nick were off for ice cream. Did she want to come? She did, but she refused, pleading work. She watched from the window as they crossed the street to Maude's.

Then she dug back into work.

THURSDAY WAS ONE of the longest days Josh had spent in Covenant Falls. He knew it was because he missed Eve.

He spent the morning putting the finishing touches on the living room. He painted the woodwork around the windows, then called Nate, who said he was free to help him move his new furniture from the bedroom into the living room.

The two of them transferred the ugly old sofa into what he termed the guest bedroom. Then they moved the new furniture into place—a big leather sofa, lounge chair, two large bookcases, a coffee table, a desk for his stereo and laptop and the small dining set.

"Looks great," Nate said with admiration.

Josh looked around. The furniture changed everything. It was a home now, not just a run-down cabin. He needed a rug in the living area, a bright one to give it color. Maybe some piece of pottery for the mantel. An odd satisfaction flowed through him. *This was his.* The first place ever really his.

He was thirty-five years old and this was the first time he had lived in a house except for one year when he was seventeen and he'd bunked in the basement of his high school coach.

"The bathroom needs new wallpaper," he said. "And it really could use a second bathroom."

Nate grinned at him. "You keep going. I can use the work."

Hell, who was he fooling? Himself, apparently. Rehabbing the cabin, turning it into the house he'd wanted so fiercely as a kid, had become a drug.

Amos barked from the bedroom, where Josh had put him until they finished moving furniture. Josh opened the door, and Amos came inside the room. He sniffed the new sofa, then looked around and gave a short bark.

"It's in the other room," he told Amos. Amos followed him into the guest bedroom. He walked to the old sofa, then performed his intricate maneuver of crawling up onto it as if he was a thief sneaking up on a prize.

"The new one is more comfortable," he said, but Amos didn't move.

"Okay," he said. "Be that way."

Nate laughed behind him. "I like that dog," he said.

"Well, you can't have him. A beer, though, is a different matter."

They went outside and drank the beer on the back

doorstep while Nate regaled him with tales of Covenant Falls people that he might meet on Saturday.

When Nate left, Josh tested the new lounge chair. He felt like a kid at his first Christmas. Until he realized he didn't have anyone to share it with. He'd always been just fine with his own company before, but Eve, Nick and a growing number of others were changing that.

He went to the kitchen and made a sandwich, then wandered outside with Amos beside him. He could see the park from the road, the park where Nick played ball and where the town had held the fundraiser. He imagined there were children playing on its beach.

Was this the kind of life he wanted? He'd never thought so.

But he already missed Eve. He looked forward to seeing young Nick again and watching the huge grin spread across his face when he saw Amos.

He smiled when he thought of Fancy and he looked forward to meeting the other members of the motley crew. He liked Stephanie and Nate and Mrs. Byars and Maude. He even found himself appreciating the unconventional police chief.

While he was being honest with himself, he had to admit pride in the cabin. He thought David would approve. He wouldn't mind rehabbing other structures. Even build them from the ground up.

Thoughts piled on each other. He'd never allowed himself to think about the future before, not before or after his injury. He hadn't been able to see one outside the Rangers. Now he saw Eve, and her warmth and humor and strength filled some of the holes in him.

The question that haunted him was what he could bring to Eve and Nick except a violent past and a present haunted by ghosts.

CHAPTER TWENTY-THREE

FRIDAY WAS NEARLY half over before Eve drove up to Josh's cabin.

He had just finished applying the wallpaper to the bathroom and was cleaning up when he heard the unmistakable sound of Miss Mollie approaching. Eve had said she was bringing Nick.

He opened the door as she and Nick stepped out of the vehicle, Nick pulling a reluctant, scarred pit bull behind him.

Amos quietly joined him. When the dog saw Nick, his tail started to wag, but he went still when he saw the dog try to hide behind the boy. Eve watched anxiously.

"Say hello," he told Amos. Those were words Dave had used when introducing new members of his team to Amos. Amos used to offer his paw to whomever his alpha wanted him to meet. He hadn't offered it since Josh had adopted him, but maybe that was because Josh had never used that expression. Or maybe because Josh hadn't been big on commands with him. He'd given too many for years.

With Amos at his side, he walked over to Nick and the timid pit bull that broke his heart because he so reminded him of his first glance at Amos in the kennel at Lakeland Air Force Base. Then as Stephanie's Sherry had done to Amos, Amos did to Braveheart. He walked over to him, sniffed him thoroughly then licked his ear in an invitation to friendship.

Braveheart stopped shaking. After a moment, he started sniffing Amos. His stub of a tail tried to wag. Nick's face lit. "See, I told you, Mom. I told you they would like each other."

Eve smiled down at her son, and Josh thought it one of the most beautiful expressions he'd ever seen. Her face was so full of love and joy that he ached inside.

And Amos? Josh was proud of him and how far he had come these past weeks in Covenant Falls. Maybe Amos hadn't had the chance to be just a dog. He'd been trained to be a soldier.

"I have some dog toys inside," he said to Nick. "Why don't you come in and pick out a few they might like? And maybe, just maybe, there might be a dog treat or two, as well."

Nick and the dogs went in first, then Josh held the door open for Eve.

"Rummage as much as you like," he told Nick, who moved quickly, both dogs at his side.

Eve stood in the doorway, and he relished the astonished look on her face. "You have furniture. You actually got furniture."

"Yep."

"It looks like you," she said.

"I hope that's good."

"Oh, yes. It belongs here."

So do you. He wanted to say the words so badly but resisted. He put a hand on her shoulder, his fingers touched her cheek and she leaned into his palm. Seconds passed. Magical seconds. Filled with unsaid words and an intensity that shook him to the core. Suddenly he knew she wanted him as much as he wanted her.

What in the hell was he going to do about it?

He breathed slowly. Nothing now. Her son was in the other room, would be here in a moment. He lowered his hand. "Will you go out with me?"

She looked at him for what seemed forever. "Yes," she said simply.

"When?" He felt awkward.

"Tonight. I'll see if my in-laws can keep Nick after practice."

"Where do you go on a date in Covenant Falls?"

"Well, there's Maude's," she said with a grin.

"I have a better idea. I can buy a couple of steaks and cook them outside," he said. "I cleaned that darn barbecue pit and haven't used it yet."

"And I have a bottle of good wine and can make a salad."

Their gazes met, and emotions swirled. Attraction rippled between them, so heated he had to take a step backward. He took a deep breath. "Done," he said. "I'll pick you up at…seven."

She gave him directions to her house. "I could just drive over here," she said.

"That wouldn't be a date," he replied.

"You're not worried about my reputation?" she teased him. "Last time I checked, I was over twenty-one and single, and right now I don't care what anyone thinks, except for my son, and I think he would approve."

The air seemed to thicken between them, and the tension was almost unbearable. A decision had been silently made, and he sensed his life would not be the same.

He stepped back and she turned away from him just as Nick, followed by the two dogs, came back into the room. He had a KONG ball in his hand and a stuffed fox with a long, long tail. "Mom, he's got more toys than we do."

Eve looked at Josh with a raised eyebrow.

He defended himself. "When I picked Amos up, I didn't know what he liked, so I bought out a pet store. All for naught. He wouldn't have anything to do with any of them."

"Maybe if you put cheese in the KONG, he would," Nick said earnestly.

"I'll give that a shot," Josh promised.

Eve laughed, but it was a shaky laugh. "And that reminds me, Nicholas, my lad, that we have to take Braveheart back home and get you a snack before baseball practice."

"But Braveheart wants to stay."

"Translation, Nick wants to stay," she said.

"I think they will see each other again," Josh said. "Soon."

"Can you come to baseball practice?" Nick asked.

"Not this afternoon." Josh discovered he wanted to go, but he had a stronger commitment. "I have some shopping to do."

"What about the game Saturday?" Nick persisted.

"Afraid not, sport. I'm working on a roof."

"Aww."

"Give me a full report," he said, "and I'll be at the next one. Okay?"

"Did you play baseball?" Nick asked.

"In the army. I ran track in high school."

She glanced down at his bad leg.

He shrugged, but he realized how little they knew about each other. The superficial stuff, sure, but not what made them who they were. Track was what had saved him.

"Take Braveheart to the car," she told Nick. Her son started to protest, then obviously thought better of it. Nick snapped the leash on a reluctant Braveheart and disappeared out the door.

"Are you sure about tonight?" he said.

"Yes." She stood up on tiptoes and brushed her lips against his.

Then she was gone.

EVE SAT THROUGH the baseball practice calmly enough, but her emotions were rioting. She talked to the other parents as if a momentous decision had not been made today. And she knew it had. She was opening the door. Opening her heart. And it terrified her.

They left the field at six, and Abby took Nick home with her for an overnight visit. It made sense, Eve said, since she had to be at the roofing party early Saturday. Abby could take Nick to the ball game, then bring him to the roofing.

She reached home at six-twenty and had forty minutes to get ready. She made a quick salad first. Lettuce, tomatoes, green onions and a little Gouda cheese with a dressing of olive oil, vinegar and herbs. It was all she had at the moment.

Animal duty came next. She checked the horses' water, then fed the dogs before letting them out for a few moments. Now she had twenty minutes. Darn, but she felt like a schoolgirl on her first date. She wondered whether she was ready for the fallout of her decision to have dinner with Josh. They had been relatively discreet until now. By tomorrow, though, she expected everyone in town would know they were dating.

It was really foolish, she knew, for a single woman of almost thirty-five to be worried about something like that. But she had worked hard to build a professional and responsible image, and she was protective of the programs she'd fought for. She didn't want anything to affect them. And her in-laws? It was one thing to urge her to date again, another to watch it actually happen, especially with someone new to town, someone who might well want to move.

Be careful, she kept reminding herself, but nothing worked when she was with him. They gravitated toward each other like lodestones. She took a quick shower, ran a brush through her hair and pinned it back with a barrette. She dithered over what to wear. Certainly nothing fancy. It was just a dinner at home. She finally chose her favorite lounging wear: an elderly but clean pair of jeans and comfortable gray pearl shirt. It was time that he knew the real Eve, who would rather be on a horse than in a city hall office. She slipped on a pair of low-heeled sandals.

She grabbed two bottles of red wine she kept for company dinners, then looked at the clock. Five to seven.

She didn't have to check for him out the window. Captain Hook and Miss Marple considered themselves the watchdogs. They started barking.

She wondered whether she should wait for his knock, decided that was silly and went to the door. She had the immediate impression that he was as nervous as she.

"Hi," she said brilliantly.

"Hi, yourself," he replied, equally as eloquent. Then he smiled as his gaze swept over her. "I like this Eve," he said, and she knew he meant it.

She thrust the wine bottles into his hands and grabbed the salad. The dogs were standing in a semicircle in back of her.

"The motley crew, I assume." He was wearing his usual jeans and a blue denim shirt with the sleeves rolled up. He'd shaved, and the faint scent of aftershave was intriguing. But then everything about him intrigued her.

She suddenly relaxed. This was Josh. The Josh she'd spent an afternoon with at the falls, who'd rescued her son, whose gentleness with Amos had touched her. "In all their glory, or lack of it," she replied.

She locked the door as they left. He had gone ahead and put the wine bottles in the car, then held the Jeep door open for her. Their hands met, the warmth flowing through her. She saw the same awareness in his face. Neither moved for a moment, then she ducked inside the Jeep and fastened the seat belt.

He went around the car and stepped inside. When he turned on the ignition, music came from a CD player, and she was surprised to hear classical music—a symphony she recognized. She didn't know why she was surprised about anything concerning him. Whenever she thought she had him pegged, he startled her again.

"I like your music."

"Me, too," he said with amusement.

"I took you for a jazz man. Maybe country."

"I like that, too. And blues and folk. Some pop."

"Anything you don't like?"

"Heavy metal."

"We're musically compatible," she said.

Then they were at his cabin. Amos was watching at the window. "I thought it would be all right to leave him for twenty minutes," he said. She started to get out of the car on her own, then noticed him limping quickly to get to her side. She waited, clutching the salad. He opened the door, offered his hand as she stepped out. He didn't let go as they walked to the cabin. She moved closer to him, the salad now clutched in one arm.

They went inside. Amos padded over to Josh and stood next to him. Protectively, she thought. She put the salad down on the table and scratched Amos's ears, then looked around. He'd added a lamp between the sofa and lounge chair in addition to the two light fixtures in the ceiling. The evening sun that flowed in from the front windows gave the walls a rich golden glow.

She looked at the room anew. She'd been distracted earlier, watching Nick and Braveheart interact with Amos. But now it had her full attention.

A few books had been added to the bookcase, along with a stereo, giving the room a more lived-in look. She liked it. She liked it very much. It was like him. Masculine. Straightforward. Minimal but comfortable. *Comfortable* wouldn't have fit two weeks ago, or even two days ago. But now she stood with him, and she *was* comfortable. There was still that edge. Maybe there would always be an edge. But she liked him. Really liked him, as well as being so physically attracted to him. There was no pretense about him. Even those protective walls of his now seemed surmountable.

"It's wonderful," she said and saw him relax.

"I'll get the wine," he said.

She watched him walk to the car, the limp barely detectable. She had seen it much worse, and she wondered whether he was working to hide it. She didn't have time to look longer because he was back, putting one bottle on the dining room table and opening the other.

"No wineglasses," he said wryly.

"Now, why am I not surprised?" she said, reaching up and kissing his cheek. "I'm learning what is important to you and what isn't. Any glass or cup will do just as well."

He gave her an approving look and went into the kitchen. She followed him and had time to look around. He'd painted it a soft yellow with white trim. The appliances, all obviously new, were white, as were the cupboards. The floor tiles were a swirling mix of cream and yellow. Sunlight flowed through a large spotless window. The kitchen was bright and happy. She wondered from what part within him it came.

He reached up into a nearly empty cupboard and took down two water glasses, then located a corkscrew. "I found this at the market. Alas, no wineglasses," he said with a crooked smile. He easily opened the bottle and poured them both a glass, handed one to her. He tapped his glass with hers in a toast. "I'm glad you're here," he said simply.

Her heart filled to almost breaking as she took a sip, her gaze never leaving his face. "I am, too," she said, but the words were inadequate for what she was feeling. She took another sip to cover her confusion. How could she feel so…full of need, so hungry for his touch? Each look, each move, caused her pulse to beat erratically.

He put his glass down and took hers from hands that suddenly stopped working. He put her glass down as well, then raised his hands to her face and skimmed the backs of his knuckles along her cheekbones. "You're beautiful," he said, his voice hoarse.

She wasn't. Never had been. She was always the freckle-faced girl next door. But at this moment, looking into his eyes, she felt beautiful. His hands moved downward, skimming her body, igniting fires wherever he touched, fires that turned into a conflagration. Her legs were rubbery, her breath faster.

Then he bent down and touched his lips to hers with a tenderness that overcame any reservations she might have had. His kiss deepened and the heat between them was like the deepest blue of a flame. Swirling eddies of desire enveloped her. Her arms went around him and held him close. She wanted to touch and feel and taste. Her lips melded with his, and her body quivered with need. Her heart thudded, the noise pounding in her ears.

She warned herself to be cautious, but she'd well

known this might happen and she had chosen to come anyway, and now warm, irresistible feelings flowed through her like a tide. She felt the tension in him, the barely restrained passion of his hands as they moved down her body.

Then he tensed and pulled back. "Eve?"

She knew what he was asking. She knew the risk. That he might leave and never come back and leave her heart in pieces. But she had lived like a nun these past years, avoiding risks, and now she couldn't afford to avoid this one. She was in love with him. It had only been a few weeks, but she knew. *There.* She'd admitted it to herself. It was hard to believe that something this powerful could happen in such a short time and yet…there it was. Tom had been right. She was going to grab what she could get.

She nodded.

He released her and handed her the glass of wine while he went around the windows and pulled the curtains and dimmed the lights. He led her into his bedroom and Amos padded behind them. Once inside he took her in his arms again. "Are you sure?"

She had not been in his bedroom before. It was monk-like with the one single bed, one chest. But then he had been army for nearly two decades, ready to go on a moment's notice. So different from her own homes.

But at this moment, she didn't care. She wanted to feel him next to her, in her, as a part of her. She wanted to invade that aura of aloneness that was so much a part of him, and make him laugh and take away the horrors he'd known, and which still obviously haunted him.

"It's not very grand," he said.

"I think this is perfectly grand," she replied and meant it. She loved this cabin and what he'd done with it.

JOSH SWALLOWED HARD when she spoke because he knew she meant it. To her, the cabin—small that it was—*was* grand. It was something else to him. It had meant survival to him. It had saved him from experiencing what so many other vets had suffered and were suffering. It had given him purpose and, along with Amos, had helped subdue the nightmares.

But now it had become something else. Something he had forgotten existed inside him. And Eve had been there, quietly cheering him on. From that first day when she had trespassed on his land, she had challenged him when he needed challenging. She'd somehow led him to care again when he'd been so reluctant to let himself do that.

He tightened his arms around her and relished her warmth, the way she felt next to him. His lips caressed hers with a possessiveness that jolted him. She was warm and alive and she had brought light into his life. Light and laughter and caring. He wanted her more than he thought possible.

"Are you sure?" he asked in a hoarse whisper.

"Oh, yes," she said. "But..."

He held his breath.

"I wish you would act with more alacrity." Her eyes laughed up at him.

"I'll try to improve," he replied with a grin.

Damn, but she was amazing. He never knew what to expect—the serious Eve or the sassy one that popped out when he least expected it. But he hastened to follow her suggestion. He kissed her again and felt her hand move to the back of his neck, stroking the sensitive nerves, plunging him into waves of sensation.

He was all thumbs as he tackled her shirt, but he finally undid the last button, then he undid the bra, thinking how perfect her breasts were. Round and firm. The nipples were already growing rosy and hard. He leaned down and his tongue ran lightly over one of her breasts, then the other.

Then she undid the zipper of his jeans and pulled them down. He stepped out of them, taking his boxers with them, and she stepped out of her slacks.

His hands went to the small of her back, turning her and guiding her down on the bed. They settled next to each other, hands joined, asking for nothing more at the moment than just being together. He studied her body. Hers was so perfect. His looked like a battlefield, but all he saw in her eyes was wonder.

She touched the various scars where shrapnel had hit him during that last battle, including the faint one on the side of his face. Then she kissed him, slowly, sensually, until he was throbbing with need.

He touched her breasts, then moved his mouth down to her body, caressing, tasting, nibbling until she was trembling and straining toward him. He felt her pulse quicken, and then he was on top of her, teasing and touching until she cried out. He turned away for a second to open the small package he'd bought earlier. Then he turned back to her, angled his body above her.

He probed slowly, taking his time, waiting until she wrapped her arms around him, letting him know she was ready.

She made a small cry. He felt her body tremble, then move instinctively to welcome him. Sensations flamed and sent waves of heat glowing through every part of him. He moved in rhythm with her, a wanton dance that grew more and more frantic until he heard her cry out. Then, still connected, they rolled to the side, each clutching the other as waves of pleasure continued to rock them. He closed his eyes, allowing himself to relish every last quiver.

They lay there silent, hands locked. He was rocked by what had just happened. He'd bedded women before. Now he knew he'd never made love to one.

"Wow," she said simply.

He kissed her nose. "I echo that inelegant but quite accurate interjection."

"Good," she said. "Let's do it again."

"Damn, but you're voracious," he said. He wondered whether he would ever stop being startled by her. Just as he had the day they met.

"Honest," she corrected him. "Some say to a fault."

THIRTY MINUTES LATER, they took a shower together.

Eve had never showered with Russ.

She loved it. The intimacy. Soaping his body and studying him while she did. The way he soaped hers and kissed her as he did. She could have stayed there for a very long time. But the water cooled, and steaks were waiting.

She had never felt quite as free to do or say exactly what she wanted. Her mother was a traditionalist. Very proper. Then as a young wife married to a high school coach, she'd learned to curb her tongue. As city clerk and mayor, that was even more necessary.

Only with her father had she felt free of rules and "standards." And now tonight.

Once dressed, she looked at her watch. It was nine. She should leave by eleven. She went into the main room, saw the back door was open. Josh was lighting charcoal in the pit.

She went back inside, topped up their wine and went outside. She studied the neat pile of charcoal and hardwood. Flame was beginning to flicker.

He held out his hand. She took it and stood close to him, silently. Words could ruin the magic.

Eve leaned against him, felt his strength. Warmth. She didn't know how long they stayed that way, watching the flames flare up in the evening light.

The moon was bright above them, as were the millions of stars that had come out. A slight breeze had taken the heat from the day. It was a perfect Colorado night.

When the fire was ready, she went inside to get the two large porterhouses that were sitting on a platter on the counter. Next to it were two new plates, two steak knives and forks. She took the salad from the fridge and could count the other items inside on one hand.

She found equally bare cupboards when she looked for salad bowls.

No sign of permanence here. Her heart sank. Why had she thought he was changing his mind about leaving? He certainly hadn't lied to her. He'd made it clear he was a loner and a wanderer.

And if she'd known he might be leaving soon, would she still have slept with him?

Yes. She'd known there were no guarantees.

She took the steaks outside. Josh tossed them on the grill.

"We need to talk," he said suddenly.

She didn't want to talk. She feared what he was going to say, that this had been nice but he would be gone next week. Or the next.

But she looked into his eyes and nodded.

"You know very little about me," he said. "You've taken everything on blind trust."

"I know a lot about you," she contradicted him. "I think maybe even more than you do."

"You might be right about that," he said with a wry twist of his lips, "but you should know what you're getting into. I've never been part of a family. Never really lived in a house until now. My life has been army barracks and deployments. When I was a kid, my mother was a drug addict and we moved from one rented room to another. Half the time I slept in the street or on a bus. She died of an overdose the day I turned seventeen."

She took his hand and held it tight. She realized he felt that his words were an indictment against him. She wanted to tell him none of it was his fault, but she didn't think it would help. Not now. "What then?" she whispered.

"I stayed out of sight when she died, hoping no one would care enough to check on an addict's son. If the authorities did, I knew I would be sent to a foster home, and I wasn't going to let that happen. I was finally attending a high school I liked. The coach saw me running one day and recruited me for track. I lived on buses and stayed with other members of the track team, bummed food from them. Then the coach realized I was homeless. He let me stay in a basement room of his house. He suggested the army, and the day I graduated, I joined. It was my home, my family, for the next seventeen years until the leg injuries took me out. You can't be a Ranger if you can't move fast."

"How did you meet David?"

"We were both sergeants when we went to Ranger

school and we were paired. It's pure hell. No sleep. Not much food. One endurance test after another. We pulled each other through and were assigned to the same outfit. The Rangers kept us together until he decided he wanted to be a dog handler and convinced our captain that our unit needed one. God, he loved that dog."

She knew the rest of the story. About the last engagement.

He took the steaks off the grill and walked inside. She stayed where she was for a moment. The emptiness in his voice told her far more than outward emotion would have.

He was back in a minute with a pail of water he poured on the ashes.

Then he put an arm around her shoulders and they walked inside together.

She wasn't hungry, but she set the table and poured both of them more wine.

He looked at her directly. "There's something else. I have PTSD," he said bluntly. "It comes at night, although I had episodes during the day in the hospital. I have nightmares and wake up yelling, and the bed is soaking wet. I think I'm back in Afghanistan. I could hurt you, or Nick. I can't do that to either of you."

"I don't think you would ever hurt anyone you care about, even unconsciously." She hesitated. "I love you."

He went still, and she saw a muscle work in his jaw. Those brilliant green eyes swam with emotion.

"I didn't believe it could happen so fast," she said. "I didn't believe the movies or the books or friends' tales. But I think I fell in love the minute I saw your scowl that day we met. And the first time I saw your smile, I was a goner."

"But—"

She ignored his interruption. "My husband died much too young and too suddenly. We had grown up together, and I thought that's how love worked. Slow and easy. Nick was traumatized when Russ died, and then again when my father was killed. I said I would never put him through anything like that again. No love, no pain. I was wrong. Love is worth the pain."

She tried to smile. "That's my little lecture. I think we should eat the steaks before they're ice-cold. You'll need your strength tomorrow on the roof." She gulped nearly the whole glass of wine.

He watched her with a bemused expression, then stood. Took the few steps to her. He leaned down.

The kiss was so tender, so achingly tender, she wondered why she didn't melt down to her toes.

One step at a time. A giant step.

CHAPTER TWENTY-FOUR

IT WAS NEARING eleven when Josh took Eve home. After the kiss, they'd engaged mostly in small talk as they finished dinner. But the air had been electrified with emotion.

He insisted on taking her to the door but did not go in. Nor did he kiss her, although that took all his willpower. He'd probably already damaged her reputation, and he'd discovered this night that when they started a blaze, it was damned near impossible to pull back.

But he continued to hear her words. Over and over again. *I love you.* Words he hadn't heard before. Words that had power. Words that terrified him far more than the enemy ever had.

It was obvious that when she loved, she loved completely, without reservation. He didn't know if he could do that in return.

Amos whined when Josh opened the door. Josh knelt on his good leg and put his arms around Amos, just as Dave used to do. He received a big lick on his face.

Maybe he was catching on to this loving business. He took Amos for his walk, passing by June

Byars's cottage. Her light was still on. The rest of the cottages and cabins were dark.

The sky was midnight blue, and the moon gave enough light that he could see the buildings in the park across the lake. This was Eve's town, her heart and soul. Could he be happy here? Nearly everything in his life had been marked by action. He'd thrived on challenge and adrenaline. He'd been good at war, at violence.

But he'd also liked books. Learning. He'd chalked up a number of hours of university credit during off time. History. Economics. Literature.

His superiors had wanted him to get a degree and join the officer corps, but that wasn't what *he* wanted. He'd just wanted to learn things.

He thought about Dave. He'd planned to drive to Pueblo to see Mabry, the attorney, but now he felt more of an urgency, although he couldn't say why. A call would have to do.

He turned back. It was well after one o'clock now, already Saturday, and in a few hours he would see Eve again.

His steps quickened.

AFTER JOSH LEFT, Eve closed the door but lingered against it, trying to steady herself. Her emotions were running wild. Her body still tingled from their lovemaking, and tears had dried on her cheeks from his careful words about his past.

He'd confided in her. She knew from his voice how

painful it was. He was a quiet man who'd learned to keep everything inside himself. Especially pain. She wondered if anyone else knew all of it. Maybe David Hannity had.

His words had torn into her heart. But they also told her that he cared for her. It had been evident in his touch, in his halting confidences...

The dogs gave her an ecstatic welcome, and she gave each of them a small treat. They promptly forgave her for not bringing Nick home. She then checked on the horses. With whinnies and head butts, they made plain their dismay at not being ridden more often. "Sunday," she promised and gave them each a half carrot.

Those duties done, she retreated to the house and turned on her stereo. She could think better with music, and she had a lot of thinking to do.

Tonight had been full of ups—spectacular ups—and downs. He had never said the word *love,* and she'd blurted it out. Three weeks—less than three weeks—and she'd thrown aside all her reservations. How could she have done that? How could she offer her full heart when he wasn't ready to do the same?

She would worry about that tomorrow. She needed to go to bed, but she doubted sleep would come.

JOSH CAUGHT ONLY a few hours' sleep before waking at 6:00 a.m. He dressed in his most comfortable jeans and one of his paint-stained T-shirts. He wore his combat boots. He figured the thick ridges would help on the roof.

He arrived at the roofing site at a little after 7:00 a.m. after taking Amos to the animal clinic. Amos hadn't been that happy about the outing until he saw Sherry. Then tails started wagging. Amos didn't seem a bit sad to see him go.

He hadn't bothered to eat. "Don't worry about coffee or breakfast," Nate had told him. "There will be plenty of food."

Although he arrived only a few minutes after seven, the street was already packed with cars, trucks and people. He had to find a parking place nearly a block and a half away.

The roofing party was at a modest ranch that needed painting as well as a new roof. The yard contained several struggling yellow rose bushes, and the grass was almost gone, although what was there was neatly mowed. A large metal bin had already been placed in the driveway for discarded shingles.

Two men were untying the cover on the back of a truck containing new shingles. A nearby pickup truck was being emptied of its cargo of ladders, nails and tools. Roof boards had been piled next to a ladder that leaned against the house. One man was walking up and down the roof as if it was no more than a sidewalk.

Josh looked around for Eve, but didn't see either her or her pickup, Miss Mollie.

Nate, who was unloading a ladder, raised a hand in greeting. "Hey, glad to see you."

Josh helped Nate position the ladder against the roof. "What's first?" Josh asked.

"Coffee, I think, and introductions. And something to eat. You have to try the cinnamon rolls. The best cooks in town try to outdo each other every time we have one of these.

"A new group of women will come in with lunch and still a third will bring supper," he added. "My mom's one of the latter. She makes a mean chili."

"What if the roof is finished?"

Nate laughed. "The guys will slow up to make sure that doesn't happen."

"Is there a boss here?"

"Craig Stokes. He's the one up there now. He used to do it for a living in Denver. When the market crashed, he decided to retire back here. He's a native. And an army vet, too, by the way. Put in his twenty."

Nate introduced him to the other volunteers. He immediately recognized the veterans by the way they greeted him with a "Hey, bro." He stopped counting after a while.

In the next-door neighbor's yard, three women tended a commercial-size coffee urn. He headed toward June Byars.

"Mr. Manning," she said in a delighted voice. "I'm so glad to see you here."

He grinned at her. "Those rolls look like they're worth a lot more than a few hours of my time," he said.

She beamed at him. Disconcerted, he grabbed a cup of coffee and a roll and took a big bite. They were still warm and so good he grabbed a second. He began to understand why so many people had volunteered. "Wow," he said.

Mrs. Byars's smile grew even broader. "There's plenty left," she said. The woman next to her was not to be outdone. "You'll have to try my honey buns, too," she said, "and welcome to Covenant Falls."

He nodded. "I'll do that next break, ma'am," he said and followed Nate back to the work site. Nate introduced him to Stokes, who had climbed down from the roof.

"Glad to have you here," Stokes said. "I saw you limp. Are you going to be steady on the ladder and roof? We need workers down here, collecting the shingles, getting tools and materials. It's just as important."

Josh didn't take offense. It was the guy's job to be careful. "I've been on a ladder rehabbing the cabin," he said. "I wouldn't be here if I didn't think I could handle it."

"Okay. Ever tear off shingles before?"

"A few. I'm pretty good with tools."

"Okay. Nate will get you a tool belt with everything you need." He paused, then added, "If that leg starts bothering you, let him know, okay?"

"Sure thing," Josh replied.

"Thanks for coming."

Stokes turned back to the other volunteers, who were gathering around him.

"The shingles that are there are warped and damaged, and they all have to be removed. Probably need to replace a lot of roof boards, as well." A collective groan came from the crowd.

Stokes continued. "For those who haven't worked a roof before, it's hard, exhausting, dirty work. Since we have more volunteers than usual, we'll swap off every hour and a half. So those who don't go up on the roof now can run the magnetic rollers to pick up the nails and go up in the next shift." His gaze turned to Eve, who was approaching.

"Sorry to be late, guys," she said. "One of the horses kicked up a fuss this morning."

"That's okay, Mayor, you're here now."

"Someone else is coming behind me," she said. Josh didn't like the forced sound in her voice.

"Yeah?" Stokes said.

"Sam Clark."

Josh felt a shock, heard a murmuring around him. Others were surprised, too. "I'll be damned," someone behind him said. "That's a first. Sam doing something for someone."

Josh saw worry on Eve's face. She took Stokes aside for a moment. He saw her say something to him, but the voices were too low for anyone to hear. He saw Stokes nod, then return to the volunteers. "We have some new people here," he said. "I'm going to put them between two roofing veterans. Mr. Manning…"

"Josh," he corrected.

"Josh, you go between Nate and the mayor. They're both expert." He called out two more people to help another first timer. The rest, Josh assumed, were roofing veterans. "Those who don't have a tool belt, grab one."

Stokes went up to the deputy, who had arrived just after Eve. "Ever work on a roof, Sam?" he asked within Josh's hearing.

"No," Sam said and nodded toward Josh, "but if he can do it, I can."

"I have enough volunteers for the first wave," Stokes said. "You can help clean up the shingles and debris until the second shift. There's coffee, donuts and cinnamon rolls next door."

Clark scowled, started to protest then after looking at the faces around him, nodded and walked toward the coffee.

What in the hell was Clark doing here? He was glad that Clark wouldn't be up on the roof with him.

Eve came to his side. "Good morning," she said shyly.

She looked more appealing than ever in jeans and a T-shirt with a dark blue cotton shirt over it. She wore a Colorado Rockies baseball cap that pulled her hair back, and well-worn tennis shoes.

For a moment he forgot about Clark, forgot about everything except last night. "Good morning," he replied, and felt like a schoolboy. Then he noticed that several other guys were looking at them. He forced himself to glance away, but Lord, he wanted to reach over....

"I'll go first," Nate said with a bemused look on his face. "You can watch while I take off the first few shingles, then you're on your own. I think you'll easily recognize any rotten or damaged boards. A red marker is in your tool belt. Okay?"

Josh nodded.

Nate scrambled up the ladder like a monkey. Josh took his time, pulling himself up the one time his bad leg failed on a rung. Then he was on the roof and inching up until he was next to Nate. He pulled on his work gloves.

Nate used a tool to scrape under the shingle, working around the edges until it was completely underneath, and pulled. Josh immediately understood why Stokes had said it was hard, dirty work when he tried to do the same.

He looked over at Eve, who had already pulled one up and was starting on the second. It took him several minutes to pull up the first shingle, then he got the hang of it and was catching up fast. They worked downward as the second group took their place on the rooftop and started on the other side.

He watched the others carefully aiming shingles at the bin below, calling out a warning first.

He concentrated on the work and wouldn't let himself glance at Eve. He was lagging behind the others in his line, but not by much. They waited until he finished the second layer, then they moved down as a group. They were more than a third of the way down when Stokes called for a break. Nate shook his head. "We can go on," he hollered down.

Stokes nodded and they continued. Josh's leg was stiffening but he ignored it. Instead, he concentrated on removing the shingles.

They worked another hour, then Stokes called them down. They were halfway down the roof.

Eve was closest to the ladder and went down first. He painstakingly followed her, making sure his good leg landed first.

He winced at the sudden pain, then moved away for Nate. Eve was looking at him with concern.

"It's okay," he said. "It just needs a minute or so to wake up."

Her heart was in her eyes, and he had to turn away. Nate was at his side.

Stokes gave him a nod of approval. "Get some water," he said.

Josh nodded. Although it was midmorning, he was damp with sweat. It was a cloudless day and the sun was bright. He judged the temperature to be in the low 90s. Nothing like Afghanistan, but hot enough.

All six members of his team made their way to the large water dispenser on the back of one of the trucks. He tried not to look at Eve, but he felt the camaraderie of the group. He felt as if he was back with his guys in the field. He was part of a team.

He took a long drink. Then Nate splashed some water on him, and they all started to do the same, including Eve, who was grinning.

Josh suddenly walked away. He'd kept his feelings at bay these many months. The shrink had told him he couldn't hold them in forever, that someday they would break out and he would be the better for it.

It had started last night, and now his emotions were streaming out. *Not now. Dear God, not now.*

He kept walking, past the trucks and the cars until he reached his Jeep. Then he stopped. He just stood there, and then he was aware of Eve next to him. Standing quietly. Saying nothing. Understanding without being obtrusive. There if he needed her.

He slipped her hand in his and she moved closer to him, resting her head against his heart. She didn't care if the world—or everyone in Covenant Falls—saw them.

"It's coming back, isn't it?" she said softly.

"It never goes away," he replied. He didn't want to hide any longer. Not from her. "I think it's receding, and then something reminds of my team, something like splashing water on each other. And it all flashes back." He hesitated. "Today was different."

"Why?"

He didn't know how to put it in words. That he felt he was betraying his friends by feeling part of something again. That he was beginning a life again when they weren't.

"Betrayal," he finally blurted out. It was impossible to keep anything from her now, not when she was looking at him as if her life were his.

"Because you lived when they died, when Dave died?" she asked softly. "You think they would feel that way? That your living well was a betrayal of them?"

He was silent.

"Would you feel that way if it was reversed? Would you not want Dave to have a good life? Isn't that why he died? Because he wanted you to live. Isn't it a betrayal to throw it away?"

He looked down at her.

"I know a little of how you feel," she said in a low voice. "When Russ died so suddenly, I felt guilty about being alive. I kept wondering why him? Why not me? Everyone loved him. Only Nick got me through it. You haven't had anyone."

Her eyes told him that he did now.

He held her tight, as if his life depended on it. He didn't care if anyone watched. After a minute he let her go. He still wasn't free of memories. He didn't think he would ever be free, but now maybe he could relive the good as well as the bad.

He swallowed hard and looked around. No one had followed them, and they were shielded by cars and trees and fences. He touched her cheek, then kissed her lightly.

"Let's go back," she said. "I haven't had breakfast."

"Then you haven't had Mrs. Byars's cinnamon rolls." His voice was hoarse.

"Oh, I have. Many times. She's a regular on the do-good circuit."

"As are you."

She shrugged. "I'm mayor."

"I doubt many mayors work on their constituents' roofs." His voice was getting back to normal.

"I want to get reelected." She reached in one of her pockets and came up with a phone. "I meant to call Tom and tell him Sam is here."

"Better here than at my place."

"Still, he should know."

She phoned Tom. When she hung up, she said, "He's sending Ryan to watch your place. As far as I can tell, Sam's just wandering about, not doing anything but getting in the way." She was distracting him, easing him back into the present, and she was doing it very neatly. He smiled, and her mouth stretched into a wide grin.

"Mom! Josh!"

Josh turned around and saw Nick running toward them. Eve hugged him when the boy reached them. "Where's Amos?" he asked.

"Staying with Sherry today," Josh said. "A little dog together time."

"Look," Nick said and held out a digital camera. "Grandpa gave it to me to take pictures for your campaign. He said to take one of you on the roof."

She raised an eyebrow and turned to Josh. "He's worried Al will win the election and chase out what people are left here." She turned back to Nick.

"That's a very good idea. I think you should take pictures of everyone and send them to the newspaper since I haven't seen any of the staff here today."

"Okay," he said happily.

"But don't go close to the house without one of us," Eve warned him. "There could be nails and flying shingles. We don't want another trip to the hospital."

"Okay, I promise."

"What about something to eat," she said to Nick.

As they walked in front of the work site, Nick took a photo of the men on the roof, then the three of them walked over to the tables in the neighbor's yard. Mrs. Byars was still there, along with a growing number of women. "My mother-in-law, Abby Douglas," Eve said. "And this is our newest resident, Josh Manning."

"Mrs. Douglas," he acknowledged.

"Good to see you, Mr. Manning," Mrs. Douglas said, and her gaze went from him to Eve and back again. Josh wondered if their relationship was that obvious.

"Coffee, young man?" Mrs. Byars said, then whispered, "I saved you and Eve my last rolls. And Nick, of course. I keep some back for my favorites."

"I'm glad I'm one of your favorites," Josh said. He took a cup of coffee and a roll, as did Eve, who gave a sigh of appreciation as she bit into it. "I love you, Mrs. Byars," she said. Nick was too busy eating to comment.

A huge plate of sandwiches suddenly appeared on the table. Then came potato salad and baked beans.

More ladies were appearing with other dishes. "That's quite an army," Josh said. "Nate told me there would be good food, but he understated it."

"So you're Mr. Manning," another woman said. She thrust out her hand. "Mighty nice of you to join us, I'm Sue Harris. I teach at the school. My husband is up on the roof now. Bob Harris."

Two weeks ago, he would have felt crowded by all the interest in him. He would have been suspicious of it. Now he saw Eve's friends through her eyes. Good, sincere, friendly people who wanted a better community and were willing to work for it.

Nate came up to him. "They are almost ready for our group," he said. "It's getting pretty hot up there and we don't want anyone up there for more than an hour. We should be finished then with the old shingles. Then an eight-man team will replace the boards. They will need us back after that to nail on the new shingles."

"Clark still here?" Josh asked.

"Strutting around not doing a damn thing," Nate said. "I asked him if he wanted to work, and he said he *was* working, that there needed to be an officer around because of the traffic." Nate grinned. "He keeps glaring at you."

"Personality conflict," Josh said.

"He has a lot of those," Nate replied. "See you over there."

Josh was ready. His mind was running amok. Too

many emotions warring against each other. Work was a good way to slow them down.

Eve told Nick to stay close to his grandmother, then walked to one of the pickup trucks where the equipment was. She took off the shirt she'd worn over her T-shirt and strapped on the tool belt. It looked well used. "It was my dad's," she said with pride.

He had always thought her pretty, but never so much as at this moment. The belt emphasized her curves and she had a dark smudge on her nose. The bill of her baseball cap framed her remarkable eyes.

They watched as the group of men came down, their shirts drenched in sweat. Then, as before, Nate climbed the ladder, followed by Josh and Eve. Then three more came after them, moving to the left side of the roof.

He felt more confident now and was able to keep up with the others. They had three more lines of shingles to dislodge. The sun bore down on them and sweat rolled down his face. He looked over at Eve, and she was concentrating on a particularly stubborn shingle, then with a triumphant cry she tore it off.

The sun was straight above when they finished. Eve was first to go down, the damp T-shirt hugging her. He went down next and almost stumbled as he reached the ground. Her hand caught his. Two weeks ago he would have felt humiliated. Now he appreciated the warm hand clasping his.

She continued holding it as they walked back to

the equipment truck. "Let's get some water and a sandwich," she said.

They were walking over to the food table when her mother-in-law met her. "I can't find Nick," she said. "I've been looking everywhere."

Eve's face paled. "How long has he been gone?"

"About forty minutes. Not that long, but I told him to stay close. After you and Mr. Manning went over to the house, he wanted to take pictures of you going up the ladder and some while you were up there. I saw him there, then he just seemed to disappear. I started looking for him. No one has seen him."

Eve turned to Josh. "It really isn't like him to wander far when he's been told to stay around. Last Saturday was the exception and he promised never to leave again without telling me."

"He's always been interested in my Jeep," Josh said. "Maybe he walked down there to take a picture."

"Josh parked on Oak Street," she said to Abby. "Has anyone looked there?"

"I didn't go that far," her mother-in-law said. "We went a block in every direction. Probably nothing to worry about. He might have seen a stray dog or…"

"Abby, why don't you take your car and drive around? Josh and I will go down Oak Street. I have my cell with me if you find him. If I do, I'll check in with you."

Josh hurried over to Nate and told them they couldn't find Nick. "Would you ask some of the guys who aren't working to look?"

"Sure thing."

"Thanks."

Josh and Eve jogged down the street and turned on Oak toward his Jeep. It was there. Nick wasn't. Josh looked around the car. Grass had been trampled, but then he and Eve had stood here an hour earlier.

He heard Eve cry out and he ran over to her. She held remnants of a camera in her hand. The one her son had carried earlier.

He saw raw fear on Eve's face then.

And he felt it, too.

CHAPTER TWENTY-FIVE

"WHERE WAS IT?" Josh asked.

"In the street, against the curb," Eve replied, her voice shaking. She couldn't stop shaking. It didn't make sense. Maybe it had fallen from Nick's pocket. Maybe he was looking for it now. But then why hadn't he returned? Nick knew how she worried, especially after last week. Maybe she was overprotective, but with what had happened to Russ...

"Is the memory card still in there?"

Why hadn't she thought of that? She looked inside the wreckage and found a battered card.

She passed it to Josh, who took a look and swore. "We need to find the same brand camera," he said. "Or maybe a laptop."

"I'll call his grandfather," she said. "He gave him the camera, and I'm pretty sure he has more at the drugstore. He's just three blocks away."

"Call your chief of police, too," Josh said in a tight voice.

She didn't question him. She punched a button and Tom's voice came on immediately. "Tom, Nick is missing. I found a camera he'd been using. It was smashed against a curb. I'm afraid something's wrong."

"When did you last see him?"

"About two hours ago. Abby was looking after him. Said he disappeared an hour ago. People have been looking everywhere."

"I'm on my way over. Is there anything else?"

"We have the card from the camera. There might be something on it. I'm calling Jim now to see whether he has another camera in stock."

"Good. I'll alert our people and be over there in ten minutes."

She called Jim and hurriedly explained. He did have more of the cameras and would bring one over immediately.

Eve and Josh went back to the roofing site and found Stokes. He'd already been alerted by Abby and had sent those not working to search the nearby areas.

Josh looked around. Sam Clark had been here earlier, but he didn't see him now. "Where's Clark?" he asked. "Is he out looking for Nick?"

"Haven't seen him for a while," Stokes said. "Guess he got tired from doing nothing," he added with a snort.

Tom arrived and behind him was Jim Douglas. He had a camera with him. "We got a good deal on these cameras," he said. "They've been flying off the shelves. Lucky we had one left. I checked and the battery's good."

He handed it to Tom, who inserted the card. He turned the camera on and flipped through the phoos. He stopped and swore. Then he handed it to Eve, who then gave it to Josh.

Josh looked at a photo of Sam Clark using a tool to break into his Jeep. A second one showed him reaching inside with something in his hand. "Clark must have seen Nick taking the photo," he said.

"You think he took Nick?" she asked.

Silence met the question.

"But then wouldn't he have taken the camera with him rather than leaving it in the street?" Eve asked.

"Maybe he didn't see the camera," Josh said. "Maybe he just saw Nick watching him."

Tom swore. "Based on the footage from the cameras at Josh's cabin, I finally got a judge to sign off on a search warrant for Sam's house today, and we were getting ready to serve it. It was supposed to be confidential. Maybe he was tipped off and decided to plant evidence. He wasn't on duty today, so I couldn't keep Ryan on him."

Josh looked at Eve. Her face was pale. He put a hand on her shoulder. "We'll find Nick."

"Damn right we will," Tom said. "Anyone see what Sam was driving?"

"I drove up the same time Sam did this morning," Eve said. "He was driving his green Chevy. He looked agitated, but then he often does. But it was really unusual for him to attend the roofing."

"Good," Tom said. "We can track the car." He turned and explained to Josh, "We have police radios in all the officer's private cars in case of an emergency."

"Wouldn't he know that?"

"The radios are fairly new. We've never used them except for testing. Our officers know the radios are there, and they may be called to help in an emergency, but I'haven't mentioned we can use them to track where they are."

"But he *could* know?"

"He could," Tom admitted. "I'm going to the office and get everything organized. Eve, you stay here in case we're wrong and Nick shows up." He moved quickly to his car and drove off.

Eve shivered as she watched him go. She wanted to run after him. Josh's arms went around her.

She looked up at him. "Why would Nick go with him without screaming his head off? Nick's watched enough police shows to know never get into the car with…" Her voice stopped.

Anyone except for a police officer.

The fear grew worse.

Eve felt helpless. "I have to tell Abby, and Craig Stokes. He'll have to find someone to…replace…" She paused, then said in a voice she didn't recognize, "There's a chance we're wrong, and Nick returns on his own. Maybe he saw Sam breaking into the car and just started running…."

Josh held her closer. "We'll find him. I promise."

She had gone from shaking to cold. She was so cold. His arms weren't a comfort, they were a prison. She had to find Nick. She broke loose and started walking, then running back to the work site. Nick would be there, snitching a sweet and keeping the ladies entertained with tales of Miss Marple and Captain Hook.

He had changed so much since the year of near silence after his father, and then his grandpa, had died. She would kill Sam herself if he did anything to hurt Nick, to send him back to that place.

Somewhere inside she knew Josh was keeping up with her despite his leg, although she didn't look back. Why had she volunteered for the roofing when she should have been with Nick, protecting him?

Her cell phone rang. It was Tom. "We've tracked Sam's car. It's near his uncle's place in the mountains. Ryan and Mike are already on the way, the other officers are behind them and I'm leaving now. Julia's going to contact the state police about a possible kidnapping and ask for an assist. She'll let us know if the car moves again.

"I'm telling everyone to use their cells, not their radios. Sam's in way over his head. He's probably still in a panic and trying to figure a way out of this mess." He paused, then added, "You might call Stephanie and put her on alert. We might need her and Sherry."

"You don't think…"

"I'm not thinking anything. I just don't want to preclude any possibilities. Is Manning still there?"

"Yes."

"Let me talk to him."

Reluctantly, she handed the phone to him. Resenting him. If only...

"Roger that," she heard Josh say after a short pause then he handed the phone back to her.

"What?" she demanded.

His gaze met hers. "He wants to make sure Nick still isn't around here. He wants an organized search. He can't be sure Sam took Nick."

The implication hit her like a sledgehammer. "You don't..."

"It's only about covering all bases," he said. He took her hand and pulled her toward the work site. She was met by Abby, who took one look at her face and put a hand to her mouth in horror.

"We can't find him," Eve said. "We think maybe he's with Sam Clark, but we don't know for sure. Tom wants an organized search."

Josh found Stokes and talked to him quietly. In minutes all the men working on the roof were in a circle around Josh and Eve. In a few sentences, Josh told them that Nick was missing and there was the possibility of foul play. They wanted every yard checked within a six-block radius.

Everyone quickly organized themselves into groups to check the various yards. Several got on cell phones to call for more help.

Eve tried to call Stephanie but her phone was out of service. A call to the clinic was answered by Lisa, her vet tech, who said Stephanie was on an emergency call to a ranch forty miles out. A mare was birthing win foals. Eve knew Stephanie wouldn't be able to leave. Twin foals were tricky and could result in the death of the mare and foals.

There was nothing more she could do here that she couldn't do on the road. "I want to go," she said.

Josh nodded. "I'll drive. Nate can take care of things here."

Eve turned to Jim. "Would you stay and let us know if anyone finds anything here?"

Jim gave her a big hug. "Of course, Eve. You do what you need to do."

"We'll stop and pick up Amos," Josh said. "He could be helpful. If you have anything of Nick's with you for him to catch his scent..."

"We can pick up something at my house," she said. She started for her truck.

He stopped her. "My Jeep is better for the mountains." She wanted to say no. Guilt was hitting her in waves. If she hadn't been so distracted by Josh, she would have paid more attention to Nick.

Still, she knew Josh was right. Without another word, she led the way to the Jeep. He drove first to the animal clinic, where he picked up Amos, then to her house. He waited while she ran in and returned with a pair of Nick's jeans. "They haven't been washed yet," she said.

He stopped at his cabin and grabbed his Glock and belt holster, then asked Eve for directions. He drove faster than the speed limit but he didn't think there was anyone to stop him. "How long?" he asked.

"If Sam is going to his uncle's cabin, forty minutes or so." Her hands were clasped together so tight they were white. "What if we're wrong?"

"This is a possible child kidnapping," he said. "There will be law enforcement—county and state— all over the place. If Nick shows up somewhere else, you'll be notified. In the meantime, my gut tells me it's Clark."

She didn't say anything. Her gut was telling her the same thing, but maybe it was because they both disliked Sam Clark. She had a hard time believing he would actually kidnap a child. He was impulsive, un- disciplined. She knew that. But violent? Why hadn't she insisted he be fired? She'd tried to keep peace but…at what price?

She called Tom again. "Where are you?"

"About fifteen minutes out," he said.

"We have three cars and six men. A helicopter and several county cars are between you and me. Do you want us to wait on you?"

"I don't want a show of force to rattle him and make him do something rash, but you're the expert."

"I agree," Tom said. "I'll go in with Charlie. He's probably the closest thing to a friend Sam has. We might be able to talk him into just giving up. I'm hoping he didn't know about the camera and has no idea that we connected him to the boy. We've kept everything off the radio."

"Okay," she replied. "We'll be maybe ten minutes behind."

She hung up and repeated the conversation to Josh, who nodded.

He reached out a hand and squeezed hers. "It'll be all right. Clark's a blowhard but I don't think he's a killer."

"But Nick doesn't know that."

"I'm not sure about that. Nick's a pretty savvy kid."

"But he is a kid. Ten years old."

He squeezed her hand again, put his hand back on the wheel. She was silent until she directed him on a narrow road that seemed to wind around forever as it went up the mountain. She knew the turn. She'd been at Al's cabin with her father several times.

"Okay," she said. "Take a left."

He turned down a rutted road and drove a mile, then she saw the large hunting cabin—three police cars were parked in front. Tom was outside and walked quickly to their car.

"Nick?" she asked.

"There's a problem," he said.

She went cold inside. And started shaking. "What kind of problem?"

"Sam admitted he took Nick after I told him about the photos. But he said that Nick jumped out when Sam slowed down to take a sharp curve. Sam went after him, but he had to park first on an incline and by the time he got out, Nick had disappeared. Charlie's inside with Sam now. Everyone else is out looking for Nick. I have at least twenty more men and women headed here," he continued. "My wife is taking over the dispatch desk, and the dispatchers are coming in, as well. The state is sending a team. I've called search and rescue, and they're sending over a couple of teams, too."

Eve tried not to scream. Nick lost. Scared. "Maybe Sam's lying."

"I don't think so. It's just dawning on him how much trouble he's in. I told him we knew he robbed Shep's place and we found all we needed in his house, plus the two belt buckles he had in his car. I told him we had a photo of him breaking into Josh's Jeep. If anything happened or happens to Nick, he knows its first-degree kidnapping and murder."

She tried to think. "He would go downhill. My dad used to tell him if he ever got lost, go down. Find a stream and follow it."

Tom's face softened. "I believe Sam when he says he never meant for all this to happen. He just wanted that chief's job, to be someone other than just Al's nephew. He wanted to show everyone how competent he was, and he kept getting in deeper and deeper. I think he's horrified at what he did today and I think we can believe that he isn't lying." He hesitated, then added, "Hell, none of that matters now. Josh, I see Amos in the car. Can he track?"

"He hasn't had that specific training, but it's worth a try." He paused. "You have someone who can move fast with him?"

Ryan stepped toward him. "I can."

Eve could tell Josh hated that he couldn't keep up through the woods, but there had been no hesitation.

Josh opened the Jeep door, and Amos stepped out gingerly, then looked around. He knew Tom and Ryan, but there were others here now.

"Where exactly did Nick leave the car?" Ryan asked.

"About an eighth of a mile from here," Tom said.

"What do I do?" Ryan said. "I've never handled a search dog."

"Eve bought a pair of Nick's jeans," Josh said. "We'll take him down to where Nick jumped out and then let Amos smell the jeans. He may be reluctant to go with you, and if so I'll start out with you but I don't want to slow you down."

They walked down the road to the spot where Nick left Sam's car. Josh knelt next to Amos. "Nick needs you," he said. "Nick is one of your pack."

Ryan stooped and held out his hand and let Amos sniff. Amos offered his paw. Acceptance.

Eve handed Ryan the jeans and gave Amos time to sniff. Amos whined.

"I think he understands," Josh said. "Duty time," he said and rubbed Amos's neck. "Find Nick. Find Nick for me." He handed the leash to Ryan. "Find Nick," he said again.

Amos looked at him, not moving. "Go, Amos," Josh said again. "Find Nick."

Eve stooped in front of Amos with the pair of jeans. "Find Nick," she said. "Please find Nick."

Amos still wouldn't move.

"He wants you," she said. "You're the leader of the pack. Ryan isn't."

"I can't run," Josh said, and she heard the despair in his voice.

"You don't have to. Nick can't be too far."

Josh looked at Amos, who was waiting for him. Eve was waiting, too.

Ryan handed the leash back to him. "I'll pace myself with you. If you have to stop, perhaps he'll go on with me."

Josh nodded and took the leash. "Let's go, Amos."

Amos started sniffing, then headed toward the woods, pulling Josh. Josh undid the leash and Amos plunged ahead. Josh had to half run to keep up with him but he didn't want to stop. He just prayed he wouldn't stumble over a bush or a log. Once he lost Amos, but the dog came back, waited for him then put his nose to the ground again and continued.

Pain started to run up and down Josh's leg. He heard Ryan and Eve calling Nick's name, but it was all he could do to keep up with Amos. Maybe he should have left him on a leash, but he hadn't wanted to slow him.

Fear clutched at him. He hadn't realized until these past few hours how much Nick had crawled into his heart. He was such a spunky, caring kid who'd already had too much tragedy in his life.

Josh didn't know how much time passed. Thirty minutes. An hour. He just concentrated on moving, knowing at any minute his leg might give. Then Amos started barking.

That was new for Amos. Amos went to alert when sniffing for explosives or enemy combatants. But there was excitement in the bark.

Then he heard Nick. Ryan and Eve passed him, and Josh leaned against a tree for a moment. Let Eve find her son.

He limped slowly toward the sounds. Amos's barking, Nick's voice answering his mother's cries, and then he reached them. Eve was bent over Nick, whose face was smudged and bruised. He had cuts on his arms. He was clutching his right ankle.

Ryan was leaning over him. He looked up as Josh approached.

"Looks like a sprained ankle. He fell down that incline."

Josh knelt next to him. "Hey, champ. We've gotta stop meeting this way."

That brought a weak smile from Nick. "I knew you and Amos would come." Amos was lying near Nick's feet and his ears perked up when he heard his name. Then he wagged his tail. Josh would have sworn he had a satisfied smile on his face.

Eve was holding on to her son's shoulders as if she would never let go.

Josh sat down on the ground, hoping like hell he could get up again. He took out his Swiss Army knife and cut a swath of his shirt off. Then he took off

Nick's left sneaker, noticing the boy's grimace and bound the ankle to hold it steady.

"You're one hell of a smart kid," he said unsteadily. "You did everything right." *Except maybe for taking photos of a crime in progress.* But that was a matter for another day.

Ryan leaned over and picked up Nick.

"Take us home, Amos," Josh said.

CHAPTER TWENTY-SIX

IT WAS WELL after one o'clock in the morning before Josh started the drive home from the Pueblo hospital with Nick, Eve and Amos.

Eve had called her in-laws and told them what had happened before the ambulance took her and Nick to the hospital with Josh following in his Jeep.

On the drive back to Covenant Falls, Eve sat in the backseat, holding her son. Nick, totally exhausted, slept. Amos sat up in front. He'd been praised by everyone and he seemed to think it his due. He sat like a prince and gazed out the windows. He had found his pack, and he had protected it.

Josh carried Nick inside. Nick had been given crutches, but Josh and Eve worried about the dogs. The Douglases greeted them at the door of Eve's home and gave Nick big hugs. "We took care of the horses," Jim said. "Abby has some stew on the stove. She always cooks when she's worried. Nick's going to make us all gain weight."

They went inside and at first there was chaos with five dogs and a cat barking, growling, sniffing backsides, meowing as they vied for attention. Eve directed Josh to take Nick to bed as the motley crew all crowded each other trying to get to Nick.

Nick's grandmother followed with a glass of milk and a plate of cookies while Eve settled her son in bed. Josh started to leave, but Jim and Abby Douglas insisted he eat first. He didn't object. In a few minutes, Eve came back into the room. "He's asleep with four watchdogs cuddled around him," she said with a tight smile.

"Now tell us everything that happened," her mother-in-law said.

Eve looked emotionally and physically spent. Truth told, they were both in pretty bad shape.

Josh took the lead and he told them about the rifle he'd found with his bike and how Tom suspected Sam of the other burglaries, suspicions that proved true after the sheriff found stolen items in the officer's house when Nick went missing.

"Al is really going to be torn up," Jim said. "He treated that boy like his son."

"Spoiled him rotten is what he did," Abby said, and disappeared into the kitchen, returning with four bowls of steaming stew on a tray. "Drink orders," she said. "Iced tea, milk, water. Wine."

"Get them wine," her husband said. "They've had a long, hard day. We've all had a long day."

Josh was suddenly aware of how dirty his clothes were. He'd washed his face and hands at the hospital, but there were stains and rips in his jeans and shirt. Eve had her cuts and bruises, as well.

They ate without additional words. They were all drained. Mentally, physically, emotionally.

Then Eve's in-laws said it was time for them to leave. "Church is tomorrow and I want to be there to say thanks, thanks to the good Lord and thanks to everyone who helped yesterday," Abby said.

"I should go, too," Eve said. "There will be questions. If I don't answer them, the phone will ring off the wall."

"I'll answer them," Abby said. "You and Nick need to relax."

Eve thought about it, then nodded. "Thank everyone for me. Tell them Nick is recuperating but needs some quiet time and to please respect that. About Sam Clark, simply say we can't say anything because of an ongoing investigation by the state."

Abby hugged Eve. "I'll do that. Thank God you found him," she said.

"Amos is the one who found him," Eve corrected.

Abby gave Amos a big hug. To Josh's surprise, Amos licked her.

"And thank you, Mr. Manning," Abby said. "Thank you for being there for Eve and my grandson. This is the second time you've rescued them. Can I hug you, too?"

Josh felt his cheeks warm. He didn't quite know what to do. He stood as Eve's mother-in-law practically smothered him with a heartfelt hug. He kinda liked it.

Then they were gone and he was alone with Eve.

They moved to the sofa. Both gravitating toward the other. Her hair had come loose from the clips and came down in tousled waves. She had a scratch on her cheek, and her hair still had brambles in it.

She was beautiful.

"Thank you," she said. "You and Amos."

He looked over at Amos, who raised his head at the sound of his name. "He did well, didn't he? His heart is mending."

"I think you mended it," she said.

"More Nick, I think," he said. "He took to Nick from day one. He hasn't done that with anyone since Dave died."

"He's not the only one who went into hiding."

"No," he admitted ruefully.

"Not you," she said. "Me."

"If there's one person who isn't hiding, it's you," he said. "Being a mayor is not exactly hiding."

"Yes, it is," she said. "I hid from loving again. From feeling too much for one person. It hurt too much when I lost those I loved. My husband, my father, even my mother. She didn't die, but she fled. I was going to be strong. I could do anything a man could. I am woman, hear me roar." She moved into his arms. "I don't mind roaring, but I don't think I want to do it alone any longer."

His arms went around her and she snuggled into them. It felt very good there, like she belonged.

He wanted her. In every way possible. He wanted

to come home to her, and he wanted to see her lean over Nick and make him feel safe. He wanted to see her smile at her cat and brood of dogs. He even wanted to be part of the world of caring she'd built in Covenant Falls. This was one lioness who roared with a soft voice and huge heart.

"I think I fell in love with you that first day I met you," he said. "I didn't want to. You scared the hell out of me. I'd never met anyone like you. You turned everything I thought I knew upside down. I never realized how empty my world was, or maybe I did and thought I didn't deserve more."

She looked up at him with her wide, beautiful eyes that always seemed to look inside him. Her lips trembled as she leaned up and kissed him with a tenderness that cracked his heart. "I love you, you idiot," she said when she drew away. "I think there's always been a very nice man in there waiting to pop out. It just took a dog to rip off the hard-ass mask."

He chuckled at the word picture she drew and a phrase he thought she'd probably never used before. "A dog and you."

"Not me, we," she corrected.

He liked that "we" part. He even liked the thought of growing old and gray with her. He suspected she would always keep him on his toes, always surprise him.

And then he realized he was actually thinking of the future. With her.

With Nick. In a small town in Colorado with a household full of animals and a woman everyone depended on. Dave would be more than a little amused.

"What are you thinking?" she asked, her fingers stroking the back of his neck. "You have a very odd smile on your face."

"Odd?"

"Maybe thoughtful," she amended.

"Thoughtful is odd?" he teased.

"You're avoiding the question."

"Dave," he answered. "I was thinking about Dave."

"I think he might be smiling up there," she said.

"It's still a puzzle why he held on to it," he said. "Why he didn't sell it long ago? I left a message with his attorney, asking if he knew the answers to any of those questions. As far as I know Dave had no family left. That's how we became friends. But also because we didn't ask questions. We didn't want to open each other's Pandora's box."

"What would I find in yours?"

"A lot of ugly stuff," he said. "But now I can put it away."

"I'll always be grateful to him for sending you to Covenant Falls," she said softly. "But can you be happy here?"

He hadn't been sure. Not until the past few days, when he realized he had been looking for a home all his life. That was why he'd carried that damn picture of a cottage so long. That was why he kept finding reasons to stay. He suspected Dave had known that. "I would be happy wherever you are." He paused. "But maybe…this is too fast…."

She shook her head. "I knew something was happening the first time you glowered at me. Then I brushed against you and bells rang like crazy. I didn't understand why or how, and I fought it, but…but I knew life would never be simple again."

"Do you want simple?"

"Not anymore," she said, looking immensely kissable. If Nick hadn't been in the next room Josh would have carried her to the shower and made mad, passionate love to her there, and then taken her to bed, where he could love her slowly and tenderly. He didn't want just bells, he wanted a symphony.

But Nick *was* in the other room, and they were both exhausted. It wasn't fair to either of them make promises, or decisions, tonight.

"I should go and let you get some sleep," he said. "We can talk more tomorrow." He kissed her again, lightly this time. She nodded and he helped her up. "When can I see you?" he asked.

She leaned her head against his shoulder, obviously as reluctant to leave him as he was her. "I want Nick to sleep late tomorrow morning. But I suspect he might be up for a picnic at the falls later. It's his favorite place, and there's not many people there earlier in the day." She didn't add that it was her favorite place, as well.

"But there might be some people?"

"Maybe," she said with smile that hinted at amusement.

"And you don't care?"

"No." She grinned. "I rather suspect that after yesterday the town thinks something is up between us."

Of course they would. They hadn't been exactly discreet during the roofing and the later search for Nick. He grinned. "What time?"

"About one."

"I'll pick you up."

"Amos is invited, too," she said.

Amos barked.

"I think he likes the plan," Josh said. "Take care," he said softly, then left before one of them started something they couldn't finish.

EVE WATCHED THE door close behind him. She wanted to run after him and beg him not to leave. But he was right. Nick was in the next room, and she needed to concentrate on him. Through the window, she watched him limp to his Jeep with Amos at his side. He turned, looked at her and gave her a crooked smile before climbing into the Jeep.

She took a long hot shower and washed her hair. He was right. She *was* exhausted, but she still tingled all over from his touch, from being so close to him. And her heart soared as she rewound the past hour in her mind.

He loved her. She knew she loved him. And he

seemed willing to stay in Covenant. If he hadn't, she knew in her heart she would go with him. How could she lose that crooked smile? Or the magic of his kisses? Or the easy way he had with Nick.

How could she lose the splendor he had brought into her life? Her fear of loss still ran deep. Until now, there had been no relationship strong enough to overcome it. Now there was. She had to take a chance.

Tomorrow. Maybe Josh would regret tonight, the words he'd said.

Maybe, as he'd said, they were both too emotionally spent to think rationally. Maybe by noon tomorrow, he would be headed out of town.

She turned off the light but didn't think she would sleep well.

NICK MADE HIS way into the kitchen after eleven. Eve had slept only a few hours and, full of nervous energy, took care of the horses and started preparing food for the picnic.

Nick moved on crutches almost as quickly as he ran. It had taken her much longer to learn when she'd fallen from a tree when she was eleven.

"I'm hungry," he said.

"That's a good sign," Eve said. "You can have some cereal."

He made a face.

"You don't want to eat too much since we're going on a picnic with Josh and Amos. If you feel well enough."

The frown turned into a wide grin. "Cereal will be great."

"I thought so."

Nick peered at the pan on the stove. "What are we having on the picnic?"

"Fried chicken, potato salad and coleslaw. And your grandma's cookies. Finish your cereal," she said. "I'm going to change. You had better take a bath, then get dressed. Clean jeans and shirt."

She watched him gulp down the rest of the cereal, pick up the crutches and hurry into his bedroom, the dogs following him. Her little Pied Piper of dogs.

How close she had come to losing him.

She looked through her closet for something to wear. She remembered the last time, when she'd purposely selected plain jeans and shirt. Now she wanted something more.

She found a full skirt of various hues of green and a white peasant blouse. Simple and comfortable but feminine. She selected a green silk scarf and tied her hair back with it. It was their first official date, other than the impromptu dinner, and he had never seen her in anything but jeans and slacks. She finished with a touch of lipstick and just a little blush. When she finished, it was twelve-thirty and she went into the kitchen and packed the picnic basket. She added a bottle of wine and several fruit drinks.

The phone rang and she picked it up. It was Abby.

"Mission accomplished," she said. "We went to the early service. Lots of concern about you and Nick.

Lots of questions about Josh. Is he going to stay? Any chance he would join the church? Everyone had good words about him. No one said much about Sam. Al's still too powerful, but he wasn't there today, and you know that's highly unusual." Sympathy tugged at Eve. She hated the fact that Sam had been forced on her, but he was Al's only heir and she knew this had to be a huge personal blow to him.

"Thanks, Abby," she said, then hesitated. "Nick is up and about. He's fine. Josh and I are taking him to the falls for a picnic."

"Marilyn asked whether you and Josh are an item. I merely asked her why she would think that and left. But are you two serious?"

"I think so," she said. "I didn't plan it. I don't even know how—"

"Eve, don't worry about us. We knew, even hoped you would find someone. You're a young woman. You need someone to love and who will love you. I saw how Josh looked at you yesterday. And Jim and I like him. Nick obviously adores him. Whatever you want to do, you have our blessing. And that's all I'm going to say. Have fun and give my love to Nick." She hung up.

Eve stood there for a moment, still holding the phone.

"He's here! Josh is here." The door slammed behind him.

Her heartbeat raced. She watched as Josh stepped out of the Jeep and approached the house. Nick swung himself effortlessly on the crutches toward him, followed by the dogs that jumped and yelped with excitement at seeing a new friend. Even Braveheart approached him.

Josh stooped down to say something to Nick. She couldn't hear, but Nick beamed. Josh scratched Braveheart behind the ears, then he was at the door and she opened it.

He smelled of soap and aftershave. He was dressed in his usual jeans, but they looked new, and a blue shirt with the sleeves rolled up. He looked incredibly handsome to her, especially when he smiled.

"Good afternoon," she said. Her voice seemed warmer to her.

"I think it's going to be a splendid afternoon," he replied, his deep, rich voice like warm syrup.

His gaze slowly ran over her and his smile widened. She didn't think she had seen that particular smile before. "Damn, but you're pretty," he said.

"You look pretty good yourself," she replied. Their gazes locked and he held out his hand. They had slept together just two nights ago, but this afternoon was different. They had said things last night that neither had expected. The feelings had been there, but so was the fear. The fear that it wouldn't—couldn't—last.

But now as she looked at him, she knew that what they had was far deeper than she imagined. So much for love being a process of growth. They had a spurt, a big one. Okay, a huge one.

She was suddenly aware of Nick standing expectantly next to Josh.

"There's a basket on the table," she said.

Josh looked at the basket and peeked inside like a small boy. He sniffed appreciatively. "You did this?"

"Mostly. Abby's cookies."

He looked at her with a question in his eyes.

"She approves."

Nick ushered the dogs back inside the house and hopped on the crutches to the Jeep. He climbed in the back with Amos.

"No ill effects, I see," Josh observed. "He's the most resilient kid I've ever seen."

"He's excited about today. I didn't take him to church. Too much curiosity."

"And you?"

"I asked Abby to say nothing could be disclosed since the whole matter is under investigation by the state, and Nick is just fine. Tom is saying the same."

"That's enough?"

"Not by half, but it's all anyone will get."

"Tough woman."

"Well, this tough woman is hungry."

SURPRISINGLY, THERE WAS only one family at the falls and they were preparing to set off on a hike.

Josh unpacked the basket while Nick found a stick and threw it for Amos. To Josh's surprise, Amos chased after it, his tail wagging furiously. He noted that Nick was careful not to get close to the edge and threw the stick toward the woods. He was completely absorbed in Amos and Amos in Nick. A sense of contentment filled him.

He took Eve's hand and they walked to where they had the perfect view of the waterfall. The sun was bright overhead, but the rainbow wasn't there. It didn't matter, though; he had his own rainbow.

Her fingers tightened around his, and she leaned against him. He felt her softness and her strength. "We were tired last night," he said. "And emotional."

"Emotion can be good."

"I thought I had turned it off long ago."

She looked up at him.

"But obviously not," he continued. "Because I want you as much today as I wanted you last night. I want you tomorrow and next week and next year and all the years after that." His grip tightened. "It's been damned quick, and I know it's probably too soon for either of us to promise anything, but I want you to know how I feel."

From him it was a magnificent admission.

She took his hand to her lips and kissed it and snuggled closer to him. "That's good," she said. "Very good. But I warn you, I don't believe in long courtships. It would be a source of constant speculation and gossip by my constituents."

He laughed. "That's one reason I love you. You never equivocate."

Her heart jumped as high as the sky. *He'd said it.* She looked up at him. "I love you," she said. "Nick does, too. I feel like I've known you forever, that I've been waiting for you all this time." She paused. "Do you… Could you be happy here?"

"I'll be happy anyplace you are. I already have some ideas. Maybe start a small construction company with Nate. I've discovered I rather like fixing and building things."

"What about your cabin?"

"A curious thing happened this morning," he said.

"A lot of curious things have been happening," she replied.

He nodded. "This morning I had a visitor."

She waited for him to go on.

"I told you last night, I'd called my attorney, Dave's attorney, asking if he had any information about David he could give me. Apparently it was a request he'd been waiting for. He said he needed to deliver it personally and that he was going on vacation Monday morning. He couldn't reach me yesterday, then he heard the news about Amos and me and the search for your son. So he called first thing this morning and drove down. I understand now why Dave trusted him. He'd been a close friend of David's father in law school."

"And?" Eve asked.

He took a folded letter from his jeans and gave it to her.

She unfolded it and started reading.

If you are reading this, you've probably decided to stay in Covenant Falls. I hope so. You once told me when you were very drunk about a picture of a cottage in the woods. You probably don't even remember, but I did.

You most likely have heard there was a mystery about the death of my uncle. If you are going to stay, you deserve to know, and perhaps I need to tell someone.

I was always happiest at the cabin. Both of my parents were workaholics. My dad was a famous attorney who worked all over the state. He was out of town more than he was in, and when he was home he was usually working. But when we came to Covenant Falls, we were a family. When Mom and Dad died in a private plane accident, my uncle was named guardian. Knowing how much I loved the cabin and lake, my parents left the cabin to me in a separate trust along with enough funds to take care of taxes and upkeep. That trust was to be administered by my dad's friend, Mr. Mabry. They also created another trust with my uncle in control of the funds. That one was meant to pay for my expenses, including college, until I was twenty-two, then the remainder would be split between my uncle and me. I understood there was nearly a million dollars in the account.

To make a long story short, he had a gambling habit and stole money from the trust that he controlled and lost it all. One afternoon he did the unusual: he suggested we go fishing in our boat.

It was late fall, and the fish were biting. When we got out to the middle of the lake, he said he wanted me to petition to dissolve the trust involving the cabin. He was desperate. He had lost everything in the trust account and owed a hundred thousand more.

I was stunned. I'd had no idea. I'd trusted him. He was one of those people everyone liked. I was eighteen and planning to go to college and he was telling me he'd stolen that money and now wanted the cabin, as well.

He said I owed it to him for him taking care of me. I said no. The cabin was mine. He'd stolen most of my inheritance, but he wasn't going to take the cabin. I called him a liar and cheat. I said I was going to report him to the authorities.

He attacked me. I think that was his plan B if I refused to help him. I dodged at the last second and he went over the side. I sat there for a minute, maybe more than a minute, then went in after him. I was a good swimmer, but I couldn't find him at first. Apparently he'd hit his head on the way over, and the cold water took him straight down.

When I did find him he wasn't breathing. I left him in the water and swam back to the cottage. After an hour, I called the police and reported him missing. They suspected me of murder, but they couldn't prove it. I knew I would always be suspected. And perhaps I was guilty. I could have saved him if I'd acted sooner. Part of me was so angry I wanted him dead. I left Covenant Falls that summer and joined the army. But I never forgot those happy days with my dad, and I couldn't quite force myself into giving up the cabin. I always thought someday I would come back.

When we became friends, I thought perhaps I could come back, claim it and you and I could start some kind of business together. But deep down I always knew I couldn't go back. That afternoon would always haunt me.

But not for you. Make it a happy place again. It deserves it.

"That answers a lot of questions," Eve said quietly.

"I think he didn't want to burden me with the story if I didn't decide to stay. So he told his attorney to give it to me only if I expressed interest in Covenant Falls and the cabin."

"And what do you want to do with the cabin now?" she asked cautiously.

He took her hand in his. "I know of a certain ranch that could use a rocking-chair porch and maybe a few more things. Of course, it would be easier if I lived there."

"And if you did?"

He grinned. "I thought maybe I would call my shrink at the military hospital, see if he knows another hard-ass who has no place to go. I seem to know of a cabin that's coming available."

Eve got on her tiptoes and kissed him. "I like that. We'll call it the Rainbow Cabin," she said.

He kissed her long and hard. "We forgot something," he said.

"What?"

"I think I need Nick's permission to court his mother."

"Heck, yes" came a voice from behind them.

Josh turned and saw a beaming Nick. Josh picked him up, letting the temporary crutches fall to the ground.

"Wow, this is so great," Nick said.

Yeah, wow. Josh held him tight with one arm and put the other around Eve.

He had found his home.

EPILOGUE

Three months later

IT HAD ALL started with a promise.

And now he was making another one.

Josh Manning stood before the flower-covered arch and waited for his bride.

It was a glorious day for a wedding, and Lake Park was overflowing. It seemed everyone in Covenant Falls was there to celebrate.

Nate had made the arch of flowers. Two hundred chairs had been borrowed from the community center. The first two rows had been reserved for Eve's closest friends and family. Tom and his wife. Nate and his mother. Merry, and Maude, who had baked the wedding cake. Even Eve's mother surprised everyone by coming.

Those who couldn't find chairs sprawled on the ground. Others brought their own lawn chairs.

He looked over the mammoth crowd and wondered at his own transformation that allowed him to stand here, be the center of attention. It was one big, grand party, and therapeutic for a community still shocked that one of its officers had not only stolen from its best-liked citizens, but also kidnapped a child. Sam was awaiting trial in the county seat, and Al was a broken man. He had resigned from the council after a public apology.

Eve had proposed a small wedding, but it had grown and grown and grown. The recently reelected mayor had so many friends they simply couldn't decide who to exclude.

It had been Nick who suggested the park. He was, after all, best man, and he took the role very seriously.

Josh wondered if Dave wasn't a mischievous angel arranging Josh's universe. If he were, Josh wasn't complaining. He hadn't known what happiness was until the Covenant Falls mayor had sassed him in a weed-covered yard.

The music started. It wasn't the wedding march, but the rich tones of a harp. The song was an old Nat King Cole one: "When I Fall in Love." Then Eve, escorted by her father-in-law, started down the aisle, and Josh had eyes for no one else. She wore a misty blue off-the-shoulder dress with a full skirt. A gardenia was woven into her hair, which had been fastened into a French twist. Stephanie was her only attendant.

That she had chosen him was still amazing to him. A smile played around her lips and her wide hazel eyes were soft with emotion. For him. He still had a hard time believing it.

She reached him, and her father-in-law gave Josh her hand. Her fingers curled around his, and she looked at him. The love in her eyes took his breath away.

Reverend Stephen Carroll, a family friend of the Douglases for many years, as well as minister of the Covenant Presbyterian church, smiled at them, then started the ceremony.

He heard himself say vows he never thought he would say. And when he placed a ring on Eve's finger, he whispered, "I love you" before the familiar "with this ring, I do thee wed."

Kaylee Bradley sang "The Lord's Prayer," then finally he was allowed to kiss the bride.

The kiss was long, so long that laughter came from the audience, and even then he didn't want to let go.

They were introduced as Mr. and Mrs. Joshua Manning, and as they went down the aisle Josh didn't let go of her hand.

It was another hour before the last guest had wished them well. There was still the reception, but they stole away as quickly as they could. Jim and Abby were waiting next to a decorated car. Eve hugged Abby. "You know how much I loved Russ."

"Of course I do. He would be smiling today, Eve. Josh is a very good man. Jim and I liked him from day one. So did Tom. You and Nick are in good hands."

"I love you," Eve said to Abby. "You, Jim and Nick are Russ's greatest gifts to me."

Abby wiped a tear from her eye. "You're going to ruin my makeup."

When they got in Josh's Jeep, she kissed him again. "Thank you for inviting the town."

He grinned. "I realize I'm going to have to share you with it. I think that's partly why I fell in love with you. That big heart."

FIVE HOURS LATER, they snuggled together on the new sofa in his cabin, a bottle of champagne and the leftovers of a Maude-created steak dinner on the coffee table in front of them. Candles flickered throughout the room.

"I'm going to miss this cabin," Eve said.

"Maybe we'll have visiting privileges," he replied, nuzzling her neck.

"And maybe we'll be as welcome as some of *your* visitors those first few days."

"Possible," he said. "Probable, in truth. But he probably won't have any more luck with that than I did."

"It's odd," he added. "I made Dave a promise I never thought I would have to keep. And it gave me you."

"Don't forget four more dogs, a cat, two horses, a son, in-laws and an entire town. You're a brave man, Mr. Manning."

God, but he loved her. Life would always be an adventure with her.

Tomorrow he would move into her home. No, *their*

home. But he did plan to add a rocking-chair porch. And an office. Next week, he and Nate would hang out their shingle as a construction company. The three of them—Eve, Nathan and himself—planned to promote Covenant Falls and bring in both businesses and people.

He nuzzled her neck some more. "I think we should test the bed I bought for the new resident," he said.

"A supremely fine idea," she agreed, and together they held hands as they went into the other room.

"I love you," he said.

"Show me," she teased.

And he did.

* * * * *

LARGER-PRINT BOOKS!
GET 2 FREE LARGER-PRINT NOVELS PLUS
2 FREE GIFTS!

HARLEQUIN

super romance

More Story...More Romance

LARGER-PRINT BOOKS!

HARLEQUIN *Presents*

PASSION GUARANTEED SEDUCTION

GET 2 FREE LARGER-PRINT NOVELS PLUS 2 FREE GIFTS!

YES! Please send me 2 FREE LARGER-PRINT Harlequin Presents® novels and my 2 FREE gifts (gifts are worth about $10). After receiving them, if I don't wish to receive any more books, I can return the shipping statement marked "cancel." If I don't cancel, I will receive 6 brand-new novels every month and be billed just $5.05 per book in the U.S. or $5.49 per book in Canada. That's a saving of at least 16% off the cover price! It's quite a bargain! Shipping and handling is just 50¢ per book in the U.S. and 75¢ per book in Canada.* I understand that accepting the 2 free books and gifts places me under no obligation to buy anything. I can always return a shipment and cancel at any time. Even if I never buy another book, the two free books and gifts are mine to keep forever.

176/376 HDN F43N

Name	(PLEASE PRINT)

Address	Apt. #

City	State/Prov.	Zip/Postal Code

Signature (if under 18, a parent or guardian must sign)

Mail to the **Harlequin® Reader Service:**
IN U.S.A.: P.O. Box 1867, Buffalo, NY 14240-1867
IN CANADA: P.O. Box 609, Fort Erie, Ontario L2A 5X3

Are you a subscriber to Harlequin Presents books and want to receive the larger-print edition?
Call 1-800-873-8635 today or visit us at www.ReaderService.com.

* Terms and prices subject to change without notice. Prices do not include applicable taxes. Sales tax applicable in N.Y. Canadian residents will be charged applicable taxes. Offer not valid in Quebec. This offer is limited to one order per household. Not valid for current subscribers to Harlequin Presents Larger-Print books. All orders subject to credit approval. Credit or debit balances in a customer's account(s) may be offset by any other outstanding balance owed by or to the customer. Please allow 4 to 6 weeks for delivery. Offer available while quantities last.

Your Privacy—The Harlequin® Reader Service is committed to protecting your privacy. Our Privacy Policy is available online at www.ReaderService.com or upon request from the Harlequin Reader Service.

We make a portion of our mailing list available to reputable third parties that offer products we believe may interest you. If you prefer that we not exchange your name with third parties, or if you wish to clarify or modify your communication preferences, please visit us at www.ReaderService.com/consumerschoice or write to us at Harlequin Reader Service Preference Service, P.O. Box 9062, Buffalo, NY 14269. Include your complete name and address.

HPLP13R